timber hollow

M PETTENGILL

Copyright © 2024 by M Pettengill
All rights reserved.

No part of this publication may be reproduced, distributed, or transmitted in any form or by any means, including photocopying, recording, or other electronic or mechanical methods, without the prior written permission of the publisher, except as permitted by U.S. copyright law. For permission requests, contact the author by authormpettengill@gmail.com

The story, all names, characters, and incidents portrayed in this production are fictitious. No identification with actual persons (living or deceased), places, buildings, and products is intended or should be inferred.

Book Cover by M Pettengill
Art by M Pettengill
First edition 2024

Dedication

This one is for all the black cat,
secretly a big softie
individuals out there.

Never change.

Content Warnings

This is an adult paranormal romance, and may not be suitable for all readers. While it is packaged in a pretty cozy wrapping, this is, as they say, *very spicy*. Please read with caution.

If you happen to be a member of my family, and ever want to look me in the eye again, skip Chapter 19.

ye be warned.

Graphic violence, language & sex. Graphic descriptions of hunting & consuming prey animals. Domestic abuse and non-explicit mentions of sexual assault. Loneliness, depression & self-destructive tendencies.

Contents

1. Street Meat — 1
2. Charger — 25
3. Stingray — 37
4. I'm Coming home — 49
5. Bloody Paws — 59
6. Fries with Gravy on the Side — 73
7. Welcome Home, Artemis — 87

Jay — 99

8. Fire Night — 101
9. A bar, Jay — 111
10. No take backs — 141
11. Lone Wolf Girl — 161
12. Hunters Moon — 173
13. Goodnight, Artemis — 199

Intertwine in the twilight — 204

14.	Rattlesnakes	207
15.	Body Bag	225
16.	Cookies	241
Cookies		261
17.	It's all fake	263
18.	Pumpkins	273
19.	Shut up, Jay	287
20.	The Forge	299
21.	Heartstrings	315
22.	I adore you	327
23.	My Pack	349
24.	Coffee	357
Concrete		369
25.	Bitch Boy Ethan	371
26.	No take backs	391
27.	Perfect	411
Artemis		420
28.	Open at the Close	423
Bonus		435
Acknowledgements		441
About the Author		443

| Also By | 445 |
| Endnotes | 446 |

1
Street Meat

ten days to full moon

You do not want this. My wolf whispers. Her claws are at my fingertips, fur rippling under my skin. She's too riled up, too close to the surface.

All I can hear is my heart pounding in my ears, my stomach twisted into knots. The off-white dress I stand in underneath the fluorescent lighting fits well enough, considering it is a sample size. It clings to all my curves just like I hoped. Silky cream fabric shines in the light when I twist my hips and shimmy my shoulders. The dress also has a long-ish train, pooling around the small podium I stand on.

It is a *beautiful* wedding dress.

But...

You do not want this. My wolf says again, golden eyes peering out at me from the dark corners of my soul. I ignore her, wincing at the clamminess of my hands as I brush them down the skirts of the dress. "I don't think this is the one," I say, catching Cassandra's eye in the mirror, and avoiding Cordelia's.

Cassandra rolls her baby blue eyes, her impeccably manicured hand that had been under her chin flopping down to her side. "We've been here for *hours, Artemis.* Can't you just pick *one*?"

"I'll know when I know! This one isn't it." I reply, trying not to snap at her.

Why did you ask her of all people to come? My wolf whispers, even closer to the surface of my soul with her long, fluffy, inky black tail coiled tight around her body.

Because I'm an idiot. I bite back.

You shouldn't talk about yourself like that, she chides. Not all shifters can converse with their beast, and it is times like this that I find myself annoyed that I can. Perks of being a Direwolf, I guess.

Whatever. I grouse back, returning my attention to the reflection in the mirror. My stomach rumbles loudly in the small wedding boutique. It's a combination of anxiety and hunger. I haven't eaten yet.

"Really? We *just* had breakfast." Cassandra says under her breath, rolling her eyes. "It's a wonder she even fit in these off the rack." She adds, turning in her seat to face Ethan's mother, Cordelia, like I can't hear them.

The entire White family had been surprised at how easily I overheard delicate conversations they'd believed I was too far to overhear in the beginning. Thankfully, they'd believed my lie about good genetics and pointedly began to make sure I was leaving the room *entirely* when they conducted business. The White family is seen as one of the most charitable families on the West Coast, along with the Carter family–Cassandra's. *I* happen to know better. The conversations I've overheard paint a different, darker picture.

And not in the delusional *I want to be a mob wife because they're actually the **good** guys* kind of way, either.

"*You* had breakfast. You know I don't usually eat that early in the morning, Cassandra." I reply, not even bothering to pretend like I hadn't heard her snide comment. I've told Ethan, his mother, the entire staff, *and* Cassandra at least a thousand times by now that I don't eat breakfast. I'm never hungry first thing in the morning. I'd determined in my teens that it's because when I shift, I hunt. Waking up to eat a baked sugary thing after wolfing out and *wolfing down* a rabbit never settles well.

Of course, it is a bit more difficult to do that these days. I'd grown up deep in the forests, like most shifter packs where hunting is easy. While some species preferred other areas like the ocean or deserts, wolves like the mountains, and the trees.

Here in the city, shifters aren't common unless they have an avian form or smaller animals like a housecat. Anything else is too risky for most, particularly for a full Moon run. Some species of wolves are small enough to pass for a stray dog within city limits, but even so not many choose to dwell here. There are no open areas to run across. No trees to sprint wildly through. No Moon to howl at. I've managed to be lucky, my fiancé lives on a ten-acre plot just outside the city. No one questions my enjoyment of late-night strolls much, there. I've had to work hard though, to keep my wolfy presence hidden. She doesn't get to hunt *nearly* as much anymore.

"Will you *pick one* then?" Cassandra hisses, rolling her eyes again, waving her finger at the dresses.

Maybe this is why I asked Cassandra to come. Because she is the only one who isn't going to be overjoyed at picking out wedding dresses, she is the only one who won't be screaming and crying the whole time because I am getting married. Or, rather, because *their baby boy* is finally getting married. Like I'd expected Cordelia to... But it seems I was mistaken. Neither of the women have seemed particularly enthused to be here with me. Which is....*fine* I guess.

Sam, the only friend I have here that I made myself, wouldn't have even bothered trying to hide her disdain at the two snobby women occupying the bridal boutique with me. For that matter, she doesn't in particular care for Ethan as a person. Unfortunately, the Whites don't particularly care for her, either. Of course, to her face, they act kind enough, but behind closed doors, I overheard them once ripping her apart for her *lower status*.

Really makes a girl wonder what they say behind *my* back.

Cassandra's family, the Carters on the other hand, has been friends with the Whites for *years*. They are both old money, Ethan and Cassandra had attended the same prestigious universities as their parents. Six-figure jobs were lined up before they even stepped foot on campus. All thanks to *mummy and daddy*.

Ethan and I had only been dating for about seven months when he popped the question. In the middle of an upscale restaurant, with all his very wealthy, powerful, and *extended* family sitting at the banquet table with us. I'd never been to the restaurant, and haven't since that night. I couldn't even remember what the food had tasted like. Just that I had been so very *very* bored before Ethan pulled the antique jewelry box out of the inner pocket of his suit, all the women at the table cooing at the romanticism.

Obviously, *because I am a dumbass,* I said yes.

That had been five months ago. Five months of planning for a wedding rapidly approaching and no one— not even I— had thought to themselves *'Hey, I think the bride is going to need a dress'* until now. The wedding is in four and a half months, the noose is slowly tightening around my neck. This is how I ended up in this bridal boutique with a pair of women who seemed like they would rather be anywhere else.

Three months ago, my mother left me a voicemail saying that she *saw the announcement in the tabloids* and *hoped I would invite the family* and *wished she was a better mom* and asked *when are you coming home, it's been years.*

I haven't returned her call. I just don't have the energy to talk to her about Ethan. It's not like she is a particularly *bad* mom... She just.... Isn't a very good one either. My mom always dealt out more guilt trips than she did affection. There are times when I can remember her cuddling with all of us on the couch, watching shows. Making soup when one of my siblings was sick. But more than that I remember how often I was overlooked, how often I felt like I was invisible to her in comparison to Athena or Apollo.

My mother has a fucking *lady boner* for naming her children after the Olympians. Sometimes I feel like an idiot, named Artemis with a sister called Athena and a brother named Apollo. Am I a twin? *No.* Are we Greek? *Also no.*

I haven't liked the way my name sounds in a *very* long time. Particularly when these people say it.

Unfortunately for me, *I* am the child that takes after Dad. Darker hair. Darker eyes. I am a constant reminder of the man she never got over. I'm pretty sure that my mother started hating him, more than she missed him somewhere around my eighth birthday. Hated him for dying, and leaving her alone. Shifters rarely marry, and for that matter are rarely *strictly* monogamous, but that doesn't mean the love isn't deep and true between them.

And for my parents, it had been as close as you could get to having a star-fated mate, outside of the novels I pour myself into. Even as a kid, I'd found solace between the pages of a book, just like I'd find it between the trees.

Tucking a strand behind my ear, I take in my reflection once again. My hair is lighter than I like it... If I didn't know any better, my tanned skin and cool blonde hair would paint me as the typical Californian girl. The very expensive stylist Ethan's mother hired to get me ready for the wedding has done a phenomenal job, I'll give him that. The ends of my hair would be fried to a crisp if he were any less talented. Of course, Cordelia had also taken the liberty of scheduling laser hair removal and the weekly mani and pedi combo. One morning when Cordelia was unexpectedly in Ethan's house, she had been *particularly* offended at the state of my nails post-shift. She goes weekly as well, though that is just because she is a spoiled bitch. Cordelia had been born with the silver spoon in her mouth, just like Ethan. I have another hair appointment lined up later next week to retouch my roots, which are a much dirtier, darker shade of blonde, edging on brown.

*You **do not** want this.*

Please, be quiet. I beg my wolf. She huffs, tucking her face under her tail deep within the confines of my mind.

"I guess it'll be the second one then." I finally say, dropping my hands to my thighs. The second dress is the one that Ethan's mom had selected while booking the appointment. It is grand, and positively screams old money with the lacework sleeves and beading. The owner of the shop had informed us the style was influenced by the gown one of the English Queens wore at their coronation. I don't care to remember or ask which one.

"*Oh*, marvelous dear. That one looked better than the others anyway. *Classy.*" Cordelia doesn't need to say anything else, the implication that the one that had been my favorite *wasn't* classy is clear. I don't know how women like her do it— make you feel about three centimeters tall with barely a handful of words.

"Finally, you're making sense," Cassandra says, raising herself off the velvet settee the boutique had sitting before the large mirrors. She calls the boutique owner over, taking care of the arrangements while she waves me off the podium like I am a dog. Cordelia pulls lipstick out of her Chanel bag, and a small compact mirror.

My wolf raises her hackles, from inside my mind where she lay dormant. But, I leave the showing area and dutifully change back into my t-shirt that is long enough to serve as a dress, tiny bike shorts, and sneakers. This is not usually what they like to see me in, but because I'm dressed on-trend no one has said anything. I'll have to change, of course, for family dinner.

The bistro Cordelia takes us to for ladies' luncheon serves salads, green smoothies, and lettuce wraps. Inwardly, I roll my eyes.

Nary a spec of carbohydrate or gluten to be seen on the thick cardstock paper that serves as the menu. My stomach rumbles painfully again as I peruse the offerings.

The two ladies at the table with me are rail thin, proudly informing me that this is their favorite restaurant as their eyes flick over the menu. It's times like these where it is hard to ignore just how opposite they are to me in every way. I have soft curves, hips, ass, *and* thighs. Muscles and strength where they do not. Not to mention the fact that one of my arms is covered in tattoos. I'd started getting them almost immediately after leaving home. Now my right arm is entirely covered in them. Some I did myself with a cheapo tattoo machine I'd ordered online, but most were done by professionals.

I quickly pulled my phone out while they were looking over the drinks, to shoot a message off to my hopeful savior.

> That was a disaster.

> Oh, like you didn't know that was going to be the case?

> Shut up. They took me to a fucking bunny bar. Emergency. NOW. I need real food.

> Code red coming right up.

I want a cheeseburger. Or a pizza. Oh, *fuck*. The taco truck just down the street smells *divine*.

My phone starts ringing seconds later. I answer it, doing my best to act normal. Sam's distraught voice comes through the phone speaker, much louder than I thought humanly possible.

"He broke up with me!" She wails into the phone before I've even muttered a *hello*. I give my future mother-in-law an apologetic look, excusing myself from the little wrought-iron table. Cassandra and Cordelia barely pause their conversation.

"Oh, *honey*," I croon into the phone, selling the *concerned-friend-bit* as I stride down the street under the guise of needing privacy. Sam continues blubbering about her imaginary lost love for another moment, her words barely coherent over the sniffling and sobbing. Once I am out of earshot— or at least human earshot— I say "clear," into the phone.

"Did they buy it?" Sam asks, voice entirely clear like she hadn't just been wailing into the phone about her pretend boyfriend dumping her.

"Yep. Like catching fish in a barrel," I say, still pacing around the end of the street like I am trying to calm her down. "You deserve an Oscar."

Sam cackles into the phone, then says "*Perfect*. You coming over?"

"Yeah, but I can't stay long. It's *family dinner* night. I'm definitely stopping first at the taco truck though. It's calling my *fucking name,* you want?" I moan a little, a breeze wafting down the smell of roasting meats and salsa.

"Boo, you whore."

I snorted. "Shut up. You want some or not?"

"Yes. Hurry up, beeyotch."

"Patience, hoe!"

"Love you."

"Love you too."

Hurriedly, I walk back to the table where Cordelia and Cassandra are sitting, a waiter taking their overly complex salad orders. Seriously, why order something if you're going to completely alter it?

Interrupting Cassandra's edits to her chicken salad, I say "I'm so sorry. I have to go. My friend just got dumped, she shouldn't be alone."

"Aw, poor thing. Do you want to take her a salad?" Cordelia asks, raising an entitled finger to prevent the waiter from leaving. *As if a fucking salad is appropriate breakup food?*

"No, I don't want it to wilt by the time I walk over there." Sam's apartment is across town, and it would take me about an hour to walk. Calling a cab is out of the question.

The Whites do not call a cab. *Ever.* And, since I have the *ugly ass piss dick* heirloom diamond on my finger— that means I can't call one, either.

"Oh, take my car darling. I'll call Stephen and he'll come fetch us," Cordelia says, fishing her Mercedes keys out of her purse. Cordelia isn't entirely horrible, but she also isn't a very *nice* lady. She picks and chooses when to show her humanity. What little bit of it there is.

"You're a blessing, Cordelia. Thank you," I say, taking the keys from her manicured hand. Never a single platinum blonde hair out of place, Cordelia is the picture of *old money*. Perfectly styled hair, designer clothes, shoes, and bags that cost almost the same as a house. Not *her* house, of course. But *a* house.

"You'll be back for dinner, won't you?" She asks, raising her mimosa to her lipstick-stained mouth.

"Of course. Wouldn't miss it," I reply, rushing from the table and into the parking garage. The entire White family lives on the *Estate*. Each child has their own home, dotted around the grounds. Cordelia and Stephen live in the main house, naturally the largest and most grand on the property. The Whites have their fingers in almost everything. Stocks, an import business, some of them are lawyers, and there is even an accountant in the family.

The main house is also where I am to marry their son in a private ceremony, only the elite few in Cordelia's circle would be granted an invitation. It's only a handful of months away now. Every week, they host *family dinners.* Anyone they deem to be family at the moment is welcome. This meant of course that the entire thing is a facade to do business deals that are too...unsavory to complete at the office. If you are invited and you don't show? You'd become a veritable pariah until Cordelia and Stephen deem you to have suffered enough, and welcome you back into the fold.

The grey Mercedes is double parked, and I cringe from embarrassment as I lower myself into the luxury vehicle. I want to scream to everyone in the garage that this isn't my car, and it wasn't *me* who parked like an asshole. Sure, it is a nice car, but it doesn't compare to some of the vintage cars Aggie took me to see, once upon a time. Or even some in Ethan's collection that he didn't even know how to drive.

I should call Aggie.

Yes, you should. My wolf replies immediately, still too close to the surface.

Slowly, I back the sedan out of its parking space and drive the loop-de-loops of the parking garage until I reach the exit. Making sure to wave dutifully to Cordelia and Cassandra as I turn onto the road, slowly driving away from the bunny bar.

Cordelia would skin me alive if she knew that I am about to pick up *street meat* in her car.

Fuck 'em.

Carrying both mine and Sam's taco orders out of the parking garage and towards her building, I feel my phone buzz in my pocket in quick succession, again, again, and again. A pause, and then it begins vibrating once more, this time signaling a phone call. There's only one person who texts like that, three times in a row and then immediately calls. *Ethan*.

I quickly shuffle the bags in my hands, fishing my phone out of my pocket.

"Hello," I say, pinching the device between my shoulder and ear.

"What are you doing?" Ethan immediately asks, catching the way my breath is uneven through the speaker.

"Carrying tacos and drinks in one hand and talking to you, why?"

"For what? I thought you were getting dresses with my mother." He says sharply, suspicion lacing his tone. I can't help but roll my eyes, passing through the door to the building held open for me by a man leaving.

"I did. Sam called while we were sitting down to eat. She got dumped so I'm bringing her tacos."

"Oh. Poor girl. I could set her up with one of my friends from the office." He offers, and I hear the wheels of his office chair creak, and the thud of his shoes on his desk.

"I'll ask her. What did you need? I haven't had a chance to look at your text, my hands are full."

"Nothing. Mother told me you left the lunch early so I called to see what's going on. Will you be home for dinner?" Again, I can't help but roll my eyes as I enter the elevator.

"Wouldn't miss it. I'll be home by the time you're off work." I glance at the digital clock above all the buttons for the floors as I mash the one for Sam's apartment. I can hang out here with Sam for at least a few hours before I have to go back to the Estate and get dressed.

"Okay. Make sure you're presentable." Ethan says, hanging up the phone without waiting to see if I respond.

"Self-important asshole," I say under my breath, exiting the elevator a moment later. There are only two apartments on this floor, a short hallway from the elevator and large steel doors offset from each other on the two walls. The building I believe was at one point a bread factory or something, this level I believe was used for storage. The two apartments mirror each other, the space for the elevator and hallway taken equally from the residences. I've never met Sam's neighbor, but from what she's told me she is a very beautiful lady, and Sam definitely has the hots for her.

I kick the bottom of her door lightly twice, waiting for Sam to open it. Her door is notoriously tricky and I don't want to tempt fate and spill everything. Sam opens the large door moments later, swinging it wide enough to allow me through and for her to peek out, looking for *Ms. Hot-stuff neighbor.*

"She's not there." I tease over my shoulder, marching over to the bar to set down our food, Cordelia's keyring clattering to the countertop. Sam's apartment leans into that warehouse feel, she'd left the brick walls painted white and steel beams exposed but it's simultaneously somehow *jungle-like*. She decorates it tastefully, draping colorful fabrics on the brick, lush pillows on every couch or chair, and art from her local artist friends hanging on the walls. But along with that, there is an abundance of shrubbery and plants dotting the large open floor plan of her apartment. She keeps it delightfully balmy in here, and it smells alive like a forest would.

I've always liked Sam's apartment. More so than I ever liked *the Estate.*

Sam slams her door shut, scoffing as she says 'ugh, you're the worst."

"Pretty much," I say, shucking my sneakers off and climbing onto the barstool, perched with one leg up. "Be useful and grab napkins, I forgot them at the truck," I say to my friend, unloading the bags that are full of tacos, nachos, and queso.

"Oh, the Corgi let you borrow her car? I feel *special*." Sam says, spotting the Mercedes key ring on her counter, grabbing a stack of napkins, and sitting on the other barstool.

I snort, unwrapping a taco. "Oh yeah. She practically threw them at me." As I take my first bite, I do a little dance because *fucking hell* that tastes good, Sam doing the same. "Fuck, that's a good taco."

"That's what she said," Sam says around a mouthful without missing a beat, making me nearly choke on the second bite I'd just taken.

"Fuck off" I laugh, prying the lid off of the queso. Sam and I eat our food while she tells me about the most recent run-in with *Ms. Hot Stuff Neighbor*. I'm convinced that one of these days, Sam will pluck up the courage to ask the woman out already. As we're cleaning up, Sam asks "Where was that truck?"

"Like a block away from the dress shop," I reply, drying my hands to then collapse on the biggest of her couches, the green one. She follows me, sinking into the cushions sitting sideways, a knee folded under her.

"So tell me, how did dress shopping go?" She asks, playing with a fraying thread of the throw blanket on the back of the couch.

"About how you'd expect. Cassandra was a witch, Cordelia... was *Cordelia*. I picked the dress that was her favorite." I shrug, feeling indifferent about the whole thing.

"Why didn't you at least pick the dress *you* like? You're the one getting married." Sam asks, rolling her eyes and taking another drink, the straw squeaking in the plastic lid.

"I don't know. Didn't feel like it was worth it." I reply, taking a sip of my soda as well. Sam hums in response, cocking her head to the side.

"What?" I finally ask, flopping my head back on the couch cushion.

"Why do you stay?" Sam asks quietly, and *there it is*. The question I can always feel lingering on the tip of her tongue. She doesn't shout her dislike of my fiance into my face at every opportunity, she just quietly hates him for the both of us.

"Because it's easier. Because they have ten acres to run across. Because I don't have to keep moving." I say, sighing. The unsaid part is that I just *don't care*. I don't care that he doesn't love me. Don't care that he doesn't treat me right on most days. I just... *don't*. I know it could be better, I see the bullshit, and yet... I just don't care. Sam is an anaconda shifter, so there are some things she understands– like the space to shift. Her entire apartment is catered to her snake-like traits. But, she doesn't understand... *pack*. The desire to belong— even if it tears your soul to pieces.

Sam hums, leaving the proposition to dangle in the air unspoken. She'd offered once before, to open her apartment to me, give me someplace to escape Ethan. I smile at her, very grateful that she hasn't let me disappear like my other friends have. Shifter, or human. But I don't take the bait.

"How long until dinner?" She asks, thumbing through her phone, accepting that nothing is changing today.

"I have like two hours before I have to leave."

"So should I order a pizza now, or wait like twenty minutes?" Sam asks, smirking.

I howl with laughter, my ribs feeling tight. "Give it like twenty. It's the Corgi's *ladies'* night. That means no gluten or cheese to be seen on the menu."

"What do the *men* do while all you eat salads and comment on your outfits?" Sam asks, switching apps to the food delivery service and selecting toppings.

I snort. "Go and pretend they are pro golfers, drinking their weight in overpriced booze."

It's Sam's turn to chortle, and she makes a serious face, pulling her voice down into a mockery of a genteel man, swinging her arms haphazardly while she says "Righto Chap. Jolly good serve there. *Four*!"

And, it's so stupid, and silly and so very *Sam* that it makes me once again throw my head back and howl with laughter.

2
Charger

six days to full moon

One good thing about marrying into the White family is that the men work during the day, and everyone else leaves *me* alone. Every day like clockwork, Ethan, his dad, and brothers leave the White Estate in their flashy, overpriced cars at 7 AM on the dot. All of them in a little parade following Stephen's Rolls Royce through the gates.

It means however, that every day at 6:10 I am woken up by roving hands and pleads of *"Come on baby, I need you before work,"* followed by five minutes of grunting, and then he's out of the house twenty minutes later without so much as a *have a good day, love you*.

So, every morning when he leaves, I can get up and move around the house without stepping on eggshells and pretending to be enamored with all of the glitz and glamor around. The first thing I do almost every day is go 'for a walk' around the Estate. Usually by the second mile, I've shifted, stashing my clothes in a hollowed-out tree. That typically takes up most of the morning. Afterwards, my routine is pretty simple. When I'm in the shower a maid will bring up a cup of coffee, placing it on the edge of the sink. After getting dressed in leggings and a tee shirt I take my mug into the library, settle myself in the large window seat, scrolling through social media and the news. Eventually, someone will come and collect my empty mug as they come through cleaning the already pristine house. When I get bored of doom scrolling, I pick up whatever book I left lying on the seat, and curl up with a blanket, emerging from my cocoon only when I need to use the bathroom, or in search of snacks.

There is a little pull chain that operates a bell in the kitchen for the cook staff. I've been told repeatedly that I can use it to have them bring anything I want up. I can't bring myself to pull on the chain, though. The house is huge, but the kitchen is only a set of stairs away. My mother always called me lazy as a kid, but even I can manage to descend the stairs for a good *snacko*. Ethan? Not so much. If I am considered lazy, then Ethan would be... worse, *much* worse. Every time Ethan uses one of the chains that are littered throughout the house I have to suppress the way my lip wants to curl, the disgust unfurling in my belly.

Ethan's house is large, but even with the various rooms and the massive lawns, the library is still where I spend most of my time. The July heat has nearly given way to August, bringing with it the even hotter breeze, and the potential for forest fires. The cooler temperatures of fall are still a long way off, but even so, the west coast doesn't get nearly as cold in the fall as home. However, with the smallest chill in the air in the earliest hours of the morning, the grounds staff has already warned me against going outside so frequently in the fall and winter months. Already advised to find a new hobby for the morning, rather than my walk around the grounds.

And already, I want to scream. My wolf feels as restless as I am.

Of course, my plain black leggings and comfy t-shirt are not considered *acceptable* attire in the White family. So every day at 4:15 I trudge back into the closet and choose one of the ensembles that was carefully chosen and selected for me by Cordelia's stylist. My wardrobe has dwindled to a handful of leggings, big t-shirts, and the stray black dress I'd managed to hang on to. Cordelia does not approve of many of the pieces, and what the matriarch of the family says, goes. So within the first few months of dating Ethan, the majority of my wardrobe was slowly donated, new pieces that made me want to light myself on fire replacing them. The Whites are hosting a fundraising dinner tonight for homeless shelters in the county, which means I have to select my outfit from the side of the closet I'd been told was appropriate for *events*.

Starched white shirt, grey tweed skirt with threads of green, purple, and blue throughout the houndstooth stitching, and a matching blazer. Nude heels from the rack. The selections are simple. Easy. Carefully, I style my bleached hair in a loose updo, slightly side-swept with strands left out around my face. A couple of swipes of concealer, mascara, and nude lipstick complete the look.

I barely recognize myself in the mirror. I don't know who this doll with wide brown eyes staring back at me is. With a small shudder, I leave the closet and dutifully make my way to the entryway. Truthfully, I am running a little late, but only by a minute or two.

That's nothing compared to the additional ten minutes I spend standing at the end of the stairs in the entryway, waiting for him. I hear the engine first, Ethan's Dodge Charger whipping into the driveway through the large windows. When he parks the car, he leaves the driver-side door open as he walks into the house. A butler opens the oversized door to the house for him, Ethan doesn't even break stride.

My fiance's watery blue eyes hungrily roam over my body, an ugly, self-satisfied smirk on his face. Then he's roughly pulling me into a bruising kiss the moment he's within touching distance. His hands grip the back of my head, tangling in my hair and wrinkling my shirt.

"How was your day?" I ask when Ethan releases me, straightening the hair he's mussed up, attempting to smooth my shirt, knowing Cordelia will eventually say some snide remark about it when we get to the main house.

"A day. Are you ready?" He answers, barely looking at me as he turns back around and begins walking out the door, tugging me with him. "Mother is waiting for us, we'll be late if we don't leave now," Ethan says like I am the sole reason we are ever late. He's still wearing the khaki suit he wore to work, though the navy blue tie is loosened.

I roll my eyes at his back, and say "Yes, of course." My heels click against the hardwood as I follow him out of the house, and into the Charger. Ethan is already seated by the time I land in the passenger seat, the engine rumbling. He peels out of the circular driveway nearly as soon as my door closes, throwing me back against the seat. The drive to the main house takes all of two minutes and is done in complete silence. Ethan never likes to talk about work when he comes home and never cares to ask what I do all day while he's gone, so there is nothing really to talk about. Honestly, I would have preferred to walk over, but arguing with Ethan is like talking to a brick wall. Regardless of what I say, he'll do what he wants. So I don't bother anymore.

My wolf stays silent too, pacing within the confines of my mind. I am not looking forward to going to the main house and rubbing elbows with people who by all rights should be good, kind, and generous. That is what their public persona would have you think. Behind closed doors, they take off that mask. Ethan, of course, does not see it that way. He's known all of these people his whole life, so to him this really is *family dinner*.

"Watch your mouth tonight. Father has invited the Senator." Ethan says as we pull into the manicured drive of the main house. There is a humongous wisteria tree that shades the drive and the entryway, though the flowers have all gone now. When Ethan first brought me, it had been in full bloom, massive tendrils of flowers swaying lightly in the breeze.

"Won't say a word." I declare, clenching my jaw, anger burning in my belly. Ethan does nothing, just throws the shifter into park, and exits the vehicle, the car door slamming behind him. My door closes much softer, solidly thunking as I follow Ethan to the door of his parent's house.

"Ladies first," He says as his parent's butler opens the door for us, and for a moment— one single shining moment my anger dissipates. Then, Ethan swats my ass as I enter before him. The urge to shift and rip his fucking hand off rises up my throat like bile. As Ethan enters his parent's house, his entire demeanor changes. Ordinarily, he's at best only half interested in what I have to say, or what I'm doing.

Inside these walls, I'm a novelty. A new shiny toy he gets to parade around, something he gets to rub his brother's noses in.

It is no secret that Ethan likes me best for my body. I'm well aware of that fact, and usually, it doesn't bother me. These dinners, though, where Ethan and his brothers get together, get deep into their cups, and start talking about their wives–my hackles rise. Like Cordelia and Cassandra, Ethan's brother's wives are all rail thin, vapid, and petty. John is married to Vanessa, Phil to Karina. Beyond the fact I don't like being shown off like a show pony, a bright shiny penny, their spoiled rich boy attitudes are despicable. And it's not like I need any help making my future sisters-in-law hate me. They seem to manage that all by themselves, even if I hardly say a word.

"God I love that fat ass of yours," Ethan whispers in my ear as he throws his arm over my shoulder. "I'm gonna bend you over the Charger later. Fuck you against it like the dirty whore you are." He says, pressing a kiss against my temple as we enter the sitting room. Disgust makes my lip curl. His family—extended and not— are milling about, cocktails in hand. The person who must be the Senator is next to Cordelia and Stephen, a gaggle of older women and men circling the trio. His brothers all cheer as Ethan enters, clearly already on their second or third drink. He immediately steers us over to them, and I silently begin to count the minutes until food is served, smiling and nodding at the conversation I'm only half listening to.

It's not like I'm expected to say anything.

When dinner is served, it is *of course* a drawn-out, multi-course affair. I'm seated between Ethan and Karina. She's not half bad unless you count her absolutely abhorrent attitude when one single drop of alcohol splashes her tongue. Luckily for me, she's sipping wine tonight and hasn't yet broken into Stephen's scotch. She'll still be a miserable cunt, but she won't immediately start hurling insults at me. No, that will be later when the ladies start gathering in the sitting rooms when the expensive Port wines come out.

Servants first bring out little crab cakes with hollandaise sauce drizzled over the top, the breading on the cakes perfectly crisp and delicate. I eat the whole thing, mopping up the extra sauce with my last bite of crispy delicate crab. My plate is cleared before almost everyone else, and Ethan's punishing grip on my thigh reminds me to eat the next course a little more *demurely.* Karina eats maybe one bite in between sipping her wine and gossiping to Vanessa.

Then, there's a soup that looks more like baby food than a broth. It tastes like a lovely summer squash, peppery and creamy though. As I take sips of that, Ethan strikes up a conversation with his dad about the account they're working on, the Senator joining in with interest. It wouldn't take a genius to understand that whatever business deal they're cooking up is definitely not above board. The three men don't use explicit language to talk about the deal, but they don't specifically try to *hide* what they're discussing, either.

The Senator thinks he's so clever, referring to the capitol as the "home office" and veiling his words behind *"Well this is for the good of the American people"*. He's convinced himself that there is no wrongdoing in his underhanded dealings with the Whites. He wants them to get him re-elected for another term. And, in return, the Whites will have exclusive first dibs on the oil drilling that the Senator plans to approve. The Whites help him, he helps the Whites. I only get down half of my soup before my stomach turns, listening to the men.

After the soup, there is a light Caesar salad, greens cut from the small garden on the grounds, and crispy crunchy croutons sprinkled on the top. I'm beyond ready to leave, barely able to restrain myself from performing an old-fashioned lobotomy. I think a fork to the eyeball will probably do it. If nothing else, it would end the evening. Dinner takes entirely too long with these people.

And to think, I *get* to do this for the rest of my life, week after week. Month after month.

3
Stingray

two days to full moon

It's been a month since the Senator last attended *family dinner*. He's coming again tonight, bringing his sons with him this time. Ethan has been home all day, riled up about whatever deal would be solidified at tonight's meal.

I've been the recipient of all his focus, all his excess energy all day. At any given moment, he'll walk up behind me, grab me, and immediately start pawing all over my body. Sliding his hands under my shirt, tugging my leggings down. Denying Ethan takes more effort and willpower than just accepting his advances. So I let it happen. Let him use my body, because after he'll leave me alone for a few hours at least. I stay out of my library selecting a few volumes to read early in the day before he wakes, settling in the Sunroom. I don't want to... *taint* my only haven in this monstrosity of a house.

Looking back, I'm not sure how I missed all of the glaring red flags the man waved in my face. How I grew to care about him at all. Because I do, I love Ethan. He has his moments. It's what is under the straight-laced exterior that I missed. The *rot*.

When it comes time to prepare for dinner, I try to avoid going, telling Ethan that I have a migraine. A little while ago, he joined me in the Sunroom, talking *at* me even when I had a book in front of my face.

"I've got something that will cure you, Princess." Is Ethan's only response to my migraine, and he fists his cock through his lounge pants, waggling his eyebrows at me from where he reclines on a sofa.

"Stop it, I'm serious," I reply, rubbing my temples. I really do have a headache, My neck and shoulders are *painfully* tight. If I had to guess, I would say that being around Ethan today– *all day* has caused it.

"No, you've got to come with me. I can't be the only one without some ass on my arm." Ethan says dismissively, his attention firmly returned to the phone screen.

"Of course." I sigh, slowly rising from my chair to begin the process of dolling myself up. Can't wait for an evening of being absolutely ignored. *Fantastic.*

Ethan smacks my ass as I pass by, saying "Wear the red outfit. I want all of them to be jealous of my Princess' fat ass."

I grit my teeth, saying nothing as I make my way upstairs.

I'm going to bite his hand off someday. My wolf growls from the darkened corner of my soul where she rests.

Someday I might just let you.

My backpack is heavy. So is the suitcase I toss into the back of the car. I've already loaded the trunk. There are so many different models in here, I wonder how long it would take Ethan to notice which one I've taken. If he'd notice at all.

Not all the cars within Ethan's collection are antiques, even if many of them are. He has a McLaren over in the corner, and he is always bragging about owning a supercar- even though he's only driven it around the loop of the Estate, never out on the road. The beautiful thing doesn't even have plates on it. Tonight he'd been particularly braggadocious about the hunk of metal, and I have to fight back the urge to fucking smash the windshield and dent the hood and rims.

I end up choosing the Corvette Stingray- flashy, even if it is entirely black. The Stingray is a stick shift, though not the convertible—that is across the garage, sitting amongst an array of drop tops. I couldn't find those keys, and I am too impatient to go and look for them again. In any case, the lowered top would cut into trunk space.

I'm ready to leave. To get the fuck out of here.

Ethan doesn't know how to drive a stick shift and despises the fact that I can. So—the Stingray—one of only a few models in here with a standard transmission, it is. The plates are only on it because it was all handled by the dealer, driven over here by a salesman with slicked-back hair. I remember the day it was delivered, how Ethan had sat in the driver's seat out in the driveway, cooed about the rumble of the engine, and smoothed his hands all over the interior. Then instructed a servant to park it. He just hoards the beautiful cars because he can.

Unbeknownst to him, the next day before he came home from work, I took it for a spin. Drove it down the highway, steadily shifting through gears, windows down. I have been itching to get back in it since.

He's an asshole. My wolf grumbles.

No argument there.

Earlier I'd watched Cassandra smooth the lapels of Ethan's jacket down with a small secret smile on her lips. Then she straightened his tie.

From where I stood at the balcony's edge of the grand staircase after family dinner I'd felt sick for just one moment, and then, *nothing*.

Ethan had long disappeared from where all the women were congregating. Cordelia wanted to look through the album containing all the previous generations of White weddings again before her *baby boy's* wedding. Ever the dutiful daughter-in-law to be, I went up to the library and got it for her, and then put it back again when they were done. While I was gone, apparently everyone began moving from the parlor where Cordelia had been holding court with her circle of old money women to wherever in the Estate they fancied. The Senator's wife has that same sort of predatory glint in her eye that Cordelia does.

It is almost like I am invisible to them unless I am on Ethan's arm. Servants see me, of course. I am the stranger amid the White Estate. But no one else ever even glances my way, unless Ethan is beside me. So, naturally, no one saw me at the top of the staircase, watching what was unfolding between Ethan and Cassandra in a darkened corner of the mammoth house.

I'd worn the red dress he'd asked me to. Apparently, Cassandra had also gotten a similar instruction. Hers bares the entirety of her back, and dips below her sternum. Someone might say that she was *overcompensating*.

Unable to look away, I watched Ethan's gaze track her lips, and roam down her body hungrily. The way he pressed her against the wall, pulling her leg up to his hip tells me they'd done this multiple times. There is *familiarity* in the way he dips his hand beneath her blood-red skirt, and kisses up her throat.

There is experience with the way she claws at his shoulders, tilting her hips, unzipping his pants.

I'd expected tears.

Rage.

Something.

Anything.

But no, there is just ringing silence in my brain.

Relief.

Immediately, I turned around, took the servant's staircase, and left through the back patio. I didn't even know if Ethan was aware of its existence, or if he knew that *I knew* of its existence.

The Whites even have a small driving range on the grounds, golf carts parked under a small overhang. I took one back to the house Ethan had moved me into. If I shift, I leave my clothes and shoes behind. I don't need to leave breadcrumbs for them to follow.

No one saw me or paid any attention to me as I packed up what little I'd come here with, well, what was left of it anyway. The clothes I *actually* wear all fit in one suitcase. There are a few items I've accumulated that I didn't want to leave behind, my laptop, headphones, books, and a handful of jewelry that would be handy if I needed money. And I *may* have raided the safe that I know Ethan never locks. He is too lazy.

Twenty grand in bills would come in handy. They'd never miss it, anyway. I doubted they'd miss me either. At least I wrote them a note. It is a complete lie, but I still wrote one and left it on the fridge in the house Ethan and I had shared.

I'm going to the spa. Pre-wedding pampering. See you soon! Kisses.

The highway is dark, but it doesn't matter. I can see as easily as if it was broad daylight. The Moon is high, almost full but not quite. There are only a few days until the full Moon, to leave the city and find somewhere safe to shift.

The Moon is full, bright— and lonely. She hangs low in the sky, the tops of the Sequoia trees partially obscuring the face of the Full Moon. The Sturgeon Moon. Perhaps I'll find a river to fish in tonight. Pay homage to the great hunters of the past.

When I left the White Estate, the first destination I had in mind was the forest. I know the Pack that lives within the Yosemite forests. Sam introduced me to them when we first became friends, she does graphic design work for the Packs coffee business. The Alpha had invited me to join their ranks, even if it was only for full Moon runs. He said *"A wolf needs a pack. We'd be happy to have you within our ranks. A black wolf is a thing of rarity."*

I declined. At the time, I'd merely said I'd think about it, but I never had any intention of joining the Yosemite Wolves. Just like I never had any intention of joining any of the Packs I'd visited years ago on my way to California.

None of them had felt like home.

Standing on the remains of a petrified Sequoia tree— the trunk as wide as I am tall—my breath steams as it leaves my lungs, black fur rippling in the breeze. Fall has not arrived yet, but within the trees, you can feel it. Autumn will be here soon, bringing with it even colder nights.

I tilt my head back, letting that single, lonesome note free.

And then, with a burst of speed, I'm moving. Tearing through the underbrush, darting around massive trees that are hundreds, if not thousands of years old. I run without a true destination, feeling the wind through my fur, tracking all the wildlife with ease.

I catch the scent of blood. Elk. A feast waiting to be devoured. Turning my nose towards the scent I easily follow the trail. In my shifted form, the tips of my ears hit the four-foot mark. I'm a few hundred pounds heavier, stacked with pure undiluted power. But even so, taking down an elk by myself would be a challenge.

Nevertheless, I follow the earthy musky scent of the elk's blood. Almost as soon as I begin following the animal, I find the scents of the Yosemite pack. They're hunting the elk, too.

As easily as I found the scent of blood, I turn away from it. I guess I won't be feasting on elk, after all.

Hours pass, the Moon inching across the sky as I race under the canopy of trees. The Pack never finds me, but I know when they take down the elk. I hear the beast scream before it cuts off abruptly.

I can't help how my jaw aches, saliva dripping out of my maw. My wolf and I are hungry. Had I joined the Pack on their run, we would be feasting already. Sinking our teeth into the hot, wet meat. Our paws helping to tear chunks free. I could see them all in my mind's eye, ripping the carcass apart in a frenzy. Blood coating their muzzles and dripping off the fur.

My stomach rumbles almost painfully. Still, I keep running. Running and running through the trees. Eventually, when I find a river I stop, wading into the cool waters where rocks make small rapids and wait for the fish. It doesn't take long before the animals are throwing themselves up and out of the water to move upstream.

I catch one between my teeth, devouring it on the spot, holding its triangle-shaped head between my paw and the rocks to rip it apart. It's gone too soon, so I catch another, and another.

I gorge myself on fresh fish, ears moving like satellites, looking for any sign of other wolves. I wouldn't be run out of the forest by the pack, but that doesn't mean I want to talk to them.

4
I'm Coming home

eight days to full moon

The television inside the gas station has Ethan's family plastered all over it, the gossip reporter gushing about them. Nightfall is imminent, the last rays of light streaming above the dilapidated building. Neon signs inside boast nachos and beer, and I'd availed myself of the former. It was just bagged tortilla chips and yellow cheese sauce from a machine that looked like it was from the Seventies, but I inhaled them nonetheless.

Wedding of the century. The White family and the Carter family, to be joined at last! The glass door covered with dozens of cigarette brand stickers of the gas station is propped open, letting the voice of the woman on the TV out into the waning day, and the cooler night air in.

Well, that was fast. They only waited a few weeks. I say to my wolf if only to pass the time. Something about pumping gas tonight feels like the slowest activity on the planet.

Did you really expect any less?

No... I wonder if she got pregnant.

My phone already has several missed calls from my mother on it. None from Ethan. Not that he is even able to call me. I'd immediately blocked each and every member of the White family, and as a rule, I do not answer unknown numbers.

Sucks to be her. My wolf remarks.

Yeah...

I've been staying in motels, eating my weight in pizzas and takeout since leaving. I'd stop at a rest area now and again in the middle of the night, letting my wolf out to prowl. Full Moon had been challenging, but I'd ended up running from Yosemite down to Sequoia, trying to stay away from all the other packs. Though, not far from dawn I did finally let loose the mournful howl that had been building in my throat all night. Every single wolf that was out in the park howled back.

Where are you? We welcome you. Come, Come. An invitation to run with their Pack. Something had cracked inside me that night.

A wolf isn't supposed to run alone. After a time, they say it can break something in you. A Wolf doesn't go rabid or anything, but we are told that if you run without a Pack for too long, your wolf will change. When I'd first left Timber Hollow, I bounced from Pack to Pack, moving through the land like a ghost. I hadn't managed to find anywhere where I fit in. Sure, there were friends in those places I'd regretfully had to leave behind, but they weren't *my* Pack. At this point, it's been two years since I've joined a Pack Run.

My wolf is the same as always though, so I don't know how much I believed the tales anymore. But still, the way the Packs howled back to me in the last hours of the night under the full Moon had tugged at something in me. Cracking through all the walls I'd slowly built up around myself.

I've been roaming, wandering since leaving Ethan because I didn't have an exact destination in mind... Until now. *Now* I know where I want to go.

Where *my wolf* wants to go.

She misses home. Misses the trees. Misses our *Pack*.

I left home right after graduating high school. Disappeared one day, and never looked back. I have no idea who still lived there if my old friends had moved on. Or if I even really wanted to look up my old friends. I'd only kept contact with one person, my Dad's sister, Aggie.

Others had my number, like my mom. I never manage to pick up their phone calls, though.

Aggie had been supportive of my choice, once I'd called her- *three thousand miles* away from home. Even if it meant more risk of exposure for me, without the safety of the pack, Aggie supported me. She understood my desire to leave and had done it herself when she was much younger. However, her trip didn't take her nearly as far away from home, *and* she hadn't stayed away for quite as long. Hadn't disappeared without warning. While hunting wolves isn't as common these days... There are still poachers out there who would love nothing more than to have a great big wolf hide on their wall.

Grabbing my phone from my back pocket, I call her while I lean against my stolen ride pumping gas. I am going to miss this car whenever Ethan comes looking for it.

It is only a matter of time before he comes for the car, one of his treasures for him and him alone to touch... And, I am surprised no one has come looking for the heirloom diamond that currently sits inside its box somewhere in the depths of my backpack. I'd been told that the ugly gemstone had been in the family for generations when it was presented to me in that restaurant. And since Ethan's sisters-in-law *apparently* hadn't wanted the large canary diamond cut into a baguette with chocolate diamonds on the side, (*couldn't imagine why, the thing vaguely looked like a piss dick*) Ethan had been allowed to give it to me.

Hopefully, I'd be within shifter territory by then. It wouldn't change much, other than making me feel even minutely more in control. My rambling thoughts are cut off when the ringing ceases.

"Artemis, my love," Aggie answers on the second ring.

"Hey, Aggie." I've called her Aggie ever since I was a kid because I couldn't pronounce Agnes. At this point calling her anything else seemed like calling her by something that wasn't her name. She is Aggie. Simple as that. Not that my mom had ever stopped trying to get me to call her *Aunt Agnes*.

"Awfully late for a chit-chat, isn't it?" She says, and I have to do the mental math to determine what time it was back home.

Where am I anyway?

Nevada.

Shit, it is 2 AM over there.

"Yea. But I have a good reason." I say, feeling the gas pump kick off, signaling the full tank.

"Oh yeah, what's that love?" She sounds curious.

"I'm coming home," I reply, replacing the gas pump to its holster. I'm glad I've already gone inside for road snacks, Aggie can talk in circles like nobody's business.

"Oh, how nice!" She gushes, and I can practically feel her vibrating with barely restrained glee at the mere prospect of my return.

"I need a place to stay. I'm *not* going to Mom's." I say before she can begin her tirade. I love her, but god sometimes she'd talk you into the grave.

"How long until you get here?" She asks, and I hear her shuffling papers in the background, probably looking for the classified ads. Aggie lives in a tiny little cabin, just big enough for her.

"Four or five days? Depending on the weather."

"I'll see what I can do. Do you need a job too? I have a friend in Somerville that needs a bartender. Nights." Aggie asks all business.

I sigh, running a hand through my hair. "Yeah, might just as well." I have some money saved, but I don't want to live off of it... *anymore* that is. I should probably dye my hair too. Get rid of this fucking bleached mess.

"Everything okay?" Aggie asks, the simple question feeling far heavier than it would any other day.

I sigh again. "Yea. Everything's fine." Well, I am returning to the place I'd sworn never to return to with my tail tucked between my legs, but *everything's fine.*

"You know you can tell me anything, right?"

"I know, Aggie. I know." I try to keep the exhaustion from my voice.

"Well let me make some calls, you be safe okay? Don't take any risks you shouldn't." A.k.a. don't shift if you don't have to. The Full Moon is a ways away yet. I'd be within the shifter community soon. And then I could shift all I wanted to. *Whenever* I wanted to.

"Okay. Thank you, Aggie." I say, lowering myself into the front seat after shuffling a bag of sweet chili Doritos, a bottle of Gatorade, *and* a Redbull out of the seat. I'd just tossed them into the car through the open window before pumping gas.

Aggie ends the call, likely noticing my distraction, after saying her goodbyes, *see you soon*, and *I'll have everything sorted by the time you get here.* That was what I liked about Aggie. She never hovers. She knows I can take care of myself. Knew I'd been doing it since Dad died.

Driving away from the gas station, I can't explain why I feel like going home is…

Like surrendering.

5
Bloody Paws

Full Moon

My first stop once I am back inside the official town limits of Timber Hollow is Aggie's cabin. It's about dusk, cars leaving shifter territory one by one as they venture out into the bigger city we neighbor, Sommerville. The nightlife of Timber Hollow is nearly non-existent *unless* you count stripping naked in front of your friends and running through the trees in wolf form.

Personally, I feel like that should count.

The town is a safe place to live though, tucked away in the woods. Protected in more ways than one.

Aggie's cabin has a brightly painted door, a bold streak of pink in the forest that is otherwise slowly turning its green leaves orange and red one by one. I know Aggie is inside, bustling around her kitchen. Pots and pans clang together audibly even out here.

She's expecting me, so I just open the door, striding on in. Dear Aggie presents me with a freshly baked loaf of banana bread as soon as I step foot into her little one-story cabin. Her place has always felt like home, sometimes more than my own house did. Arms laden with *more* banana bread, she steers me towards the kitchen table. She hasn't replaced it, or even sanded it and revarnished... All the little dings and scratches from the past are still visible in the wood. A bowl of deep purple grapes sits centered on the wood surface, a stack of papers and a set of keys beside them. Once seated in the high back chair, I descend upon the bread, smearing butter across thick, warm slices while she gives me directions to the bar where I am supposed to be working for the foreseeable future.

I have no idea how long it's been since I've had something baked like this... *Intentionally* for me, because Aggie knows I love *her* banana bread. She doesn't ruin it with chocolate or nuts. Not to mention the fact that the White household doesn't cook things like that. Gluten *and* sugar in one dish? The Corgi would blow a gasket.

"It's in Somerville, just off of the old mine route. It's been there ages, you know where I'm talking about?" Aggie asks me, and then keeps talking, seeing me attempt to open my mouth and respond, even if it is stuffed full of banana bread. Honestly, I am only really half listening. I pay attention to the important bits, like when I am supposed to report for my first shift. And that Coyote Bill- *the original,* and his family are Shifters. That's how Aggie knows the owner.

Coyote Bills. I'd heard the older crowd talk about the place as a kid. It is supposed to be *the* place for entertainment if you are under the age of sixty. The bartenders there are all girls, and *naturally* once a week the bartenders do a dance routine- in chaps, on top of the bar. Sometimes they even light it on fire.

Or, at least that's what the rumors said.

When I left Timber Hollow all those years ago, I made my way across the States by bartending. I stayed in the forests for as long as I could, seeking out packs nearby. They found me jobs, usually at their establishments. At first, it was just little hole-in-the-wall dive bars where all they served was draft and bottles.

Those packs weren't nearly as large as Timber Hollow's. Eventually, I made my way up to the fancier places– and larger packs. Some of those places had a dress code and overpriced mixed drinks on the menu. For *years,* I did it over, and over again until I landed in Malibu California, and into Ethan's lap. Coyote Bill's wouldn't be any different than any number of those bars.

Well. Maybe a little different. I've never danced on top of the bar while it was on fire.

That's not true. My wolf remarks, barely a whisper of thought through my consciousness.

You know, I think you're right.

I'd forgotten about the seedy little bar in Denver, run by one of the many packs that could be found in the wastes that define the Midwest. I definitely did end up dancing on the bar there, but I hadn't *lit* the fire. *That* had been a *complete accident.*

Sure, A complete accident that you dropped the flaming zippo onto the alcohol-covered bar top. She snorts again.

Okay, sure... But, that was because Cindy Lache was flirting with my at the time *friends with benefits situationship*, that *she* had set me up with. I'd seen them kiss while I was hopping up on the bar.

Yeah. Complete accident. I agree.

When I ran into Ethan at an antique car show *everything* changed. Of course, we had been there for separate reasons—he was *shopping,* and I was killing time until I had to go to work. Which, coincidentally, had been the first desk job I ever had. Nights at a 1-800 customer service line were a previously undiscovered circle of hell. I'd pay good money to subject a few people to that fate.

After a few weeks of messing around with Ethan, and then spending all day together, *all the time*, I thought I'd been in love. And then he proposed. And then his mother told me not so subtly that the women's job in the White family was to make connections, and birth sons to their husbands. Then Ethan started encouraging me to leave my desk job.

Of course, *like the dumbass I am, I listened* to him.

Which meant 24/7 at the White Estate, something I now determine to be another undiscovered circle of hell. The fucking *worst* of them. Sure, there were unending amounts of things to do- you could go ride horses, or play golf, or tennis or basketball, or fucking racquetball, or any of the other multitude of other bullshit sports things rich people do.

But, go for a 5-mile walk by yourself every day? You're batshit *insane.*

What it had meant, however, was that while my TBR was endless- so was the funding to purchase those books. *That* had been the hardest part of leaving. At first, I'd only gotten myself the stray paperback, and then months went on and no one said anything about the deliveries of books that were seemingly endless, so I said *fuck it*. In the year of my engagement to Ethan, I had amassed a small fortune worth of special editions, and multiple sets of some of my favorites. Too many had been left behind. What had fit in the trunk were my *absolute* favorites–prized possessions even. And, of course, a dismal few from my TBR.

My saving grace in leaving Ethan is that he has no idea that I had saved every single coin I could manage before we got together. I've amassed a nice little sum of money, enough for someone like me to live on for quite some time. What I'd nabbed from Ethan's safe is just icing on the cake. Not to mention that cash is far less traceable than using the sum of money in my bank account. Now that I'm home though, it would be fine.

With a mental nudge from my wolf, I tune back into the conversation with Aggie.

"You'll be staying over at the old Grimes place. You remember?" She pauses, grabbing a grape from the bowl in front of us. I nod in return. My best friend from high school lived there. "Well, it's an apartment now. You'll be in Marcus' room, but I can't get the keys until the Monday after next, so until then it's just like old times." Aggie says, smiling brightly at me. I used to come to stay with her when my brother and sister were ganging up on me.

Even staying on Aggie's pull-out was better than going to Mom's. Marcus was my cousin- *loosely*. There are a handful of shared relatives between us. While in school we hadn't talked though.

Nothing like going from living in an *almost* mansion to having roommates at 24.

Satisfied that I knew where I was going to live and where I was going to work, Aggie launches her gossip tirade, giving me all the ins and outs of the town while I dig into the second loaf of banana bread. It's still warm, and so delicious I know I won't need to hunt tonight. My wolf has all the calories she needs, now.

I learn that Marcus is going to be gone for a few months on an oil rigger, and Aggie has swooped in at just the right time. Barely home an hour, and I have a job and a place to stay.

Do I have a plan?

Nope.

Do I have any idea of what I am fucking doing?

Double nope.

Maybe Aggie had said who my roommates are to be, and I wasn't listening, but I guess it doesn't really matter anyway. From what I understand, we will have opposite schedules. I am about to start working nights, and they all have day jobs within the village or the town over.

I'm back home, in Timber Hollow with a fancy car that isn't mine, and the past nipping at my heels.

"Why aren't you running tonight?" I ask, directing the conversation off of myself. The Moon calls to me, even now. I want to *run*.

"These bones are too old to keep up with you youngsters." Aggie winks, and immediately I understand why. She might be telling *part* of the truth, but I know she truly stayed behind to see me.

"Did you already go out?"

"Yeah, when the Moon first rose. Caught a rabbit." She says, then adds "Your mom went with me, has been for some time now."

"So she won't be out with the pack?"

"No, she and Athena still go together. Your mother developed a conscience I guess and doesn't want to let me go by myself." Aggie snarks, and I huff a laugh, wondering if that conscience would extend to me.

Finally, when Aggie lets me leave, stuffed full of *three* loaves of banana bread, I exit her kitchen and walk around back using the pavers she'd laid in the grass when I was barely old enough to shift. Clovers grow between the stones, rather than grass. Seeded at the same time as the pavers. It smells vaguely like vanilla back here, the last few of the yellow flowers slowly shriveling, drying up in the early autumn chill.

Shifter babies are supernatural even as toddlers, we grow up with our wolves inside. Thankfully, though, the shift never comes until we're around nine. By then the kids are all half feral with the need to *run,* and chase the Moonlight between the trees.

The first shift is always the hardest. We're clamoring to run, full of energy. But the instinctual surrender to the wolf takes time, to let it come forth, freed from its cage. My first official shift had been born from loneliness- and had been earlier than my siblings. With Dad gone, no one knew how to talk to me anymore.

Timber Hollow was surrounded on three sides by state land- *shifter* land. Just walking the path, my wolf rises. She's clawing at my soul, clamoring to be let *out* as I rip my oversized hoodie over my head.

She knows these lands, these trees.

Home.

We are home.

For me, it has always been easy. I'd never been afraid of her. Inhaling the crisp air, then I sink beneath the soft, dark fur that belongs to my wolf. Even now, shifting for me is a *surrender*. Surrender of control, of desires, of *everything*. Once a shifter surrenders that control, the beast emerges.

Surrender and submission come with razor-sharp teeth, and snarls in the face of death. There is nothing to fear when the wolf emerges.

The actual transformation is brutal. Limbs snap and rearrange. The skull shifts, breaking. Teeth elongate and sharpen.

It's excruciating, *exquisite* pain.

And then, *freedom*.

The Quaking Aspen tree that used to be only as thick as maybe my bicep is now nearly the size of my thigh, and triple the height.

The white bark still has a blue jay roughly carved into it, plump breast speared by an arrow.

I drop my hoodie at the base of the tree, kicking off my boots with a toe. When I toss my phone down, the screen illuminates for a moment revealing 3 missed calls from Sam before it disappears within the wrinkled fabric. Leggings are shucked off, underwear is dropped in the pile as well.

Inhale.

Exhale.

Surrender.

My wolf comes rushing forward, a flurry of transformation, cracking, splintering pops coming from my bones, and then I am covered in fur, driven by the need to run. To chase the Moonlight between the trees.

With the Moon as my guide, I retrace decades-old footsteps and darken the places my heart still pangs for within the trees. Like the stream that sometimes runs dry in the very hot summer months, and the pool of water below.

I run and I run, until I feel like my lungs will burst and my paws are bloody, hoping that my time at Aggie's will disguise my scent enough to remain undetected for just a little longer.

The wolves of Timber Hollow come in all shades of brown, and grey, and some even with a reddish tint to their fur. My wolf is entirely black, much to the surprise of my mother. My siblings have bleach blonde hair, their wolves varying shades of white and grey. While my hair is still *technically* blonde, it is darker than all of theirs. Just like Dad's. I still remember when my wolf emerged, black as the night sky, nearly blending into the darkness between the trees.

Just like Dad.

I don't think I'll ever forget the keening howl that ripped from my mom's throat that night, and how the Pack had echoed the mournful sound into the morning. It's branded into my soul.

Timber Hollow, of course, isn't exclusive to wolves. There are a few coyote shifters and even a lynx family here too. Probably more these days. The Pack has grown, likely only noticeable to someone who's been gone for so long.

The Alpha, though, is a wolf. Magnus Temple runs the pack. He is also sort of our mayor, but his control runs deeper than that. The Temples have been the Alphas of Timber Hollow since the pack's beginning. They started the logging business, way back when the town was founded. That business now funds the majority of the town's expenses. Government contracts for the environmentally conscious logging combined with the handmade- wood carvings that nearly every wolf in Timber Hollow worked at – at least once in their life- make up the majority of the town's income. The Temple family also has a Forge, where at one time they made horseshoes and weapons for the town. Now it churns out handmade gold and silver jewelry, each piece worth a small fortune.

Leaving Timber Hollow wasn't against the rules- it was recommended that every wolf gets a taste of the wide open areas of the world, before choosing where to start their own pack. We're all told that we'd be welcome within the arms of other packs, that even if you were just visiting it is important to join the monthly run. They hadn't told us what to do if the Pack didn't feel right, though. If the thought of running with another Pack felt like betraying your own soul. Like ripping out your own beating heart.

I'm pretty sure that I am the only one to stay gone for more than half a decade. And have absolutely *nothing* to show for it.

6
Fries with Gravy on the Side

seventeen days to full moon

Aggie gave me the keys tonight after dinner, and I promptly loaded my meager belongings into the car. Of course, that ever-present itch to run, to slip between the trees, calls me into the forest first.

So, at two am when I finally darken the doorstep of my new living quarters, I'm glad a mere piece of paper greets me. It's taped to the post at the bottom of the stairway, informing me which room is mine.

With just a backpack and a duffle, I silently make my way up the stairs, groaning at the sight of the unmade bed. There is a pile of sheets folded neatly at the end, though. I close the door silently, then make my bed and climb into it.

Sleep overcomes me like a sheet pulled over my eyes.

When my alarm wakes me, the house is still silent. Empty. *Fine by me*.

It barely takes me twenty minutes to shower and get dressed before slipping out of the door and into the Corvette that I had parked across the street. In the light of day though, the lot in front of the house looks big enough for a handful of cars. And there aren't any potholes, so the Stingray should be fine. Before I go to work, I stop at the gas station, and then the supermarket to pick up a couple of things I can stock up on now.

Living out of a hotel room isn't half bad, but it does get old after a while. My trip to the supermarket is quick, I don't buy anything that won't last in the car until my shift is over.

When I pull up to the bar, the parking lot is packed, dusk descending through the trees. The front doors are open to the night air, and a pair of bouncers are out front checking IDs. Winding my way through customers towards the bar, looking for someone who looked like a manager. Instinctually I know it's going to be a *long*, long night. It's packed with patrons, and it seems like one of the two bartenders... Doesn't exactly know what they are doing.

On top of that, bottles of liquor are strewn and thrown haphazardly on the shelves, mixers are left out of the coolers. Dirty dishes piling up on the bar.

When I give my name to a human by the name of George, he in turn gives me directions on how to operate the POS to ring in drinks and food. How to clock in, what to do in the case of a fight- holler for the bouncers first, cops second. The boss is out for a few, but he'll introduce us shortly. The whole time, the guy is shouting to be heard over the jukebox, voice straining and crackling. I wish I could have told him I could hear him fine, *without the shouting* -thanks.

George showed me where the backstock of beer and liquor was, where the bathrooms were, and the location of the aluminum baseball bats beneath the bar, should I need it. And then, he promptly began gathering dishes and left me to it.

One bartender had on the same black t-shirt with the logo on it as George, though his looked practically new in comparison. I noticed everyone had the same branded bottle openers tucked in their back pockets.

The blonde bartender behind the bar with me had on a bikini top and jeans, her Coyote Bill's t-shirt cut wide around the arms, cropped short. Her blonde hair was curled with cowboy boots on her feet. She was beautiful, with her bright blue eyes and creamy skin, not a single freckle in sight. She appeared to know what she was doing, with how fast she was slinging drinks out.

Aggie hadn't mentioned a uniform last night so I'd shown up in cut-off jean shorts, and a white cropped tee, despite the autumnal chill in the air. Trusty checkered vans on my feet to get me through the night. The addition of a bottle opener didn't really *feel* like an official uniform, but *whatever*. Maybe I'll get the T-shirt later, but regardless I am glad to not be in pants tonight, with how thick the air feels.

Well, nothing to it, but to do it.

Fighting my way through the crowd to get back behind the bar, I start my first shift. This part of bartending is always the same.

'What are you drinking?' 'That'll be four fifty.' Over and over again, I take orders, dutifully hand out change, and open up tabs. Mix drinks behind the bar. Smile at the patrons of Coyote Bills.

I am taller than each of the other bartenders, by a few inches. A woman with an apron on came and got glassware, disappearing out back again within seconds. The blonde and I worked pretty well together, and I'm also pretty sure George told me the names of everyone already, but I must not have been paying attention.

I don't imagine you happened to have been paying attention? I ask my wolf.

Nope.

When it is my turn for a break around nine-thirty, I grab my small backpack and head out the back doors beyond the small kitchen to the parking lot, asking the cook for an order of fries, *gravy on the side please* as I pass.

A single hand raised into the air tells me he heard my request.

The air is crisp, and invigorating. September has cooled the August heat. Even as a Leo- a summer baby I love when the air turns, changing the greenery into a landscape of orange, yellow, and red. The colors of the fire that live in my gut.

Or so the astrologers say.

The night air is a perfect balm for the sweat coating my skin. Breathing slowly, I absorb the light of the Moon.

She is new, barely visible. Just a small crescent shape hanging high in the sky. Another few weeks until she's Full, and the Pack run.

My luck so far has been great. The Pack has not sniffed me out yet, despite my frequent runs through the forest. It'd been long enough since I left, I guessed, long enough that there was no one left who would recognize my scent.

Even so, *someone* must be aware of my presence here. I'd left a literal blood trail to Aggie's doorstep.

Until someone makes me go see the Alpha, I'm merely biding my time. Timber Hollow had once been my home... I'm not sure if I can still say that about the town. The forest, though...that would *always* be my home. Once upon a time, no one in the Pack had known these trees better than me.

The door to my left creaked open, the older cook holding a tray of fries with a side of gravy out to me, like a peace offering.

"Thanks." I smile, taking the tray from him.

"Sure thing, Darlin'." The old man has the voice of someone who grew up in the South but had managed to travel enough that the majority of the southern drawl has vanished. It is always there on the *'Darlin's* he'd handed out like candy to all us bartenders though. The cook wears a black apron that covers him from neck to shin, leathery skin full of faded tattoos. I'm sure he has a name, but I've only heard him referred to as Cook. Nothing else.

The door slams shut when he ducks back inside.

I have another fifteen minutes to eat these fries, and then I have another four hours of bartending to get through.

And another run, right?

And another run.

As it turns out, George doesn't need to introduce me to the owner, as the door creaks open once more.

I'd learned the owner of the bar is named Ivy from the blonde bartender, Angel. I am taller than her, but it isn't by much. Ivy has dark eyes and dark hair loosely braided down her back. The turquoise earrings dangling from her ears look to be handmade. She wears leggings and a Coyote Bills tee, feet tucked into lavender Converse.

"Hey, I'm Artemis. Want some?" I greet her, holding the plate of fries out to her like an offering. She laughs, taking a french fry from the plate and dunking it into gravy.

"Ivy. You're Agnes' niece, right?" She replies, putting the whole french fry in her mouth.

"That's me."

Wasting exactly zero time, Ivy launches into what must be her new hire speech. "Ground rules? Don't fuck the patrons while you're on the clock okay? Fights break out and shit gets busted, and then I have to fire people. Don't steal, don't lie, and don't be a dick to your coworkers. Simple, right?"

"Exceedingly," I answer.

"We're usually closed for the full Moon- so don't worry about losing control or anything like that."

I blink in surprise. Even the bars that I worked at all those years ago were open on full Moon.

"You're a shifter too?" I ask, expecting her to agree.

"Obviously. Black Bear. You?"

I grin. "Black wolf."

"From Timber Hollow? That's rare." Ivy sings as if I'm not aware of that.

"I've been gone for a while," I say, directing the conversation away from the shade of my fur.

"Agnes said as much," Ivy replies. Hearing someone call Aggie by her full name feels foreign... Strange.

"How do you know Aggie?"

"She was a friend to my Uncle. Came to the funeral when he passed and helped me out a little with getting my bearings with all this." Ivy says, gesturing behind her, and the exterior of the bar we lean against.

"Aggie's good like that," I reply, and Ivy makes a sound of agreement in her throat, taking another french fry. My phone buzzes in my pocket, and when I take it out it reveals a weather update for the evening.

"Shit," I hiss, seeing the time on my phone, and realizing that it is well past time for me to return from break. My plate of fries is barely half eaten, my stomach still painfully empty. "I have to get back in there," I say to Ivy, pushing off of the wall.

"No, you don't. New hire orientation with the boss." She winks at me, snagging another french fry. "I have more fries coming out too."

Right then, I feel it in my soul that Ivy and I? We are going to get along *great*.

Angel, the blonde, was supposed to close down Coyote Bills with Ivy, but she had some family emergency so I offered to help Ivy do it. I've done it countless times at other bars, so how different would it really be? Overhead lights illuminate the space, walls decorated with vintage signs and license plates. Neon signs with the bar's name are now dimmed, their humming silenced. Music still plays, though at a considerably lower volume than during business hours.

I collect bottles and cups that remain scattered around the bar, depositing them next to the sink where Ivy is washing and rinsing.

After I pull bags out of trash cans, I take them out the back exit, remembering the dumpster underneath the power line from earlier. We had deposited the paper tray and remnants of our fries into it hours ago.

A row of floodlights encircle the entire bar. They look new, and the hum of electricity from all the lights shining at once is practically deafening in the otherwise silent night. When Ivy and I had been out back here, they'd been considerably less bright. When I go back inside, I find Ivy out from behind the bar, a rag in one hand, and a spray bottle in the other.

"Bright as shit out there," I say to Ivy, chuckling as I walk over to the sink to wash my hands, they'd gotten sticky from the bottles I'd picked up from a hidden corner on my way back in here. Fuck if I knew what the fuck had been on them if it wasn't just beer or juice.

Whatever the stickiness was, I don't want it on my hands anymore.

"I don't want any of the human women feeling sketchy outside in the dark. That's all." She replies, shrugging while she wipes down tables. We've already restocked beers in the coolers, wines, and mixers.

Yep. That makes sense. "I thought they looked new. Nice." I say, just to make sure she knows I'm not trying to be an ass. I've never worked at a bar that was illuminated so well while I closed. The other two bartenders are also human, so I appreciate Ivy's efforts to keep her staff safe.

I grab a rag from the pile, and the other bottle of sanitizer and set about wiping the other half of the tables. Ivy had told me earlier that we don't need to touch the bathrooms. She has a cleaning crew come in every morning before opening because she *hates* cleaning bathrooms.

Thank fucking god. I hate it too.

And that is it for my first shift at Coyote Bills. I learned that the original Bill was a coyote shifter- *big surprise,* and had left the bar to his favorite niece, Ivy. She has some plans for the place, weekly events like fire night to keep the business fresh, and to increase the revenue on nights that *weren't* fire night. She doesn't want the bar, her uncle's legacy, to remain a little hole-in-the-wall dive bar forever. She wants to update the decor a little, less cobwebs. Small things like those, would potentially help the business thrive. I think Ivy is a genius, and I want to help.

So, with butterflies in my stomach, I suggested slap shots and had the delight of explaining what they were while we were wiping tables.

Patrons line up for a slap in the face and a shot from a hot bartender. Maybe throw in a little praise for good measure. Ivy *loved* it. We are going to do it tomorrow night at Fire Night, as a soft launch. I have such a good feeling about this place. About Ivy.

I leave Coyote Bills much, much later after closing. Ivy and I have so much in common, that it had been hard to stop talking, once we got started. So many hopes and dreams in common, and similar tastes in books. All her ideas on how to turn this place into something *more* inspired me. Made me think that maybe Timber Hollow wouldn't be so bad, after all.

Now, I am pulled over on the scenic overlook just outside of Timber Hollow. I feel... Hopeful. More hopeful than I've been in a long, long time.

Hope is a silent killer. I could only *hope* that it won't come for me.

Guided by the Moon I shift once more, surrender to the beast inside, and run through the trees. Down the path to the waterfall, through the clearing. Around the small lake, tucked away in the woods.

And even later, standing on a rocky outcropping I hear the pack.

My pack.

Howling into the night. Running with joy, *together*. All of them out there, happy…Without me.

Something cracks, something fragile breaks loose deep within me.

Will they even accept me back? After all this time?

7
Welcome Home, Artemis

new moon

The sound of someone sneezing downstairs rouses me from a deep, *deep* slumber. Probably one of the maids.

The room is gloriously dark, warm arms cradle my body. Slowly, awareness of my limbs comes to me. A leg was thrown over Ethan's hip, the other wedged between his legs.

One hand is wrapped around my front, pressed against my throat, thumb resting on my pulse point. The other is dipped below the waistline of my underwear, fingertips hooked on my hip bone. Heat spools low in my middle. Breathing slowly, deeply, I shift, snuggling back into the large, warm frame of Ethan, smirking when I feel his cock pulse against my hip.

Ethan?

I jolt awake, adrenaline spearing through me as I whip the blankets off. Who the fuck I am next to—*on top of*—I can't say. Whoever it is, though, is half naked, and *gloriously* hung, if the impression of his thick dick against my hip is any indication. After work, I had crawled into my bed in only an old threadbare tank top and underwear. Apparently, I had been tired enough to forget to lock my door.

"Who the fuck are you?" I screech, reaching down under my pillow as I spring off of the bed. On instinct I flip the knife open, holding it so that the blade is tucked against the inside of my arm, out of sight.

"Who the fuck am I? Who the fuck are *you*?" The man says in a gravely sleepy voice, throwing covers off of himself with a heavily tattooed, muscled arm. *I know that voice.*

"Oh, fuck me sideways," is all I manage to croak as I lock eyes with the one person I haven't let myself even consider running into. He isn't supposed to be here.

How was he **here**? *In my fucking bed of all places?*

Jay's hair is stuck up at all angles, and sleepy eyes that can never really decide if they want to be blue or green are staring straight through me. Like they always do.

"Artemis." He says my name, clearing his throat and I am instantly transported back into the terrified body of seventeen-year-old me, listening to him talk to his friends about me. About *us.*

A heartbeat passes, and yet it feels like I'm reliving every single moment I've ever spent with him.

We were always running hot and cold, constantly fluctuating between friends, and *more.* The truth is Jay had been my best friend before he was anything else. Anything *more.* Even when it was more, we were on, then off, then on again like the world was on fire.

Fighting, kissing. Laughing. Running. Fucking.

There was that summer when my mom had paid attention to me long enough to see the bite mark on the back of my shoulder from Jay. We'd been running in the fields together, and I'd made him chase me. The result was that my shoulder had the imprint of his wolfish teeth for *weeks.*

Sometimes, I swear the silvery scars are still there when the light catches my skin just right.

My mom, dear Darla, had warned me that what we were doing was *more* than just teenage love. I never did tell her that I'd bitten him back, and had drawn blood.

And then there was that winter when I was sure he hated me. The year I ran around town with the boys he wasn't friends with. I'd never seen Jay as jealous as the year I hung out with Brody Williams.

I'll never forget Graduation weekend. I hadn't even walked across the stage, shaken hands with the principal, or thrown my cap up in the air with everyone else. I'd been long gone by then. Dropped contact with everyone—except Aggie—and disappeared into the night like smoke.

"Jay." I croak. Those fucking eyes are like a sucker punch to the gut. Tattoos crawl up his arms now, spreading across his chest and up his neck. Even his face is decorated with them close to his ear. The marking almost.... Looks like an arrow.

"What are you doing here?" Jay asks, shifting on the bed. The now entirely *too small* bed.

"This is my room." Adrenaline still courses through my veins. An air conditioner compressor kicks on somewhere in the house, filling the silence with dull roaring.

I am *positive* Jay can hear my heart thumping in my chest. The muscles on his jaw feather, and his Adam's apple bobs.

My mouth waters.

"This is *Marcus'* room, and he's gone for a few months. How'd you get in?" Jay corrects, eyes flicking down my body and back to my face. A flash of heat goes straight through me, pebbling my nipples under the thin tank top I wear. I fight the blush that rises to my cheeks.

I don't think I am successful.

"I'm renting," I reply, feeling like I am poised on the edge of a blade, placing all my weight down. Letting the blade bite into my skin, rather than choose which way to go. With just my name, tumbling from his lips Jay reopened that old ragged wound. I hadn't realized it would reopen so easily.

A slow, lazy smile stretches across Jay's face, and I can't decide if I want to wipe it off or see where it leads. Once upon a time, trouble followed a smirk like that.

Raising on all fours, he crawls across the small bed, putting his feet down on either side of mine, where I stand with my back flush against the still bare bookshelves. I stay still as stone, watching him with half-lidded eyes. My heartbeat ratchets up, and my lungs feel entirely too small.

What is he doing?

Then, Jay reaches out with both thick arms, bracing them on either side of my face on the shelf behind me. Instinctually, I raise my knife, holding it against his neck.

Jay doesn't slow his advance, just keeps coming at me, letting me decide if I am going to let him move, or if I'd stop him with the blade at his throat. I let him come, only stopping him when he put his face so close to mine that I could smell the tequila on his breath from the night before. A single drop of blood wells at the tip of the blade.

"Welcome home, Artemis." Jay finally says, flicking his eyes down once more before he pushes away. Then he is gone. Gone like smoke between my fingers. I deflate, letting the bookshelf take all of my weight.

"Fuck." I bang my head against the bookshelf twice for good measure, then push off of it. I need a *motherfucking shower*. And then, I have to get ready to go to work.

The shower does nothing to cool my heated skin. Does *nothing* to relax the tension in my shoulders, in my core.

My wolf is restless. Now more than she'd ever been, even within the confines of the city. She is *excited* about the tension between Jay and I.

As I dress, I keep racking my brain as to *how the hell* I woke up in Jay's arms. Clearly, he knows this was Marcus' room, even if Marcus didn't have so much as even a poster on the wall. So *why* was Jay in the bed?

My hair is still wet, the bleached ends of it making me grit my teeth as I dutifully apply eyeliner, the wing sharp enough to cut a man. Mascara on curled lashes, bronzer, and highlighter to accentuate my cheekbones.

Then I clip a silver chain choker around my neck. A quick rough blowdry is enough to make my wavy hair manageable. It'll air-dry the rest of the way.

I need to pick up hair dye though. Like, *immediately.*

Tonight is fire night, where George lights the bartop on fire with the cheap liquor. On those nights there is a *slight* dress code. Pants and boots are required. On my first night there, I quickly discovered that Coyote Bills had shit for air conditioning, just a few fans in prime locations. October seems right around the corner, but Summer has risen for one last hurrah, scorching the Earth for the last few days. It is going to be fucking *hot* in there tonight, even without the fire.

So in accordance, I just grab a little black bodysuit that is entirely backless but is high-necked in the front. It leaves most of my rib exposed and will dip beneath the waistband of whatever pants I choose in a v shape.

Eventually, I settle on black jeans, sliding my already socked feet into combat boots, tucking the laces in so I won't have to replace them.

I haven't been able to dress like this- like *myself* in a while. Cordelia once told me that the Whites do not dress like harlots, and forbade me from wearing outfits like this while I was in public with one of them. Which meant having my wardrobe pre-approved by Cordelia's stylist. Only then could I choose my clothes.

Looking back, I want to shake myself. What *in the actual fucking hell was wrong with me*? I let them change so much of me. Had let them consume everything that made me, *me*, allowed them to mold and push me into their image of perfection.

I am sure that if Cordelia had been aware of the specific outfit I'd been wearing when her son asked me out, the engagement would have been called off in a millisecond. As it is, she'd have a coronary just picturing the short, tight black dress with mesh inserts all down the sides I wore to our date. Perhaps I'd have to dig that dress out and wear it if I ever saw the old hag again.

Turning away from my reflection I make my way out of the little room, into the house itself. According to the rental agreement, it is a *shared space*. My room is my own, but everything else is shared. I've only really come in, slept, and left. I hadn't even bothered to snoop around because of exhaustion.

Amazing timing for morals, Artemis.

The kitchen is full to the brim with bodies. Jay, a pair of men I'm not familiar with- *and* Jay's brother. A shower is running somewhere else in the house, so apparently this isn't everyone.

A glance at the clock on the wall tells me I need to rush to leave to get to work on time.

Fuck.

Everyone freezes as I move into the kitchen. I really don't have time for introductions, so I just make my way through them. Or try to anyway.

"Hellloooo, if I could just scoot-" I say, skirting around the tallest one with curly blonde hair and amused green eyes peeking out beneath the messy locks. He doesn't move an inch, making me brush the bare skin of his chest as I go past. He's leaning against the island, somehow taking up *all* the space around him.

"Asshole," I mumble, someone snorts and then starts coughing. My eyes snap to Jay's as he mops coffee off of his shirt.

"Well, hello, Tiny. *Nice to meet you too,*" The blonde says, chuckling. A half smile stretches his face, the bulging muscles on his arms are covered in ropy veins. A thin sheen of sweat covers his skin, but he smells clean, like the Sun. Not freshly showered clean- but he didn't reek like alcohol like Jay had either.

"Fuck you, I am not *tiny*," I shoot back, opening the fridge and disappearing into it to find the Red Bull I'd stashed there last night. Jay groans behind me, and I ignore the shiver of pleasure, the reminder of what it felt like to be wrapped up with him in bed.

"Oh, *yes* baby." I coo, unearthing the can of liquid crack from under a plastic takeout bag, popping the tab, and immediately sucking down a few mouthfuls. Almost all eyes are on me as I hip-check the fridge door closed.

Jay, his blue eyes trace down the line of my ribs.

The blonde wears a wolfish grin as he leans against the counter, corded arms crossed in front of his bare chest.

And the silent one with close-clipped black hair, a three-day beard covering his chin, and skin the color of midnight has mischief dancing in his grey eyes.

Jay clears his throat, raising a hand to introduce me. "Guys, this is Artemis. She's subletting from Marcus while he's away."

The two nod their heads, murmuring a "Hello."

"Artemis, this is Saint and Dante," Jay says, gesturing to the blonde first, then the other one. "And you remember my brother Alex."

"Alex, nice to see you," I say, smiling sweetly at him. Alex and I hadn't interacted much when I was in high school. He'd been in a higher grade, and far outside my circle of friends. Still, I hope it will make Jay annoyed that I am being so nice to his brother and ignoring him. Jay is in the dog house until he tells me what in the fuck he was doing in my goddamn bed.

"Nice to see you too. Didn't know you were back in town."

"Yeah, nobody really does," I reply, and ignore Jay trying to catch my eye at that remark.

Alex and Jay don't look alike, not really. The differences are clear enough to someone who knows them. The brothers have similar builds, and hair in a close shade but that's where the similarities end. Alex's eyes are dark blue, and consistently one color. Not indecisive like Jays.

"Well, this has been....*fun*... But I have to go to work. *Toodles*," I say, giving a little finger wave.

Spirit Fingers, yahs.

I don't give anyone the chance to object or call me back before I leave the kitchen, breezing out of the house. I can't stay inside for one second longer, with Jay's eyes on me like that. Hell, with *any* of their eyes on me like that. Every one of those boys are hot. I'm willing to bet they were walking red flags, just like Jay.

Well, not Alex. The ring around his third finger is obvious.

Fuck.

Welcome home, indeed.

At least the Corvette sounds nice when I speed away from the apartment.

Tiny Victories.

8
Fire Night

twelve days to full moon

The atmosphere in Coyote Bills on Fire Night is *wild*. Untamed, chaotic- *frenzied* energy fills the space. Everyone is dancing, grinding on one another to the music.

Earlier, before we opened, Angel had given me the rundown of what was expected on fire night while we counted our cash drawers. She'd demonstrated a handful of moves that they all do in sync and made sure I had the basics down. It is a fairly simple routine, a sort of line dance with a bit of little dirty dancing flare thrown in. I practiced the moves while I finished my opening duties, fairly confident that I could follow along with the others. Or, at least be able to dance to the music with them.

Around nine I open the slap shots booth for a bit, honestly just killing time. Midnight is the money hour, when Ivy and Angel truly kick off Fire Night by dousing the bar top with alcohol, dropping a lit match onto it.

Dancing on the bartop with flames licking at my legs, and music blaring feels almost as freeing as running through the trees.

Almost.

All of the patrons watch the four of us perform on the bar, cheering and singing along with the music. The die-hard regulars even know the routine– some better than I do.

Angel- the blonde is in front of me, Ivy behind me, and the other bartender that I haven't had the chance to talk to yet behind her.

George is behind the bar with a couple of fire extinguishers, just in case. He also is running the small side well for simple drinks orders- beers or sodas only. He *apparently* doesn't know how to mix drinks. I expected there to be some unhappy Karens in the crowd, unwilling to wait through the performance to get their mixed drink. There's always at least *one* person. I've worked at enough places like this to know it.

I suppose that the clientele of Coyote Bill's are advanced forms of humanity though, because there isn't a single Karen to be found.

Maybe that's just a side effect of watching hot women dance on a flaming bar top though.

The four of us bartenders dance and dance, linking arms and doing high kicks- just because Angel shouts "Hey, let's do the can-can!" With a grin plastered across her face. The blonde's laughter is infectious.

Our soundtrack is a sort of mash-up of a few different hits, longer than the average song but *just* long enough for the routine.

When the flames die down without the help of George's extinguishers, I hop off the bar. Angel and the brunette go over to climb down using a barstool located at the very end. I'm not sure if it is because they were that short or if they just don't trust themselves to jump to the floor. When they are down, they each grab a rag and the special cleaning spray to wipe down the mess from the fire. Ivy still stands atop the smoking bar, waving patrons in and making an announcement that Slap Shots will be set up again in fifteen.

My little idea has been a hit with the patrons of Coyote Bills. I can't say if they'd seen other places do it, or if the customers that haunt the doorsteps of Coyote Bills are suckers for pain or praise. I make sure I tell each of my customers that they take it *so well for me*. I've already started to recognize faces, and repeat customers of the Slap Shot.

I really do owe the Renaissance Faire I'd been to a while back—before Ethan— an enormous thank you. One of their bartenders had given me the idea in the first place.

I set up my little station next to the well George had been at, so I could wash shot glasses when I ran out. When I'd done a test earlier, I hadn't brought enough shot glasses over here, resulting in having to close the booth down much earlier than we'd expected.

Already, a line is forming within the crowd before me, eager for a Slap Shot. This area of the bar had been wiped down by Angel while I'd been getting my shot glasses, so there is nothing else to be done, except to open up the booth.

"Care for a Slap Shot?" I ask the first person in line, a barely legal college kid by the looks of him, a snapback hat on his head backward, a polo shirt with the collar popped, and a thick, gaudy gold chain hanging around his neck.

"Yeah, My buddies told me about this. I pay you for a shot and you slap me?" The frat bro asks, the tone of his voice conveying he thinks he's hot shit. He's lucky I don't *actually* slap the shit out of him.

Wouldn't want to kill a patron on my second night.

Look at you, deploying survival skills. My wolf snarks, golden eyes hovering at the edges of my subconscious.

"Yep. That pretty much sums it up. Are you buying or not? There are paying customers behind you, if you're not," I say, not giving the douche even an ounce of my energy.

Just the way he holds his head, chin raised, attempting to look down his nose at me tells me *everything* I need to know about him. I bet his mom asks for the manager for ridiculous reasons, like this douchebag looks to be about to do. Ivy would kick his ass to the curb so fast his head would spin.

"Nah, who's gonna pay for a little bitch like you to slap them?" He says, pushing away from the bar and disappearing into the crowd. I stare daggers into his spine.

Then, I shout "Who's first?" into the waiting line, patrons all rushing up to be the first. "These lovely people will pay a bitch like me to slap them!" I jeer into the crowd, making them laugh.

I feel eyes on me, my wolf suddenly restless in my mind– almost like she recognizes *someone*. But it only lasts a moment and is quickly forgotten in the clamor before me. Music starts up once more as I begin taking orders, the other bartenders doing the same down the bar from where I stand.

It's around the 15-minute mark that my hand starts to sting, so I swap hands when I smack my patrons. Left, right, left, right. Almost immediately, I realize that offering the full menu for slap shots will be a *huge* detriment to speed and efficiency. Patrons have come up and ordered a full mixed drink or a pitcher of beer, either not realizing they were in line for slap shots or not caring. Motioning to Ivy, I serve everyone who comes to my end, but she needs to help me separate the lines so I don't get bogged down.

Oh, and to make a menu or something over here.

Ivy recognizes my issue immediately when she jogs down the bar, hopping on top of a bucket to get the attention of the crowd, separating the lines quickly and efficiently. She also writes "shots only" with an arrow pointing at me on a torn-off bit of cardboard, taping it to the post at my end.

"Thank you!" I shout to Ivy as she gets off the bucket. She gives me a wave as she walks away.

Another hour passes before I'm ready to close the slap booth. My hands are now cherry red, and my stomach is practically eating itself. After one last customer, I move the tip jar to the back of the bar and wipe down the wood surface. More than a few patrons made a bit of a mess when my palm connected with their cheek.

Task complete, I start to walk away when a patron says "Don't go!" from somewhere in the crowd.

It makes me laugh, so I shout "I'll be back!" Then I slip out from behind the bar while the others continue slinging drinks. Angel and Ivy are *clearly* better than the brunette. But it's time for this blonde to get some *grub*.

Still, my wolf paces.

The double doors with a circular window at eye level for the kitchen considerably quiets the booming of the music. Combined with the roar of fans, the grill loaded with sizzling meats, and bubbling fryers.

"Hey, Darlin'," Cook greets as I cross the threshold into his domain.

"Hey, Pookie," I reply, making my way over to the large sink to wash my hands. They smell like gin and cleaning solution.

"Need some grub?" He chortles, flipping a burger on the grill and pulling a basket of fries out of the bubbling oil. I guess he doesn't mind my impromptu nickname.

"Please," I answer, sitting down on the stool next to where a mound of potatoes is piled high on the table, grabbing the peeler where it had been discarded.

"You ain't gotta do that Darlin'. You just sit there and let ol' Cook fix you some eats." He says as I begin to peel potatoes. Cook effortlessly drops another batch of fries into the oil, turning to grab a roll from the shelf of fresh bread from the bakery in town.

"The way I see it, Pookie, you help me, I help you," I reply without looking at the much older man, not even bothering to hide the wide smile on my face. He grunts but doesn't say anything else.

I manage to peel six potatoes, sending them through the slicer one by one by the time Cook is done with my order— a meatball sub and a handful of french fries. Cook places them down on the table before me, sprinkling the potatoes with a healthy dose of salt and pepper.

"*Bone apple teeth*," Cook says with an entirely straight face, though there is a twinkle in his grey eyes. Unable to contain myself, I throw my head back and cackle.

9
A bar, Jay

nine days to full moon

Rolling out of bed feels like an astronomical task. Starting the shower feels just as daunting. I'd rather do just about anything other than go to work today. Well, that is until I am clean, dry, and dressed.

Then I feel much more alive. Coherent.

Standing in front of the mirror, applying eyeliner I hear Jay's distinct footsteps coming up the stairs. How do I know it is Jay? Instinct. Well.. and his scent permeates the air ahead of him.

The door is open, and I am already dressed for work so my decision is made. Our contrasting schedules makes this whole escapade *manageable,* but I'd like answers now. I am usually gone when he comes home, and vice versa. Which also means I haven't had a chance to ask him exactly *how* it had been possible that I woke up with his dick pressed against my spine.

Not that I completely hated the experience.

No, I examine every minute detail of that morning *every single day*. Almost as if the moment is on a loop in my brain, it replays over and over and over. It has been so very, *very* long since I've woken up in a man's arms and still felt....*safe*. I'd grown so accustomed to the proprietary way Ethan had always touched me. Like he *owned* my body. The contrast between Jay and Ethan has made it impossible for me to forget the moments when Jay's hands have been on me.

And how very *different* his hold feels.

"Are you going to tell me what you were doing in my bed, Jay?" I shout as he walks past without turning from my reflection in the mirror, still applying eyeliner.

He barely makes it a step past the door before he turns, halting with an arm propped on the doorframe, watching as I cap the thin tube. Jay doesn't answer until I turn and look at him.

"It's not like I'd expected *you* to be there, Artemis. Marcus didn't tell anyone he was subletting." Jay says, and I ignore the sinking stone in my gut, the acrid sting of rejection.

"Mhm. Answer the question, Jay." That is all I fire back. Marcus told *someone*. I have his keys, there was a note at the stairs when I blundered in here.

"My brother and his girl are back in town for a while. I gave them my bed. I expected yours to be empty. Honest mistake."

Well, now I feel a little bit like an ass. "Oh."

"Won't happen again. I'll sleep on the couch until they go back home." Jay says, brushing the back of his head with a hand.

He is just as uncomfortable with this conversation as I am. Jay's intense gaze sears into me, searching for *something*.

I wonder if he found it.

"Where are you going?" Jay asks, changing the subject abruptly.

"Work" Is all I manage to grate out.

"*Where* do you work, Artemis?" Exasperation is clear in his tone, but there is something *else* there too. Jay's eyes track my legs, the curve of my hips, the dip of my waist. A smirk pulls at my lips, watching his slow perusal of my body.

I wear a cropped tank top and jeans, and boots on my feet again. It isn't nearly as devastating as last night's outfit, but it was Fire Night. Ivy told me last night at closing that the night *after* Fire Night is usually slower, and taking advantage of the natural ebb and flow of business, Ivy made the day *after* FN a reduced-hours day. I go in an hour later, and come home two hours earlier—which is how Jay and I managed to cross paths today.

Ivy's profits and margins are much better this way, or so she'd explained.

Something about the way Ivy talks about the bar makes me *really,* really excited to go to work with her. And that is a foreign concept all by itself. *Enjoying* going to work? Who am I?

"A *bar,* Jay," I reply when his eyes come back to mine. While I gather my keys and wallet, I ask "How long is your brother in town?"

"Long enough." He grumbles, and I snort. There had always been some rivalry there, some unspoken opposition between the brothers for as long as I could remember. Jay has always been bitching about Alex in some capacity. I had wondered if the older brother moving away had eased some of that antagonistic nature between them, but it seems *not.*

"Well. Thanks for ...this," I say, waving my hands around at nothing. "But I have to go.. gotta get gas..."

Well, now that I've gotten word vomit all over Jay, I think it's time to go. The only problem is, Jay's in the doorframe, not moving an inch as I approach it.

"Have a nice shift, Artemis," Jay says, his voice raising the hair on the back of my neck. The warmth of his body presses against me as I pass, forcing me to duck under his arm.

The entire encounter makes my wolf want to rub up against him. He smells *so* good.

I make it three steps down the hallway before Jay speaks again.

"Nice ride, by the way, it's sweet."

I chuckle, turning to look at him over my shoulder as I descend the staircase. "Yeah, too bad she won't be mine forever."

"What does that mean?"

"It means I stole it. *Toodles.*" I give him a finger wave over my shoulder as I stroll out of the house, the light of the fading day turning everything pink and orange.

Leaves crunch under my boots as I walk the pavers to the lot on the side of the house. The Moon is over the halfway point, which means it is almost time for the Pack run.

Pack run *and* Full Moon.

I still haven't decided what I am going to do on the full Moon. Haven't officially made any declaration to the Alpha of my presence, let alone if I am going to stay, or not.

I know Ethan is going to show up eventually, and his return is going to mean drama. Do I want to wait around for him to find me? Wait around and let him drag the Pack into our mess?

Or am I better off cutting my losses and leaving right after the full Moon? One run beneath the canopy of trees I called home, with my Pack before stuffing everything in a backpack and leaving in the middle of the night?

Fuck, my chest aches just thinking about it... No... I *want* to stay... Want to run with my Pack for more than just one night. Which means, I have to see Magnus Temple.

Which probably means talking to Jay. Telling *him* I am sticking around. Double Fuck.

My thoughts keep tumbling around and around as I drive to the bar, making everything pass by in a blink.

Coyote Bills isn't packed like the previous nights, but it is still busy enough that the first few hours of my shift pass in a blur. I order myself my usual lunch order- a plate with fries piled high and gravy on the side. A Dr Pepper completes my meal, and I hold it clutched under my arm so I have a free hand for the door.

I am making my way to the back of the bar, to go outside to eat and absorb the light of the Moon before the rest of my shift.

The door back here is also where I take trash out at night, and where our parking is. In my opinion, the best part of being in the back lot is that it is away from the front of the bar, and where patrons go out to smoke. Music filters through outdoor speakers for the patio that only a few people are using, the *thunk* of darts being thrown into dartboards permeating the music, their laughter accompanying it.

October's chill has descended, fog creeping in along the tree line. The Moon already hangs in the sky, nearly at its fullest point. Goosebumps crawl up my bare arms as I settle on the top of the picnic table, setting my food down and pulling out my phone. Thumbing through messages and doom scrolling to pass the time I eat my french fries– barely paying attention to the contents of the screen. My mind wanders back to my most pressing issue, despite how much I try to refocus on the glowing screen in front of my eyes.

The Full Moon is nearly upon me, and I still haven't talked to Magnus. Will I be able to stay away from the Pack when the Moon rises, and when I hear them thundering through the trees next to me? I don't know. It had been hard enough on my first night here not to run straight into their midst.

What I do know is that these fries are *fucking delicious.* Cook had sprinkled them generously with salt and pepper fresh out of the fryer, the outside nice and crispy just as the inside is soft and steaming. I can tell that the gravy is from scratch, likely made from the beef au jus that is also on the menu. It is thick, savory and *delectable.* A perfect snack to get me through the rest of the evening. I'll probably end up wanting something else before I leave, otherwise, I'll end up catching a deer and having venison breath for the foreseeable future.

Before Cook leaves for the night I'll get something from whatever food had been prepped and unused for the night. I'm not picky. Well... for the most part.

Ivy told me before I went to my break that they were going to set up the slapshot bar again, enough patrons had asked about it that she wanted to see how much profit we could bring in on a slow night.

The tip jars placed on the bars are already nearly full, and there is still half the night to go. Any tip handed directly to the server is theirs- no contest, but whatever is put in the jars is split evenly between bartenders and Cook. Slap shots are special- since they were my idea I keep a larger share of the jar, and the remaining tips are distributed to the other bartenders. It is a bonus for them to work the same shift as me. So far, even split between that many people, the patrons of Coyote Bill's tip *very* gratuitously. I've left with at least a rack each night I worked.

If I have to slap around some patrons every night to get a grand, *shit,* there are worse things to do for money. Ivy had extended the offer to any other bartender who wanted to be in the booth with me, but no one else jumped. Naturally, I don't mind.

Lone wolf, *awooo.*

You know lone wolves are a myth, Artemis. My wolf stirs, her inky black fur as dark as night within the confines of my mind.

Not true. We are. I am pretty sure only Direwolves communicate with their wolf this way... Almost a separate being, a distinct part of myself, but also *herself.*

We are Artemis.

You know that is not what you want. I can feel her, her eyes more golden than my brown staring at me from within the bounds of her beastly confinement.

I know nothing.

She snorts, the puff of air through her ephemeral nose makes her fur shift. I continue munching on fries, passing the time by mindlessly scrolling through apps on my phone.

When I finish my last fry, scooping the last bit of gravy up with it, I hear the group playing darts outside hoot and holler. They've been periodically making all sorts of noise, from booing to cheering and badly singing song lyrics that pour from speakers.

I listen to them, cheering and jeering alike. They sound like a family. Like a pack. Suddenly, my fries aren't settling very well in my gut.

Am I ever going to feel like that? Like I belong *somewhere*? Will I ever belong with *someone*? The old wound reopens, a ragged hole in my chest.

Probably not. But that won't stop my poor, hopeful heart from wishing. Shattering into teeny tiny pieces I never have any desire to pick up. Walking around like a ghost. I can feel the cracks now, the splinters that dug under my skin, festering and aching away.

Maybe that is what the old stories meant about it *changing* your wolf. Maybe it's just a broken heart.

Well, that's a cheery ass mood to go back to work with. Fuck.

With that extremely depressing thought at the forefront of my mind, and my food gone, I walk back through the door to Coyote Bills, dropping my plate at the food window. I don't use an apron for slap shots, since I've learned that leaning over the bar so far usually leads to the strings getting caught on bottles or something else. I almost broke a bottle that way just the other day.

The music changes, going from one being played by the jukebox to the PA system that Ivy is in control of. The song change is intentional. We've decided on a slapshot soundtrack so to speak, a song that will indicate to everyone that I am at the booth.

Her voice comes over the PA system a second later, beckoning patrons over to my side of the bar. Before I forget, I grab a piece of gum from the Pack sitting on the back counter, between the taxidermied snake, and the bottle of Añejo that is half empty. Hopefully, the cinnamon will help settle my stomach.

Men and women alike flock over to my well, after Ivy's announcement, choosing their order. Last night at close we'd gone over what did and didn't work.

There are now three rules for the slapshot booth. Your drink *has* to be from my little menu, freshly printed and laminated this morning. Cash *only*, and no fighting.

Simple, but effective.

So, tonight I ask them for their order one after another as they walk up to my little section of the bar. Ivy had also found a practically ancient-looking neon sign made to resemble a hand swinging. Where it came from or what its original purpose had been I didn't know. I'd have to ask Ivy when we close.

Hours pass, and all the while I say "What's your drink Darlin'?" over and over. As I pour their liquor, I'd ask "Pick your poison, praise or degradation?" Consent is important, after all.

Then, one after another I tell them *Oh, you're doing so well!* Or if it is a guy that wants to be degraded, I'd call them princess, and tell them to drink up. There is a careful balance to maintain. Somewhere between attainable and completely off the market. Flirtatious, and focused on my customer but not so far as to invite trouble.

The implementation of the menu, the sign, and Ivy's announcement on the PA system have made a difference in the stream of patrons at the bar. Angel and the brunette are likewise behind the bar, slinging mixed drinks and beers out in tandem. I throw myself into work, focusing on the next person in line and what their order is, so much so that by the time I spot Jay, Saint, and Dante in line, it is *far,* far too late to turn and run away.

Fuck, fuck, fuck. Saint is in line first, his shaggy blonde hair haphazardly thrown into a sort of bun at the back of his head. He swaggers up to the bar, and leans on his elbow as he grins and says "Hey, Tiny."

"What's your drink of choice?" I ask, trying to ignore the familiarity in his tone, the way his chest looks from under the dark blue button-down shirt he wears. The top few buttons are left open, and even in the dim lighting of Coyote Bills, he looks entirely too attractive for his own good.

"Aw, it's like that? I'll do three Añejo then." Saint pouts.

My eyebrows shoot into my hairline. A single shot of that is twenty-five bucks. It is only on the menu as a top-shelf option, and no one has ordered it yet. Turning from him to grab the bottle I say, "A man with expensive taste, I see. How do you want it? You want to be told you're a *good boy* when I slap you?"

"Please?" Saint's green eyes round, making it look like he is giving me a puppy dog pout. I consider it for a moment, pouring his shots into fresh glasses.

"I do like it when you beg," Molten heat blooms low in my belly, my heart racing only a little.

Careful. My wolf paces within my mind, stirred by the tension that is spiraling through me.

Saint slides a crisp one hundred dollar bill across the bar from me, and says "Keep the change."

I quickly cash him out, depositing his *change* into the tip jar.

Saint goes to grab his shot glass, to hold it but I stop him. "Not yet. When I say. Ready?"

He nods, and I grin. The crack of my palm on his cheek made the crowd gasp, and then laugh.

"Good boy, drink," I say, sliding Saint's first shot across the bar towards him.

He downs it easily after tapping the bottom against the bar. Saint slams the small glass down, letting out a roar of pleasure. He looks *electric, mouthwatering.*

Get it together girl, shit.

"You're doing so well. Ready?" Saint nods again, and without a moment's hesitation, I slap him once more, on the other cheek. The right had a perfect impression of my fingers outlined in red, now the left would match.

Saint downs his second shot while I murmur to him in a baby voice "You're so good. Such a good boy." It's an effort to keep myself from laughing since he *is* a Direwolf and I am giving him very dog-like praise. He swipes his third shot from the bar, guzzling it down, then howling.

I can't help but laugh at him, letting Saint get away with his slap-less shot.

Dante looks almost annoyed at the whole situation, but I notice his shift, the quick adjustment he makes while his hands are tucked into his pockets.

I grin. "You're next, *Dante*."

"Johnnie Walker. Double." He says without preamble, sliding another crisp one hundred dollar bill across the bar. I assume he means for his change to go in the tip jar as well, and he doesn't say anything to deny it when I dangle his forty dollars above the jar either. So, into the jar, it goes.

"How do you want it?" I ask, counting out his double in my head. Dante is ordering the same amount of alcohol as two shots but in one glass rather than two.

"Don't say anything," Dante says, then taps his cheek twice, waving me on to begin. Well fuck. That seems...*boring*.

Well, it's his hundred bucks. If he doesn't want me to say anything, I won't.

So, I shrug, wiping my palm against the rag hooked on the edge of the bar. Then, I smack the shit out of his jaw, the impact forcing his head to the side. I couldn't hit a human like this. Saint and Dante aren't *human* though. My palm stings, the flush of his dark skin nearly imperceptible.

Dante's eyes close, the muscle in his jaw feathering. He shakes his head, the muscles of his arms bunching. Then, he chugs his alcohol down in one gulp.

"Thanks for your business." I cheer, giving the brightest and wildest smile I can. "Next."

And that is exactly when I realize that Jay is next, his blue-green eyes swinging into focus as he shoulders Dante out of his way. Jay wears a dark tee shirt, stretched across his shoulders, a and hat on backward. It's the small smirk on his face that makes my pulse jump when he says "Two Añejo," Sliding a crisp bill across the bar.

And, it seems that is exactly when all sense leaves me because I ask "What will it be? Praise? Silence? Degradation? How do you want me, *Handsome*?" as I pour out his liquor.

Internally, I am turning around and perishing on the spot. What the *fuck* am I doing, flirting with Jay like that? Outwardly though, I keep my grin plastered across my face, my feet still. The two shot glasses before me are full to the brim, waiting for him to place his soft lips on the rim and drink down the tequila.

All three of these fuckers have paid in hundreds, leaving whatever their change was as a tip. Shit. I don't know if the money is of their own making, or if it had come from their portion of the pack's profit share. Either way, they are paying a pretty penny for the honor of being slapped by me.

Doesn't *that* just make your pussy purr?

Jay pats his cheek and says "Do your worst" with a sly smile. Well, mother fucker. *Giddy up*.

I don't waste any time before I smack him with just about all the force I can muster. I *may* have put more force than was strictly required for the hit. Jay's eyes shift, the silvery sliver of his wolf peeking out from under his lashes for a split second.

My wolf paces in my mind, a low whine slipping from between her teeth. She's not worried— she's *excited*. A muscle in Jay's jaw feathers, but he does nothing other than hold my gaze as he drinks down the tequila.

When I hold his second shot out, he nods, and I slap him– but this time he groans. My mouth waters.

"Another," Jay says, setting his two shot glasses down much gentler than Saint or even Dante had.

"What's your poison?" I ask as I watch him pull out yet another hundred-dollar bill, depositing it into the tip jar. My eyebrows scrunch together, and his smile turns wicked and sharp, no longer lazy or sly.

"I'll let you slap me again, but I want something not on the menu in return."

"What's that?" The galloping of my heart has turned my palms clammy.

"I get slapped, then you kiss me," Jay says in a dark voice

I raise my eyebrow. "You're gonna let me slap me again *just* for a kiss?" What is he playing at?

Jay's blue eyes meet mine in the dark club, and I track the movement as he bites his bottom lip. "Mmhm. For old time's sake." His voice is low, growly. It makes me want to shift on my feet, ease even a little of the tension cording my body. My wolf paces relentlessly in my mind.

Finally, I reply. "Fuck it." Leaning over the bar to drop a kiss on the side of his mouth, lingering for a heartbeat. Without warning or preamble I smack both sides of his face one after another. His eyes don't leave mine once as my palms connect to his cheeks, but he does murmur *"fuck"* under his breath when I am done.

"Enjoy your night, Jay," I say to him, ignoring the way my heart pounds in my chest, indicating for the next patron in line.

I learned the brunette's name, Jill, as we swapped the empty keg down in the basement. Refrigeration keeps the entire floor at a chilly 35 degrees. One of the more recent upgrades to the old bar. Jill is also relatively new here, a friend of Angel's. Jill is shorter than the rest of us, petite enough that I know without a doubt she is human, like Angel. Her teeth begin chattering almost immediately as we descend in the service lift.

Since I've swapped many a keg in my day, and Ivy had shown me where everything is down here when I closed, I volunteered to go down with Jill when she noticed the tap was empty. Coyote Bills boasts a very large selection of on-tap beers, an entire wall of the basement double stacked with the containers. Jill is barely tall enough to reach the coupler, so I tell her to shut the gas line first, and she grabs a stool to stand on top of on her way back over. I'm going to tell Ivy that someone else should change kegs, Jill just isn't big enough.

"So are you from around here?" She asks, watching me disconnect the old keg and join a new one to the lines.

"Yea. Haven't been home in quite a while though." I respond, making sure all the connections are tight. Jill grunts in response, putting her stool back in its corner. Ivy told us to use the service lift, taking the empty keg to the back where the vendor will pick it up tomorrow. The original *Coyote Bill* had the lift installed in his later years when he couldn't manage to bring the kegs back upstairs on his own. I'd be willing to bet the refrigeration and the lift were installed simultaneously.

Ivy intercepts Jill and me as we're exiting the kitchens after washing our hands.

"Just the two I was looking for. I need a word before you both go back behind the bar." Ivy says, and my gut sinks. Before either of us can ask what she means, Ivy presses on. "A reminder on ground rules. No *fraternization* with patrons." *Ah, fuck.* She doesn't need to look directly at me for me to know that she'd seen the kiss I dropped to Jay's mouth.

Fuck, fuck *fuck*. My face heats, more with embarrassment than shame.

Of course, she'd seen it. Of course, she'd seen me practically throw myself at Jay.

Jill rescues me without even knowing it. "I'm sorry, he asked for my number and he seemed like a nice guy. I didn't see the harm in it."

"I know. But what you don't know is that after he left the bar, he went outside bragging about how he got the bartender's number without any effort, and then all those guys came inside and began harassing Angel for hers. See how it gets out of hand so easily?"

Jill ducks her head and mumbles a *yes*. Ivy meets my eyes and raises her eyebrow like *'Care to add anything?'*

"I'm sorry, I didn't think that applied to my boyfriend." The lie slips out easily. *Fuck.* This is an incredibly stupid solution.

Ivy's eyebrows raise. "Boyfriend? Oh. Didn't realize you had one. No, the *rules* don't apply to boyfriends but try not to kiss him again while you're behind the bar. Please." Ivy says, and I immediately feel guilty for lying to her.

"Consider it done," I reply, tying my apron around my waist. Won't be happening again anyway. That particular lapse in judgment *cannot* happen again.

"Jill, can you go buss some tables? George is getting behind out there." Ivy orders and Jill scurries away without any more encouragement.

"Anything else?" I question when Ivy continues staring at me, my gut laden with stones.

"Yeah. Your *boyfriend* is out there asking for you." Again, that eyebrow of Ivy's is raised, and I swear that she can tell I'm lying.

I nod my head, pressing my lips together. "Ah. He's a little..." I don't finish the sentence. I don't know what to say. Thankfully, Ivy nods and waves me off.

It doesn't take long to find him among the crowd. Jay, Saint, Dante, Alex and a woman I presume to be Alex's wife are all crowded around a booth, plates of apps and fries scattered across the table with an assortment of drinks. Dante sits on the edge of the booth and spots me approaching first. He taps the table in front of Jay, tilting his head in my direction.

The weight of Ivy's eyes on my back is tangible, watching Jay and I interact. This is so dumb. So incredibly *stupid*. I didn't have to lie to her. Silently, I'm screaming— begging Jay to play along. I'm totally fucking fired if she catches me in a lie. Particularly one as blatant as that had been. And I need this job. *Want it.*

Jay stands up when I stop in front of their booth, and he says "Hey, Artemis,"

Before he says anything else I interrupt him." Hey, you're my boyfriend. Okay?" Jay's eyebrows scrunch together, but he must have seen something on my face because he immediately smiles that lazy self-assured smile he'd worn after discovering it was *me* that he woke up next to.

"Sure, anything you want." That is all Jay has to say, but his eyes flash. A glint of *something* in the blue-green depths.

"Great." I gulp. With my heart pounding and fingers trembling I take that final step towards him, stretch the tiny distance to his face, and kiss him full on the mouth.

Jay doesn't hesitate. Immediately, his arms band around my ribs, hands fisting in my hair. I lose myself in the feeling of Jay—for one single heartbeat. Jay groans into my mouth, pulling me closer to him and I whimper back, a sound he swallows greedily–and then, it's too much.

I pull away, stepping *away*, and say "Thanks..." I have to clear my throat twice before my voice sounds normal. "Uh.. I'll see you around?" Jay lets me go, even if his eyes shift, that sliver of wolf peering through—for only a moment.

Fuck.

Fuck.

FUCK.

After closing the bar down with Ivy, I collapse into the driver's seat of the Corvette and dial Sam's number. She answers on the third ring. The Bluetooth connection to the car is automatic, so I just drop my phone into the cupholder when it clicks over.

"Hello?" She answers, her music chirping softly in the background. It's easily after eleven there, but Sam is a night owl, practically nocturnal.

"You will never believe the fucking day I've had," I begin, shifting gears and driving away from Coyote Bills. It's a quick trip from the bar to the old Grimes place. Enough time to rant to her before I get home. "No, let me rephrase. *A couple* of days."

Sam laughs, then says "Tell me." A crunch through the speaker tells me she already has snacks.

"Okay so first of all— you'll never guess who I'm bunking with— and who I woke up with in *my motherfucking bed.*"

"*Who?*" Sam gushes, then *crunch crunch crunch* on her snack.

"Jay *motherfucking* Temple."

"*The* Jay?"

"Naturally." I grouse, rolling my eyes even if she can't see me.

"What happened!" Sam demands, I can tell she's practically frothing at the maw to get answers out of me.

"Nothing that interesting. It was intense— but nothing *happened*."

"Okay, boring. Don't think I missed how sad you sound about that by the way, but please– go on." Sam drawls, saying "What else, then?"

"So tonight at work guess who shows up?"

"Jay *motherfucking* Temple?" She chirps cheerfully.

"Jay *motherfucking* Temple!" I agree. "And do you know what he did?"

"Haven't got the foggiest." Sam snarks, making me chuff a laugh.

"He and his friends all ordered top-shelf shots, and tipped very *generously*."

"Okay, what's the problem there?" *Crunch crunch crunch,* Sam says everything around a mouthful of whatever she's eating.

"*Then*, Jay put a hundred dollar bill in the tip jar and said I could slap him if I kissed him."

"HE DID NOT!"

"He most definitely did."

"Tell me you did it!" Sam hisses into the phone, and I know she'd fly out here to strangle me if I said no.

"Of course I did it. Not full on the mouth, just the corner. But I still did it." The entire world beyond the reach of the headlights is dark. Quiet. Sleeping.

"Fuck thats hot."

"Shut up. That's not all."

"*Oh?*" I swear Sam is going to slither straight through my phone speaker to gossip with me.

"My boss saw me, because, *of course,* she did. And because I'm a fucking *imbecile* I lied to her when she prodded about it, saying that Jay is my boyfriend because *fraternization with the patrons* isn't allowed."

"Oh boy, okay… so that's not bad. No one has to know— you can go in tomorrow and say you broke up." Sam offers, and I feel even more dumb.

"Sure. That would have been optimal. Except that Jay had been asking for me, and of course, Ivy watched me go up to him."

"And?" Sam asks, and I feel like I have ice in my veins, adrenaline flooding my system just thinking about the kiss. Still, I navigate easily through the streets. I'm nearly back to the apartment now.

"I walked up to him and said *'Hey you're my boyfriend'* and fucking kissed him!"

Sam squeals into the phone, exploding with laughter. Had I been holding the device to my ear, I would have been deafened.

"Stop that! This is not funny!"

"Yes, it is. This is FANTASTIC!"

"Sam!" I chide, needing guidance.

"What? You're doing *amazing* all on your own." She replies, offering absolutely nothing else. "Ethan has been asking about you by the way. His bribe to give you up is to set me up with some *rich* friend of his." She tells me, and her voice drips with disdain.

"I'm sorry he's bothering you," I reply. Guilt weighs heavy across my shoulders, sinking into my gut like acid. I never wanted her to be pulled into Ethan's focus.

"I don't care. You're clearly doing much better away from here." Sam says softly, and I wish that we could have this conversation in real life. It would be much more fulfilling face to face, rather than three thousand miles apart.

"How long until he tracks the car, do you think?" I ask as I turn down the street to the old Grimes place.

"I'm not sure he's aware that he has that ability, to be honest." Sam chortles, making me laugh too.

"That does sound about right." I agree, pulling into my parking space at the apartment. There are a few cars here already, but the house itself is dark.

"I am happy for you, you know. You sound…. *so much* happier."

"Thanks, Sam. I think you'd like it here too, ya know." I reply, tracing the leather stitching on the steering wheel.

"You think so? Maybe I'll come visit."

"You should, but I think I'm gonna let you go. I'm itching to go for a quick run before I crawl into bed."

"You do that. Bang any hotties you see on your way."

"Shut up. Love you."

"Love you."

10
No take backs

eight days to full moon

The next morning when I emerge from my room, I find Jay waiting. Wearing jeans and a red flannel, his hat on backward Jay stands propped against the wall, that infuriating smirk already on his face.

"So what was that about?" Jay quips, blue eyes roaming down the bare expanse of my legs below the oversized hoodie I had thrown on.

"What was *what*?" My hackles are already raised, set off because of lack of sleep. Now that I know *Jay* is sleeping mere feet away from my room, I haven't been able to get farther than dozing.

All I can think of laying there in the dark, is his hands on my body. The way it had felt waking up with a man in my bed, and not because they'd woken me for morning sex. I can't even remember the last time I'd slept in the same bed as someone and not been constantly groped or poked and prodded at. I honestly don't know what to do with the memory. Fuck, I'd been *splayed* across him, it would have only taken a quick tug, freeing me from the confines of the lace panties I'd been wearing, a shift of his hips- and then his cock would have been inside me. Filling me.

Jay Temple had always known how to make my body *sing*. And now, dammit I fucking remember it and can't get it out of my head.

"I'm your boyfriend now?" Jay asks, the smirk blooming into a full-blown smile. It is the same one he'd worn at Coyote Bills last night, seeing me behind the Slap Shot bar. And that look in his eye was the same, and it is that one that had made me lean just a little further over the bar, dropping a kiss to the side of his lips before I'd smacked him right across the face.

Jay hadn't broken eye contact with me before shooting back the liquor. And then he'd dropped another bill on the bar and said *another*.

And now all I can think of is how he'd say that word between my legs.

"Oh, that. Uh... Well. I only told Ivy that because she's my boss. I'd be fired for doing what you asked me to do to a normal patron. So in name only, and only while you're at the bar, yes you are my boyfriend." I stammer, moving my hand in a placating wave. Trying to ward him off. Jay shifts, moving off of the wall to invade my space. I nearly *had* been fired, if I am being honest with myself. "Uness we have a big fake fight and break up outside the bar."

"And I'm not *normal?*" Jay fires back, and I can *see* his wolf rising in the depths of his more blue than green iris. He completely ignores my solution to the mess we're in.

"*Ugh*, you're so fucking *frustrating!* That is *not* what I said." I growl, feeling my wolf pace inside my mind. She wants *out*. She wants to *play with Jay*.

Wants to run in the fields with him like we did a lifetime ago.

"It's *okay*, baby girl. You adore me." Jay replies, grin pulling his mouth apart. Flashing too white teeth at me, resting his tattooed arms above our heads on the doorframe.

"Yea? Who told you that?" My heart skips a half beat, his scent filling my nose. Pine. Leather.

"You did," Jay replies easily, so sure of himself. That lazy smile still plastered across his face.

I narrow my eyes at him. "That was a long time ago, Jay." I finally answer, pushing way past him, and knocking his shoulder.

"No takebacks!" He hollers after me, letting me walk down the hallway. I give him the finger over my shoulder.

Today is my day off, and the Full Moon is almost upon us.

The Hunters Moon Festival is this weekend as well, and Coyote Bills is closed for the event. Realistically, today would be a good day to go find Magnus Temple.

Fuck, Fuck, *Fuck!*

Jay is already under my skin, asking to go see his dad is only going to earn me more teasing. He fucking *has* me and he isn't even trying. I really should cut my losses and go look for somewhere else to live. There is bound to be another apartment to rent in Timber Hollow, right? *Right?*

Going down into the kitchen, I open the fridge to see what options for a beverage there are. I can't eat yet, still too restless for an appetite, but I want caffeine. Need it really, if I am to have a battle of wits with Jay all day.

Lucky for me, it seems there is another caffeine junkie in the house because, on the second shelf, there is a row of the original flavor of Redbull, and a row of blue cans next to them. I grab one of the blue ones, intending on thanking whichever one of my roomies is the culprit, and paying them whenever I figure out who it is.

I hear Jay's footsteps down the stairs, following my trail into the kitchen, and to the fridge.

"Can I ask you something?" I ask Jay when he crosses the threshold for the kitchen like we hadn't just had a moment in the hall upstairs. Unable to stand still, I hop up onto the island counter, the cold granite biting into the backs of my bare thighs.

"You can ask me anything," Jay's reply comes easy as he opens the fridge and roots around inside. When he emerges holding a can of original flavored Red Bull, I can't help the soft smile on my face, feeling my wolf pace in the confines of my mind. His iris flashes when we lock eyes, there and gone again in a blink. His wolf is hovering close to the surface of his mind, too.

I clink my can with his, popping the top and taking a deep sip of the bubbly, blueberry battery acid-flavored liquid before I voice my request. Of course it is Jay, to stock the fridge with caffeine. *Of course.*

"Will you take me to see Magnus?" I ask, picking at the skin around my nail with my thumb.

"Why would I do that?"

"You know why."

"No, I don't."

"Yes, you do Jay."

"I really don't. Enlighten me."

I sigh, then reply "You're going to make me spell it out, aren't you?"

"Yep." Jay deadpans, his full lips making a pop. And now I'm just thinking about his lips, and fuck me—Jay knows how to kiss. I can still feel his mouth pressing into my skin, moving against my own. Can feel his hands on me in the dark confines of Coyote Bills. In the darkness of my room.

"So I can officially declare my intentions to rejoin the Pack. I want to stay in Timber Hollow."

Jay's blue-green iris bore into me, clawing down into the depths of my soul as he remains silent across the kitchen from me. I take a sip of my drink, if only for something to do with my hands.

"Yeah, I'll take you. Go get dressed." Is his eventual reply.

I nearly spit out my drink, not anticipating his easy acceptance. "Just like that?"

"Yeah."

"Why?"

He shrugs, his mountainous shoulders rising to his ear. "You're Pack."

I try to ignore the butterflies in my stomach, the way that my heart begins to race at those two words. I really try. But if Jay still considers me Pack, then maybe that means Magnus would too.

Leaving my Red Bull on the counter with Jay, I all but sprint up the stairs to pull pants on my legs, run a brush through my hair, and throw a t-shirt on over my head, oversized hoodie forgotten on the floor, immensely grateful I'd decided to shower last night before bed.

It's been a *long* long time since I'd seen the Alpha, and the last time I'd been in front of him in the Packhouse, the fifteen-year-old version of myself had been proudly spouting off facts from science class telling our very large and powerful leader that *Alpha wolves are bullshit. It's a human concept, and does not occur in the wild so why should I have to listen to his crusty, dusty ass?*

I can still remember the way that Jay had a coughing fit trying to cover his laugh. Magnus' response, of course, was *"magic, girl"*, sending teenaged me to my knees with his Alpha power. The mystical magical part of being a shifter had fascinated me, once upon a time. Before I'd lost interest in those sorts of things. Before I hated being reminded of Dad, who had been Magnus' Beta before he died.

This is going to be a fucking *shit show*. I try not to dwell on it too much as I fly out of my room, still buttoning my jeans.

Jay is standing at the bottom of the stairs, both of our drinks in hand, keys dangling out from under the cans. He waits very patiently for me to slide my feet into sandals. "Where is everyone else?" I ask, taking my drink from him, and leaving through the door he opens for me.

"Packhouse. Alex and Helena are going to have a baby, so the whole family is up there." Jay replies, crossing the lawn and opening the passenger door of a sky-blue Nissan Skyline GT.

"Oh. Well, this will be interesting. Whole family huh?" I say, sliding into the seats, anxiety rippling in my gut. Jay closes the door behind me, then walks to the other side, easily turning the engine over. I can't help but admire the flex of his fingers on the shifter, and his grip on the steering wheel. Beyond Jay's brother though, I haven't interacted with his family... like at all.

Sure there had been the occasional event that the Alpha spoke at but I hadn't ever been in the spotlight.

Jay had been as much of a mystery to me then as he is now. Maybe even more so.

"Yup," Jay says, turning the music on and advancing us down the street with practiced ease. It's been a long time since I've been home, but even so, I remember the way to the Packhouse. The hulking building is situated in the center of town, opposite the *town hall* which was only used for obtaining official documents one needs to merely exist on the planet. We drive down the side streets until we're at the main intersection, passing the entrance to the logging yard where all the large machinery is stored.

I don't *need* Jay to go see Magnus, but having at least one person with me before I beg to come back into the Pack feels better than going by myself. "How come Alex and Helena aren't staying at the Packhouse?" I ask, slipping my feet out of my sandals, and folding them up in the seat with me.

Jay's blue-green eyes cut straight through me as he shifts gears, tracking my movements. "How come *you* aren't staying at the Packhouse, Artemis?"

My cheeks heat. "*Because* then everyone would have known I'm back immediately."

"Were you not going to stay?"

"I don't know."

Jay lets the silence stretch for all of about forty-five seconds before he says "So, you know this whole *dating but not really dating thing* could work in both of our favor."

I swear the switch was flipped on gravity. "What do you mean?"

"Well. It's been a long while since I've seen parts of my family, and since they will *absolutely* be up my ass about being single, having a-" once again his eyes cut to me as he shifts gears. "-*girlfriend* for the first time in...a *while* would take some of the attention off of me."

"Ahh, so you want arm candy? Or do you want the full *girlfriend experience?*" I sass, just as the light turns yellow, and then red, bringing us to a complete halt. Jay's undivided attention swings to me in this little car.

Again, I wonder where gravity went.

"Darlin, I want everything."

Nervous laughter bubbles up, and I fight for words for the entire red light. "So what does being your girlfriend-*fake girlfriend*-entail?" I eventually manage to ask.

Jay answers immediately."What does it entail for me to be your *fake boyfriend* when I come to see you at Coyote Bills?"

"You're going to come see me?" At this point, I'm all but turned sideways in my seat, entirely focused on Jay, and not the drive—or our destination.

"Answer the question."

"You first," I demand.

"Nope."

"*Jay.*" I huff, barely able to keep the smile from my face.

"*Artemis,*" he responds. Jay is smiling though, and once again I am transported back into the body of seventeen-year-old me. I don't know how to reconcile the two versions of Jay.. or myself.

"I don't know. It entails acting..." I flail for an answer for entirely too long before I decide on saying "like a boyfriend would."

"Are you going to kiss me again?" Jay asks just as we reach the Packhouse, pulling straight into an empty spot in the back of the building. You need special access—the Pack code to enter the doors back here.

"Not... Not uh, if you would rather not...I'm sorry if I crossed a boundary the other night." I say, bracing for the rejection.

Suddenly, the texture of the dash is the most interesting thing in the world.

Jay remains silent, exiting the car and coming around to my side. He opens the door, going so far as to reach in and unbuckle my seatbelt. As the strap rolls away, Jay all but growls in my ear "No, I'm *counting* on it." Then he recedes, dutifully holding the door open for me.

This is a bad, *bad* idea.

Jay and I aren't alone, there's a group of people out back, gathered around the open door for the kitchen. Saint is among them, his shaggy blonde bun visible even over here. Looks like I'll be crossing a gauntlet already.

Was that planned, did Jay want an audience for our entrance?

"So does anyone know we're *not actually* dating?" I ask, gathering courage as I exit his vehicle. My wolf is content as can be right now, practically comatose within the inky confines of my mind.

"Nope. Saint and Dante probably suspect, but Alex and Helena have no idea what happened." Jay says, and his eyes shift silver for one single moment.

"Hmm," I hum, unsure of what to say next.

Jay's eyes turn sharp as he cages me against the side of his car. "Did *you* tell anyone that we're not *really* dating?"

I gulp, the crisp air of October feeling like ice in my veins. "No one on this side of the Mississippi river."

Jay smiles, that lazy self-assured stretch of his lips over his teeth that I have no idea how to handle. I have no idea how to handle *Jay* anymore, either it would seem.

"By the way, you would." I blurt, breaking the silence I have no idea how to navigate. Jay's eyebrows scrunch together.

"What?"

"Get a car that matches your eyes."

I am rewarded with Jay's full, bright laughter that draws the attention of at least a few people gathered by the kitchen, that silver flash of his wolf running against the current of his mind. He takes another step towards me, his body fully pressing me against the car, his hand coming around to grip the back of my neck. My hands land on his broad shoulders, not pushing him away but not gripping him tight either. I'm very aware of our audience, and there is absolutely nowhere to go, nowhere to hide.

"If you were *actually* my girlfriend I would kiss you right now," Jay says, tightening his grip on my hair, exposing my neck, and running his arm down my side. His hand lightly grazes the back of my hip, down the line of my thigh. And then, when he lowers his mouth to my pounding pulse, lightly nipping it Jay asks "Are you prepared for that kind of attention?"

"And what is this, right now?" I ask breathlessly, my fingers tightening on his shirt.

"A show. If I don't act like *myself* then they're going to question it. So it's either keep it a secret from everyone, or we loop them in. Which is it?" Jay murmurs against my neck, the grip on my hair as firm as ever. His tongue darts out, licking before his teeth close over the spot– and I have to stifle a moan.

"You're going to do this in front of your family?" I pant, and he pulls away from nuzzling my neck. I hate myself for regretting the loss of contact.

"Make me laugh like that, and maybe. Is that a problem?" Jay gives me the time to consider, even if he is only centimeters away from my face. I'm sure from where his friends are standing, this looks *a little* different.

"Why?"

"Consent is sexy, but you'll get forehead kisses regardless," Jay replies, watching my face. I'd be sent straight to hell for lying, but I will never *ever* admit just how hard my heart skipped a beat at those three words.

"Well... I'd hate for anyone to think something was amiss." I finally answer, widening my legs a fraction, his thigh slipping between my own—just a little.

"So it's a *secret* that we're not really dating?" Jay murmurs, eyes flicking down to my mouth.

"I suppose. Why?"

"So I can kiss you whenever I want?"

"When we're in *public together.*" I retort.

Jay lowers his face towards mine a fraction, his eyes never leaving my face. "And are we in *public* right now, Artemis?" I wish I could read his thoughts, and see what is going on behind those mercurial eyes.

"Yes, Jay. I suppose we are." I simper, trying to hide just how hard my heart pounds, the thrill that has shot up my spine when he says my name again. The moment stretches, and I endure it, feeling all the world like my heart is going to pound straight out of my chest.

Jay drops a kiss on my forehead, and then steps away. The cool autumn breeze rushes back in, raising goosebumps along my arms. "Let's go." He says, reaching his hand out for me to grab. When I immediately don't lace my fingers through his he says "It's a *hand* Artemis, not a snake."

"Shut up," I reply, ignoring the outstretched limb and my sudden *rampant irritation* as I make my way through cars to the door everyone is congregating around. Jay's laugh skitters against my spine. "I am *so fucked*." I mutter under my breath, anxiety bubbling up. Just thinking about being in front of the entire Pack again is making my skin crawl.

"Not yet you're not," Jay answers immediately, having caught up to me easily.

"*Shut up*," I repeat, practically snarling at him. Without warning, Jay grabs hold of my arm, slamming me against the rough brick wall of the Packhouse. My hands once again grip his shoulders with trembling fingers.

"I know it's been a long time since you've been home, but-" Jay begins.

"Don't patronize me, Jay."

"I'm not. If you would be quiet for a minute-"

"Fuck you." I snarl in his face, moving to push out of his grip.

"Anytime, Gorgeous." Jay snarks back at me, pushing my spine firmly against the brick, that same lazy self-assured smile back on his face. I shift on my feet, ignoring the way heat has unpooled low in my belly, the way my wolf has begun pacing in my mind again.

Another snarl rips free of my throat as I think of ways to get out of his hold that won't immediately signal to those just out of earshot that we are *definitely not* dating. The tips of his ashy brown hair tickle my fingers, and I am tempted to thread my fingers through the strands and pull his mouth to mine. The kiss from the bar flashes through my mind again and again.

"Are we making out or fighting, Artemis? I'm getting mixed signals here." Jay asks, his eyes flicking to my mouth and back up in a heartbeat.

I narrow my eyes at him. "Fighting."

Jay smiles, a full, wide smile like he used to. Not lazy and self-assured, not sly and devious. "For now."

And damn me straight to hell but I want to change that.

I'm so fucked.

"Why do you say that?" I ask, completely ensnared in that blue-green gaze.

"Because whenever you get bratty, you get *heated*. You don't think I remember it?" Jay whispers in my ear, nibbling on the lobe, trailing hot kisses down my neck, scraping his teeth against my skin, pushing his hard thigh between my own.

Fuck him and his *fucking memory.*

"Wha-what are you doing?" I mumble, hips surging towards him. Jay's hands grip my waist, spanning my ribcage. He might be holding me similarly to the ways that Ethan liked to, but there is a thrill down my spine— not dread—when Jay does it.

"I told you, a *show*. Now listen to me." Jay begins, speaking against my throat, capturing both my hands behind my back. "It's been a while since you've been back, and some things have changed."

"Like what?" I can barely focus on what he is talking about. Half of me wants to bolt, run away again, and never return. The other half wants to climb Jay *motherfucking* Temple like a tree and ride him until the Sun goes down.

I need to fucking get laid. That's what the problem is.

"Magus... is not nearly as lenient as he used to be," Jay says, crossing the hollow of my throat, trailing little kisses along my skin.

"What does that mean?"

"For you? I don't know. Just be careful." Jay says as he pulls away from my skin to look me in the eye, still holding my hands captive behind my back.

"Never."

11
Lone Wolf Girl

Jay leads us through a side door, not the one that the kitchen staff are gathered around after inputting a six-digit code. Saint disappeared inside while Jay was giving me his *be careful* speech, because when Jay finally lets me step away from the wall, Saint is gone. I don't have a choice in holding Jay's hand as we walk inside, since he hasn't released his grip on me. I am *acutely* aware of the amount of pressure he applies, and how loose I keep my fingers.

It's an internal battle not to white-knuckle grip his hand.

It's been a long time since I've been home, but it's been even longer since I've been in the Packhouse. My brother and sister had both hung out within its walls and used the game rooms and gym much more frequently than I ever had. But then, they were much more popular than I had been in school.

I wonder why, Artemis? My wolf takes this opportunity to snark at me.

*Because I spent more time as **you** within the trees.*

Sure, Apollo and Athena had been more popular than me in school, but they could never find me when I didn't want them to. Resident hide-and-seek champion, thank you *very much*.

The inside of the Packhouse looks almost identical to the last time I'd been inside. Sure, the electronics have all had modern upgrades, but the atmosphere has that same feeling. Like everyone is welcome. The interior walls are also made of brick, tasteful decorations are hung on all the walls. There used to be coin-op arcade games in various rooms, at one time I had a high score on one of them. Maybe I'd go take a peek before we leave.

Jay leads me through the large building, waving and doing the dude head nod thing to members of the Pack. When I'd left, Magnus still hadn't replaced his Beta... my father... since his death. I never imagined that Jay would end up in his position, but maybe I'm wrong.

Everyone seems to respect him here.

"Athena and Apollo aren't here, are they?" I ask, suddenly terrified that I'd not only have to face Magnus but my siblings, as well.

"Nope. Last I knew Apollo was back at college for his masters or something, Athena lives next to your mom though."

"Awesome. And I imagine *someone* in there is friends with Athena, right?"

"Yup." Jay chirps brightly, and I drop my head back, groaning with despair.

"Well, that's fucking unfortunate." I find Jay's piercing eyes on my neck when I pick my head up, that silver flash of his wolf again. "What?" I ask, my throat suddenly dry as the Sahara.

"You shouldn't make sounds like that while we're in public, Artemis. I might not be able to restrain myself, since you've given me free reign to kiss you whenever I want."

My stomach drops, and my face heats. Jay *motherfucking* Temple. That lazy smile stretches across his face again as color rises to my cheeks, his attention snagging on my lip caught between my teeth.

"I don't think that an empty hallway counts as public, Jay," I whisper, even if my heart is galloping away.

"No? Not even if at any moment someone could walk through?" Jay replies, pulling me a step closer.

"Nope. Let's go, handsome." I tease, feigning confidence, pulling him down the hallway with me.

Jay Temple is having *entirely* too much fun with this. The *rat* bastard. Silently, I remind myself of why I left, of why I disappeared from this town without a trace.

Him.

This hallway, I know, connects to the large banquet hall, in which I can hear dozens of people talking and laughing. The Pack is just through these doors, and if I let myself pause, to think about it for even another heartbeat, I'll bolt. So I just keep charging ahead, Jay's hand in mine. He squeezes it tight as we pass through the archway.

Jay takes the lead right away, somehow sensing I don't know where I'm going anymore. He leads us towards where I can see Alex, and Dante, Saint's big curly head peeking out above everyone at the bar.

I'm going to need a drink, or maybe five.

When Jay's brother pulls him into a brief hug, Jay doesn't drop my hand, instead returning the embrace with one arm, thumping Alex on the back. Dante gives Jay the head nod thing, giving me a small smile and half wave. I return the gesture.

The 'silent and broody' label seemed to be plastered across Dante's forehead. How much of it is an act?

"Nice to see you again, Artemis. Last time I saw you, I didn't have the chance to introduce you to my wife, Helena." Alex says, the shorter, brunette beside him smiling softly.

"Hellooo-" I chirp, giving a wave not unlike I'd given Dante.

"So I'm told you've been gone a while?" Helena asks, stepping towards me, pulling me out of Jay's grasp as his brother pulls him into conversation. Helena takes me to a high-top table, resting her elbows on the surface.

"Yeah. I left right before graduation. Why?"

"I'm just curious about you. You're a mystery." Helena proceeds to lay her accusations out efficiently and succinctly. "I know you *were* engaged not that long ago. Your beau was wealthy. You've parked a fancy car in the driveway of the Grimes place every night. Why are you back, and why are you pulling Jay into your drama?"

Helena looks soft as a kitten, but she cuts to the heart of the matter without any bullshitting. I can at *least* appreciate that.

"Well. *You're* a jolly ray of fucking Sunshine." I chortle with false brevity. "I'm back because this is my home. Me and Jay, are *me and Jay*, not Artemis, Jay and Helena, but thanks so much for your concern." With that, I push away from the table, looking around to see if anyone I actually want to talk to is around.

Of course, everyone in Timber Hollow is practically a stranger to me these days.

"ARTEMIS HUNT." The Alpha's booming voice fills the Packhouse, vibrating through my bones. Well, nothing to it, but to do it.

"Alpha!" I put on my best cheery smile. "Just the man I'm looking for."

"What does the lone wolf want with an Alpha?" Magnus replies, stepping around tables. The focus of the entire hall is upon us, now.

Oof. Okay, there's a sore spot there, apparently.

You don't say? My wolf snarks back at me, awoken by her Alpha's appearance. In the seven years I've been gone, I hadn't once committed to another pack. I'd visited plenty. Hung around probably far past my welcome as a *drifter* on some occasions, but I never joined. Perhaps that would work in my favor.

"Well, normally people say *hi*, first, but I was going to come ask to rejoin the pack. I'm home." I shrug, feeling once again like a teenager.

"Hmm. So the lone wolf thinks to come into our Packhouse on the arm of my son—the *Alpha's* son— and expects to be welcomed back into the fold, just like that?"

"I..what? What does Jay have to do with this? Why does *everyone* seem to think I came back for Jay? No. I came back because Timber Hollow *is* my home. The entire time I was gone I didn't submit to any other Alpha. I didn't pledge to any other pack. Not once. It's been years since I've even gone on a Pack run." I admit to the Alpha, and... to my pack.

Silverware clatters as it's dropped, and people suck in their breath. Hushed whispers of *she hasn't been on a Pack run in **years?*** rippling around the room.

"So not only have you gone against our ways in going rogue, you've broken your wolf too, and you expect us to welcome you back? A charity case?" Magnus says without feeling, without inflection.

"*My wolf is fine*" I growl, feeling her rise to the surface of my soul, her fur brushing my fingertips. I could shift right here and prove it, but I think that it might be frowned upon at a baby shower.

"Your wolf is *fine*, you say? Okay. We'll see about your rejoining the Timber Hollow pack. *Sure*. But you will earn your place within this Pack again, Artemis Hunt. Blood debt to your father or no— you will not be granted access to this pack's resources without contributing, *girl.*"

I grind my teeth, accepting that I'll have to prove loyalty somehow. It is the way when complete outsiders wanted to join too. Submit to the Alpha's orders, and you're in.

"I didn't expect to access anything, *sir*." I retort, only barely concealing the burning anger I feel.

"Do you have a job?"

"Yes." I practically hiss.

"Where." Magnus doesn't ask the question like he's curious. It's flat, like a demand.

"Coyote Bills."

Magnus grunts, considering. "Agnes set you up with it?"

"Yes. And I'm renting Marcus's room while he's away, though I'm sure you knew about that already." Magnus doesn't answer, just crosses his arms and stares down at me.

"Why not stay in the Packhouse?" Magnus asks, and inwardly I groan for not having thought of a better answer when Jay asked in the car.

"Because, I didn't know if I would be permitted to, or if there would be a room. I...wanted to make sure I had my own space." I stammer, my entire Pack silent, waiting for the Alpha to determine my fate while my blood roars in my ears.

"Well, lone wolf girl, if you want to rejoin the Pack here are my terms. You'll work again in the foundry for a week. Anything you make will be sold in the store, but *you* will not see a penny from the sale. And, since you wanted to be a lone wolf, not even joining on sacred Pack runs, well. You'll go one more full Moon without the comforts of this pack. One month. No one is to join her. Not for a single run, for any purpose. Artemis Hunt, the Lone Wolf, home at last." Magnus hands down my sentencing, addressing the rest of the crowd as he instructs them against running with me.

Like a thousand spiders crawling over my skin, I feel the eyes of each Pack member in the room. Feel them examine me from head to toe, and hear their whispering.

"And, Artemis, go see your mother. She knows you're home." Magnus Temple says before turning on his heel and walking away, presumably to where Dante and Helena are sitting.

I don't give anyone the time to say anything to me before I similarly spin on my heel and leave the Packhouse. I don't know what happened to Jay, and I guess it doesn't matter. I have my orders.

12
Hunters Moon

one day to full moon

"You coming, Artemis?" Jay asks me from just outside the door to my room. I left it open once I'd retreated inside with my book, several hours earlier after waking up and taking a shower.

I ignore him, turning the page. The story is admittedly *very* dirty, and *right now* is the absolute worst time for interruptions.

"Artemis," Jay repeats my name, and I lift my eyes from the page for one moment, seeing him above the edge of the book. I give him a glare that says *leave me alone*, returning my attention to the page before me. "Are you really going to ignore me?"

When I say nothing, Jay climbs across the bed, gripping me by the hip. Then he tugs me down off the pillow. It only takes a second, and I shriek with surprise, unable to stop him as he snatches the book from between my hands. With a firm grip, Jay holds me still with my thighs bracketing his hips, his groin flush against me.

Every single thought flees from my mind as I blink up at him, my heart racing.

"What are you reading, baby girl?" Jay asks as he easily finds my place in the book, and begins to read it out loud.

> *"Oh, you're doing so well for me, Little Demon." I shift my hips, driving even deeper down her throat. She moans, her shoulders twitching like she wants her hands free. "I'm going to take this call, and you're going to keep going. No matter what I say. You keep that cock in your pretty little mouth, and maybe I'll let you cum," I tease, pressing the button on the screen to accept the call.* [1]

Jay clears his throat before he says "I think I'm going to need to borrow that one when you're done with it. Tell me which chapters are your favorite, okay? Book club."

"You're going to read it?" I ask, watching him carefully place my bookmark between the pages, and set the book on the nightstand.

"Yeah. Why not?"

"No reason I guess." I am entirely *too acutely* aware of the fact that neither of us has moved from our very intimate positioning, how much of our bodies touch. Jay lowers himself a little, resting his weight on his arm, braced above my head somewhere.

"Are you coming to the festival?" Jay asks, changing the subject, his hips surging forward.

My breath leaves my lungs. "I wasn't going to, no."

"Change your mind."

"Why?"

Jay searches my face for something for a moment, then says "Why not?"

"I don't know." Looking up at Jay resting between my thighs makes me feel half-crazed. My skin *itches* with the urge to touch him.

Jay smirks again, the silver flash giving me the barest of warnings before he picks me up, throws me over his shoulder and leaves the room, holding me still with a large hand banding the back of my thigh. "Jay! What are you doing?"

"Changing your mind."

"*Jay Temple* put me down."

"Can't do that Darlin'."

"Why?" I practically screech at him, even if I am secretly admiring how easily he holds me up here, how the muscles of his back ripple with each step we take down the stairs.

"Because if you want Magnus to believe *you want* to rejoin the pack, then you need to be seen *interacting with the pack.*"

Jay barely breaks stride as he grabs my boots from next to the door, exiting the house with me still thrown over his shoulder. I'm thankful, at least that I had showered this morning, and put on more than just a t-shirt since I'm apparently spending the evening out. Leggings, a tank, and a flannel aren't much better but it is something.

"Really? Not even stopping for me to put on my shoes?" I glare at Jay's entirely too-defined backside as he carries me over the gravel towards his car.

"You're a flight risk, Artemis. Give you the opportunity and I'll be spending all night chasing your tail." Jay's hand flexes against my thigh, sending a shiver down my spine.

"That's not true!" I grouse while being fully aware that he is...actually right. I would have bolted out the door if he'd put me down. Clever *rat bastard*. Jay tosses me–gently–into the passenger seat.

"You don't fool me, Darlin'," Jay says, slamming the car door after tossing my boots into the footwell for me.

"Rat *bastard*" I mumble to myself as I shove my feet into boots, lacing them up with thinly veiled violence.

Jay doesn't do much more than chuckle to himself as he backs the car out of the lot, driving us towards the park. Saint and Dante follow in what must be Saint's Jeep. The setting Sun has painted the entire sky orange and pink. All of the trees surrounding Timber Hollow have already faded to yellows and oranges. I'd forgotten how beautiful the town is in fall.

The air smells like cinnamon and apples, freshly fried dough and crisp fallen leaves. The sky is dark, and since I've been reading all day I haven't bothered eating much. I'm going to need to get something to eat at the festival, probably *several* somethings. As we are walking into the town park, Saint and

Dante say they are going to go find their families, and catch up to us later. Which leaves just Jay and I to walk the grounds.

At first, I don't say much, just content with walking the pathways of the festival with Jay. Many of the displays and vendors are familiar to me, the very same from the festivals of my younger years–or at least they look similar enough. Or maybe all festivals kind of look the same. My stomach growls, making Jay chuckle.

"Shut up, I haven't eaten all day."

"Why?"

"Because I was reading. I didn't feel like getting up."

"Artemis."

"What?" I ask, feigning innocence.

"Let's go get you food."

"I can wait, it's fine."

"What do you want, Artemis?"

"I said I could wait."

"And I asked, *what do you want to eat?*" Jay's voice drops into a growl, his face looming over mine. I can not understand why he's so close to losing control of his wolf right now, just over the topic of me eating.

"I-What sounds good to you?"

"What do you want? Not me, not anyone else. What do *you* want?"

"Um, I guess I could go for a burger?" I say, spotting a vendor selling those just over his shoulder.

"Was that so hard?" Jay asks, spinning around when I nod towards the booth, hooking his arm over my shoulder.

"Yes." I grouse back, annoyed at the entire situation.

Jay laughs, leading us straight up to the food window just as two other customers walk away arms laden with a smorgasbord of items.

"I'll be with you in a moment," the cashier says, breaking open a roll of coins into the cash drawer.

"What do you want?" Jay asks, carefully looking over the menu boards plastered across the exterior of the food truck, arm still slung over my shoulder.

"Uhh, I guess just a Delux." The menu states it comes with cheese, bacon, onions and pickles, a house blend of spicy sauce on top.

"Nice," Jay says, relaying my order, and begins to give his own. I manage to untangle myself and step away from the truck, looking around at the festival. This season is not nearly as wet as some of the festivals I remember from my youth, so the park isn't a complete mud pit.

Tiny victories.

The Moon hangs low in the sky, nearly full. She looks red tonight, tinged with the colors of Sunset over the forest which is full of similarly colored leaves. A vast sea of yellow, red, and orange surrounds Timber Hollow.

Despite the drama with Helena, my anxiety over Ethan finding me— and my dumbassery with Jay at Coyote Bills, I'm glad to be back.

It's good to be home.

When Jay comes back with a burger, a large soda and a basket of fries I ask "Where's yours?"

"I already ate," Jay replies, stealing a french fry from the basket.

"Jay Temple you mean to tell me, that you dragged me over to get food and you aren't going to get anything?" I ask incredulously, a blush rising to my cheeks.

"No. I'm going to eat the fries you tell yourself you want but you only eat about five of them before you stop." Jay replies, that lazy self assured smile once again stretched across his face, french fry halfway to his mouth.

I narrow my eyes at him, taking a big bite out of my burger.

"That's what I thought, Gorgeous."

"Shut up," I say around another mouthful, fighting the heat rising to my cheeks.

It only takes a few moments for me to devour my meal. Eating more than just *five* french fries thank you, while Jay and I walk around, watching people throwing softballs at a dunk tank, the kids at the ring toss losing badly. I can't help but notice that Jay hadn't asked me what I wanted to drink but had managed to get what I liked anyway. I toss the remnants of the soda that we'd both shared away in a nearby bin when we walk by.

"Let's go pick pumpkins," Jay says, steering me and my now full belly towards the displays of pumpkins, all grown in Timber Hollow-or so the hand painted sign says.

"For what?" I ask, but let myself get steered that way regardless.

"To carve, obviously." Jay snarks, shaking his head.

"You still carve pumpkins?"

"Yea. When's the last time you carved a pumpkin, Artemis?" Jay asked, swinging his face towards mine. The Sun had set some time ago, but with all the lights from the festival, Jay's face is bright.

I struggle to remember if Jay has always had this effect on me, or if my becoming tongue-tied around him is a recent development. One thing is for sure though, I still like the way my name sounds rolling off of his tongue entirely too much.

"It's been a long time, Jay." I answer, "Probably since before I left."

"Well let's fix that," Jay says, smiling softly at me. I have to look away from his face, which is when I notice Ivy watching me from where she stands in line for Apple Cider.

"That's my boss over there." I say to Jay, "Do you think we're acting couple-y enough?" When I look at him, I can't define that unfathomable look in his eye, the sliver of his wolf peeking through.

"Probably not. I'll fix that though." Jay replies, that lazy smile stretching across his face again.

My eyebrows scrunch together. "What do you mean you'll fix tha-" Jay doesn't let me finish my sentence before he grips the back of my head and pulls me to him. For a second, I am too stunned to do anything. With Jay's mouth on mine, and his hands in my hair there isn't any room for thought or objections.

So I kiss him back. Thread my fingers through his hair and meet his ferocious kiss. Jay kisses like he is dying. Like he's never getting the chance again. His warm hands grip me around my ribs, crushing me to his chest.

The moment shatters when Saint walks up next to Jay and me, knocking shoulders. "Hey, there you two are. Was starting to wonder if you guys had run off to *shag*." He laughs, Dante chortling along with him.

"Nope. Artemis just told me she hasn't carved a pumpkin in like fifteen years." Jay says, turning to face the arrangement of pumpkins.

"Well we can't have that," Saint says merrily, striding over to choose his gourd. "We'll have to have a pumpkin carving party."

"A pumpkin carving party?" Dante jeers, rolling his grey eyes. "What are we, twelve?"

"Don't be a sour puss, Dante." Saint teases, thoroughly examining every pumpkin for flat spots, bumps and lumps. "Did you two love birds pick them out already?"

"Nope. Didn't manage it before Jay here decided to swallow my face." I tease back, smiling up at Jay. He is already looking at me, his lips pulled into a soft smile. Saint and Dante laugh, moving around the display.

"You gonna pick a pumpkin or what?" Jay asks, even if he hasn't moved an inch, either.

"Yeah, I guess," I reply, and it seems as if time itself pauses for me, halts on this one moment where Jay's eyes are focused on me. And then I move, and it's over.

The arrangement of pumpkins is only the beginning. Behind the shed hundreds of the orange gourds are lined up according to size, making it easier for customers to select their own. Unsurprisingly, Saint and Dante are already congregating around some of the larger ones, hemming and hawing over which one would make the best carving.

I make my way towards a small grouping of greyish pumpkins, the white sign staked into the ground before them showing their name, "Jarrahdale squash".

"That one. I want *that* one." I say, pointing to the largest of them in this pile.

"Miss, I'm sorry I overheard your friends-' the shop keep says, her hand outstretched towards me. "You're carving pumpkins, right?" Jay nods. "The Jarrahdale isn't very good for carving. They are best used in recipes."

"Oh. Well alright." I say, moving towards the rows and rows of orange pumpkins neatly lined up, on my way to find something similarly sized.

Jay lingers with the shopkeeper, talking to her in hushed tones. I can't even begin to contemplate what about. His friends are loudly debating the merits of seasoned pumpkin seeds, Saint firmly on team ranch, Dante on spicy. Then the overgrown puppy and his shadow both hoist their entirely too large pumpkins up, walking over to the shed where the cash register is to pay. I'm kneeling in front of two pumpkins, looking them over for flat spots and weird knobby bits when Jay reappears, his hands empty.

"Did you find one?" I ask Jay, selecting the better of the two pumpkins to buy.

"I found *the* one," Jay replies with smug confidence.

"*Sure* you did. Jay Temple found *the best* pumpkin in the pumpkin patch. What else is new?" I snark, rolling my eyes, even if I am smiling. Jay doesn't say anything back, just follows me and my pumpkin over to where Saint and Dante are still paying.

The shopkeeper finishes the transaction with the boys, saying "I'll open the shed for you boys in a moment, when I'm done with their transaction," motioning me forward.

Jay says "Add this one to mine." as soon as we're in front of her. The lady nods her head appreciatively, entering numbers into her register.

"Twenty two even." She says, Jay putting twenty five in her hand.

"Keep the change, ma'am. Can we store ours in the shed until we're done walking around as well?"

"Sure thing sugar. Just write your initials on the tops of this one and I'll handle the rest."

"Are you sure? We can carry it-"

"I've got it, you two kids run along." The lady replies, a soft smile pulling her lips up.

"Thank you, we really appreciate it," Jay says to the lady, and she walks away, pumpkin under an arm. I pretend I don't notice when Jay slips another ten into the check slot on the cash register.

"So now what?" I ask him as we walk away. "We've eaten, we've picked out pumpkins, what's next?"

"Ice cream."

"Ice cream?"

"Yea, you got a problem with that Gorgeous?" Jay asks, his face split by a wide smile, and that twinkle of mischief is back in his eye.

"Absolutely not. You'll have to tell me what I owe you for food and stuff when we get home though, since you took me out of the house without any time to get my wallet or anything." I say, following his lead down the main walkway of the Hunters Moon festival.

In the earliest years of the Pack's founding, the festival was a way to celebrate the coming of winter. They'd have a glorious party, then a wild run through the trees, hunting deer, elk, moose. You name it. Now, the festival is more for tourists, scheduled the day before the actual full Moon, and Pack run.

"Yea, that's not gonna happen, Gorgeous," Jay replies easily, turning to the sounds of Saint and Dante barreling up the asphalt to where we stand in line for ice cream.

"How dare you guys. Getting ice cream without us? The audacity!" Saint taunts, not even a little out of breath from the sprint.

"What's your favorite flavor, Artemis?" Dante asks, surveying the menu.

"Pistachio in a waffle cone, yours?" I answer, making sure that the option was on the board.

"Fireball, they don't always have it either."

"Yea, and when they don't he pouts about it for *days*." Saint chirps, stepping forward as the line moves.

"Well then what's *your* favorite Saint?" I ask.

"I've never met an ice cream I didn't like, Tiny," Saint replies with a wide grin, waving to someone across the park.

"Fair enough. Jay?"

"Rocky Road." His answer is short, and sweet.

"I'll give you a *rocky road bro.*" Saint says, waggling his eyebrows with a little shimmy shake. Laugher explodes out of me, Jay and Dante's chuckles quickly following my own.

"I'll pass on your quick ride and sloppy finish," Jay says, full mouth pulled into a smile.

Saint orders for us all, happily passing bills over to the cashier and handing out ice creams as they are given to him. Once everyone is armed with a cone, the four of us meander through the vendors, pointing out cool looking nicknacks or art pieces that catch our attention.

Saint may point at everything his eye catches, cooing over details but it's Dante with the mindset of a magpie. He starts off slow, only buying a few things here and there but by the time his ice cream is gone, he has several bags clutched in one hand.

There's a new addition to the festival—well, at least new to me— set up around the hayride and corn maze booth. Two metal bathtubs are set up, full to the brim with icy water.

"What is that for?" I ask, not directing my question to anyone in particular.

"Fundraising. Profit goes to the senior class." Dante answers, adding "You going in?"

"Absolutely not." I quickly answer.

"What's the matter, are you too chicken, Artemis?" Jay teases that lazy smirk on his face once more.

"*No.* I'm just smart enough to not go in an ice bath in the middle of October, Jay." I snark back, watching as a pair of guys lower themselves in the freezing water, teeth chattering instantly.

"I bet I could stay longer than you." He says, giving me a sideways glance as he also watches the guys hoot and holler about the cold.

"Pft. You wish." I immediately reply, even if it was all bravado. There is no way I am going to get in that ice bath.

"Nope. I know it."

"*How*, could you possibly know that?"

"I just do." He replies, that self assured smirk on his face. And *I* just want to wipe it off.

"Prove it."

Jay raises an eyebrow at me. "Prove it?"

"Yep," I reply. "*Prove it* big guy."

"Well, if you insist, Princess." Jay holds a hand out for me to approach the worker stationed at the ice baths.

"Don't ever fucking call me that again," I say to Jay as I walk up to the booth.

"Hi-ya folks. Feel like taking an ice plunge?"

"Yep. Both of us, please." Jay replies, handing cash over to the man.

"Excellent. You can strip in the stall behind me, we have a bunch of big white tees for you to put on to cover up with." Jay nods, going over to pull the curtain back, ducking inside the small changing stall. He emerges moments later, now only wearing boxers slung low on his hips.

Mother of god, Jay looks *fucking* amazing. *The rat bastard.*

He holds the curtain open for me to duck under as well. I don't say anything, not trusting myself that something absolutely asinine won't come out as I move under his arm. Like the employee said, there are stacks of shirts in various sizes on a table, Jay's discarded clothes to the side of a bench.

I quickly change into one of the white tees that still has the starch from the manufacture on it, leaving the little stall, thankful that it's not colder than it is tonight, or this experience would be positively miserable. Jay is already next to a tub, waiting for me. Still looking entirely too good for my health.

The worker goes over some safety things, like what to expect when you first go in and how your body will react. I can't pay attention. I catch a few things the instructor says, but not much in between drinking down the sight of Jay Temple, wearing nothing but boxers in the middle of town.

Gray sweatpants have nothing on what those boxers are doing for his...well *him.*

"Fifteen minutes is the max time we can allow you to stay in, though most people don't last beyond the one-minute mark. Any questions?" The instructor's voice interrupts my insane thoughts.

"Nope." Jay and I answer in unison. When I glance at him, he's already staring at me, smirking.

"Alright then. When you folks are ready." The guy says, motioning us towards the tubs. Jay steps towards the one closer to him, muscles rippling. Then, without warning Saint jumps over the edge of the other, leaving me standing here with my mouth flapping open.

Saint, while he's complaining about the cold fishes money out of his wallet, teeth clattering the entire time, handing a couple of bills over to the instructor now by his side. Water splashes out of the tub, condensation running down the metal sides.

"Hah, looks like I don't have to get in, after all. You can compete with Saint." I sass to Jay, crossing my arms over my chest, shifting my weight to one leg.

"Nope my bet is with you, Darlin. Get in the water." Jay orders, motioning towards the tub he stands in front of.

"And what? Share it?" I ask, motioning to the tub.

"Yup," Jay says, smirking.

"No. Just wait until Saint gets out."

"I want in on the action. Whoever lasts longest gets to pick what the punishment is?" Saint chatters, trying to smile.

"You mean if I last longer than you two you will do whatever I say?" I ask, admittedly very interested in the prospect.

"Yea, how 'bout it, Tiny?"

"Feelin froggy, Jay?" I ask, waggling my eyebrows at him.

"For you? Always." He says, stepping into the water. And until that exact moment I hadn't actually thought about what this would mean, that I will have to share the admittedly small metal tub with him, clad only in a big shirt and my underwear.

Well *shit*. I don't let myself think about it, stepping into the tub after him. This is *no big deal*.

Jay sits at the back, knees resting on the sides of the metal. As I sink beneath the icy, burning cold water my mind snaps into hyperdrive, even as a sense of calm descends over me.

Immediately, Jay tugs me back against him, arms draping across the top of my chest. "Are you okay?" He asks in my ear, shivering, hugging me tight. My hands grip his forearms, my fingertips turning white in the icy water. All of Jay's usual warmth has been stolen by the cold.

"Y-yeah," I say, stuttering. Honestly, the water isn't horrible, now that I'm almost fully under. It definitely *fucking sucks* but the biting cold of the metal against my bare ass is worse. I shift, trying to find a way to settle without my skin resting on the metal.

"Talk to me, what's wrong?" Jay asks, and I hate how thick his voice is in my ear, how it sends a thrill down my spine.

"The fucking metal is cold, Jay." I snark, wondering how long we've been in for.

"At least you guys have each other. I'm suffering over here." Saint says, teeth chattering even worse now.

"No one told you to join them, idiot," Dante says, rolling his eyes, standing next to Saint's tank. "Let alone told you to go in fully clothed." A bag of kettle korn is in his hand, a fistful halfway to his mouth.

"There was a bet. I had to." Saint whines, Dante just rolls his eyes again, munching on his snack.

"That's two minutes! Longest dip of the night so far!" The guy cheers, adding our time to a little whiteboard.

"You're gonna win," Jay says, his hot mouth against my shoulder now, shifting us so that we sink lower into the water, making me lay fully against him, my ass no longer resting against the frigid metal.

"Why do you say that?" I chatter, feeling every muscle in my body contract over and over again with intense shivers.

"Because Saint doesn't like pain. Neither do I." Jay says, his five-o'clock shadow scraping against my neck.

"Are *you* okay?" I ask, trying very hard to ignore the rush of heat that spools low in my belly with every word that Jay murmurs against my neck, how he feels pressed against me like this.

"I've got you all wet and laying across me. Couldn't be better Darlin."

"FUCK!" Saint suddenly shouts, jumping out of the ice and spraying the ground around the tub with water. "Fuck, fuck, fuck" Saint keeps chanting, dashing into the changing tent in search of a towel at the attendants direction.

"And then there were two," Dante says, turning towards us with his kettle korn. He takes a fistfull of it, stuffing it into his mouth, apparently content to watch and wait.

"Be nice to us, when you win?" Jay asks, his mouth once again against my neck.

"No promises, handsome." I chatter.

Jay chuckles, kissing the side of my head as he shifts us, "That's my girl." Then he stands, showering me with ice and frigid water.

13
Goodnight, Artemis

Later, after we all leave the festival and get back to the apartment, I go up to my room and change... I can't go to bed yet... There's this empty hole in my middle, yawning open, threatening to swallow me whole. So, I go back downstairs, maybe I will watch TV for a little while. When I enter the living room, I see Jay setting up his makeshift bed on the couch. Immediately, I feel like turning around...instead, I'm frozen in the doorframe for entirely too long. Eventually, I make my way over to the couch though... It's just Jay.

He settles into the cushions, patting the seat next to him. The TV has an anime show on, one I'm not familiar with, but it doesn't matter. It's effective enough to distract me. I settle into the corner of the couch, resting my chin on my knee, arms laced around my leg. The screen drones on and on, characters having a battle and I almost immediately zone out.

"What's wrong?" Jay asks after a minute, not even bothering to pretend to pay attention to the TV.

"What makes you think something is wrong?" I ask, glancing at him through my lashes.

"I know that face," Jay replies, shifting his eyes back to the TV.

"Hmm." Is all I respond. Truth is I don't know what's wrong either. Jay lets the silence stand for a few minutes, the two of us staring at the glowing screen. I have no idea what the plot of the show is, or what is even happening in this episode. I don't think I could even point out the characters in a line-up.

"Artemis," Jay demands again, making my head turn towards him.

"Hmm?" I hum back in response. I'm still not sleepy, but I do feel *settled* somehow.

"Come here." Jay orders, opening his arms. I hesitate for all of a second before I crawl across the cushion and curl into his embrace. "Relax, Gorgeous. Everything is okay." Jay says again, squeezing his arm around me.

At first, I have no idea how to manage that. How am I supposed to relax when Jay is wrapped around me, and the world is dark and quiet? How am I supposed to think about anything other than the way he'd held me in my bed, how he'd kissed me at Coyote Bills?

This is all supposed to be fake. So why doesn't it feel fake? Why does it feel like I'm already in way too deep? Eventually, though, my breathing matches his, slow and steady, muscles loosening one by one. I still couldn't tell you what the plot of the show is, but I think I might be able to point out a character or two.

I don't fall asleep, but I know Jay has by the end of the second episode. Moving as slowly as possible to rise off the couch, I break Jay's grip around my middle. Jay keeps snoring softly the whole time. After a quick visit to the bathroom, I come back into the living room and stare at his large form spread across the couch. There's no way he's comfortable sleeping on that thing all night. No way that he's *been* comfortable sleeping on it for however long Alex and Helena have been here.

Immediately, my mind is made up. Silently padding over to him, I grab a pillow and toss it onto his face.

Jay wakes with a jolt, his eyes flying open, arm reaching out to the space I'd vacated. When his blue-green eyes focus on me, I say "Come on handsome, you're not sleeping on the couch." It takes him a minute, neurons and synapses firing before he silently rises from the couch and follows me up the stairs.

"Where am I going?" He asks sleepily, his feet shuffling on the carpet.

"My room."

"Why?"

"Because I'm not letting you sleep on that tiny couch anymore," I answer simply. If I'm already in too deep, I might as well drown myself.

"It's not that bad. Where are you sleeping?"

"In my bed."

"Where am *I* sleeping?" Jay asks suspiciously.

"My bed. Unless, you…?" I haven't even considered that he might not want to. Might not want to share a bed with me.

Jay's blue eyes sear straight through me, the edge of sleepiness still visible, but something *sharper* and more predatory has come forward too. His wolf.

"Unless I what?"

"Unless you don't want to." I squeak.

"Are you going to be able to sleep?" He asks, searching my face.

"Yes. We're adults, are we not? You're going to wreck your back sleeping on that couch." I sass back, with much more confidence than I feel.

"Sure we are," Jay replies easily, And I feel like I've made a big mistake–a big, *dumb* one, but there is no backing down now.

"Then come on handsome. Let's go to bed." I order, opening my door. He groans softly as he follows me in. I don't bother with the lights, just walks in and climbs into the bed and under the covers. Jay comes and lays on top of the blankets, settling on the far edge. "*Jay*. What are you doing?" I ask exasperated.

"Laying down?"

"What are you doing on *top* of the blankets?" I almost add *you should be on top of me*. It's a tiny blessing that I barely manage to keep *that* particular thought locked behind my teeth.

"I didn't want to assume." He answers, voice rising at the end.

"Oh for fucks sake. Get under the blankets and go to sleep, Jay." I order, and he listens, grumbling to himself about *bossy women*. I barely restrain a laugh, letting the quiet settle back over us.

"Goodnight Artemis." Jay eventually whispers into the dark.

"Goodnight, Jay," I whisper back, and listening to Jay's steady breathing beside me, I fall into a *deep, dreamless* sleep.

14
Rattlesnakes

full moon

Waking up by myself has put me in a *foul* mood. I try not to think too hard about the reason for that as I get dressed in a sage green cropped long-sleeve and jeans. But, even being in a shitty mood won't be a good enough excuse to get out of what I have to do today.

Unfortunately, since Magnus decided to *order me* to go see my Mother in front of the entire pack, I should probably do that. Go see her today before she joins the Pack for the Full Moon. Sounds about as fun as going to bed in a sleeping bag full of rattlesnakes right now.

I've been home for almost a week already and haven't managed the few miles to her house. My mom will be pleasant I know, at least on the surface. There are always thinly veiled insults and jibes in her words. In how she says things. It's all passive-aggressive bullshit, or playing the victim. That's all she knows. More than that though, I know Mom is going to ask about Ethan. And, his car that I currently walk towards, trying to find music for the drive over on my phone. The engine rumbles when I turn the key over, vibrating the car.

I'm really going to miss this beast when Ethan takes it back.

This morning had been cold, frost glazing the windshield until the Sun melted it off. I'd watched the ice disappear through the window while I sipped on coffee. I wish, for one single moment, that Athena and I have a better relationship as I pull away from my apartment. Once upon a time, we'd been close, thick as thieves even. I don't know what changed, but suddenly we stopped talking every day, then every week, and then just all together. At this point it's been... *years* since I've spoken to either of my siblings.

Either way, I suppose it's time to go home. No matter how much I wish things were different. Driving over there barely takes any time at all.

My childhood home sits near the middle of town, a one-story house painted a horrifying pale yellow. My mom always liked the color, going so far as to paint the inside of the house a similar shade at one point. When I'd left home, the lot on the end of the street had been empty. Now, a new robin's egg blue house sits there. I have almost no doubt that it is Athena's house. I don't see anyone moving about inside, so I have to assume she's at Mom's.

Great.

Maybe it won't be that bad. My wolf's golden eyes peer out from the dark of my mind, her hope for me as tangible as a physical thing.

Maybe. I agree, even if I know differently.

Walking up to the door, I can't help but feel like I should knock. Like I need permission to enter. I don't, though, if only because I know that if I *were* to knock on the door I would be greeted with something like 'What, don't think you're welcome anymore?' or something similarly crass and passive-aggressive.

The door creaks now, the hinge not nearly as silent as it once was. As I shuck my boots off, I'm hit with a wave of nostalgia. The house smells like Mom's homemade chicken noodle soup. She used to make it once or twice a season, once the weather turned cold. Mom would also make it if either of my siblings requested it when they were sick. I can't say I remember ever getting the same treatment.

Athena is sitting at the bar, a bowl of steaming soup on the countertop before her. Mom has her back turned to the door, but I know she heard my entrance.

"Surprise!" I hoot, doing a little spin. "I'm home!" Mom turns at that, an exasperated smile on her face.

"Artemis! There's my girl." She says, pulling me into a hug, gripping me tight, and swaying side to side. "Oh, I missed you so much! My baby!" She hugs me like that for almost too long, before holding me by my chin, brushing my hair out of my face. "Your hair is lighter." She adds, "I like it."

"Thanks," I reply, giving her a tight smile, ignoring how it makes me feel. Of course, she'd like my hair lighter. I don't remind her of dad so much with it more like *hers*.

"Are you hungry?" She asks, already fishing a bowl out of the cupboard to fill with soup from the crock pot.

"Sure, a small bowl please," I answer, sitting on the stool next to my sister.

Athena says, "Hey. Heard you were back in town. Almost didn't believe it."

"Yeah, sorry I haven't been by yet. I started working right away and I've just been exhausted." The reasoning...*excuse* is for them both. It's not a lie, but it's not the truth either.

Mom sets my bowl of soup in front of me with a biscuit, saying "Too tired for your poor old Mom?"

My wolf rolls her golden eyes so I don't have to.

"No, I'm sorry. I should have come sooner." I answer, filling my mouth with the scalding soup, even if it burns like a motherfucker. I don't have to talk if I'm eating. The soup is admittedly delicious. Peppery with good-sized chunks of rotisserie chicken, celery, and carrots. The good egg noodles instead of the cheap macaroni elbows she used to use.

As soon as we leave we're going for a run. I say to my wolf, feeling the itch to leave under my skin already. Two minutes inside the house and I've said *I'm sorry* twice.

Deal. She answers.

"So you've come home and managed to get yourself in trouble with Magnus before you came to see me. What's going on?" Mom asks, making it sound as if I'd done something intentional to the Alpha.

"I heard you were already shacking up with *Jay Temple.*" Athena chimes in before I have a chance to respond to Mom.

"Wow. Okay." I say to them both, my spoon clattering into the bowl. I huff a laugh before I say "I didn't *get myself in trouble* with Magnus. He's mad because I ran off without telling anyone and without joining in on Pack runs for a few years. He thinks I broke my wolf."

"Did you?" My mom flat-out asks, and the look on her face makes me think that she agrees with Magnus.

"*No.*" I grate and leave it at that. My appetite is gone, but I know that if I don't at least look like I'm enjoying the food, and eat a good amount of it she'll be passive-aggressive about *that* too. So, I pick up the biscuit and dunk it lightly in the broth.

It's a fucking good biscuit, I'll give her that.

"And Jay? I noticed you didn't say anything about *that*." My mom quips, right as I'm taking another bite of biscuit. Leaving the opportunity open for Athena.

"One of my friends said they were all hot and heavy all over each other outside the Packhouse the other day." My sister says smugly, sipping on her iced tea.

I make a face at her as if to say *really? We're supposed to be on the same side!* And there's absolutely *no fucking way* I'm admitting that we're not dating, only pretending to because I almost got fired on my third shift.

"Alright, fine. I didn't know that the apartment Aggie set me up with was *also* apparently Jay's. But.. He uh..." I trailed off, not sure what to say. How could I explain that even without seeing him for seven years, I feel *safe* with Jay? "I don't know... He's Jay." I shrug, hoping it is enough.

I'm gonna kill Jay when I see him though. Murder him. Hack him up into tiny little pieces and scatter them across the forest so that they're picking him out from between the weeds for centuries.

As heat crawls up my neck and cheeks again, I have to resist the urge to make some excuse to leave in the next three seconds.

"I always wondered if you'd go through with it, you know." My mom says, smiling softly at me.

"What do you mean?"

"Marry that rich boy. Never thought I'd see my baby girl again, but I didn't think you'd marry him either." The smug look on her face makes my stomach twist. "Are you going to run off again when he breaks up with you this time?"

I choke on my spit. "*What?*"

"You don't think I figured it out? You took off right before graduation and that party you *begged* me to go to. Then Jay starts asking about you looking like a lost puppy. He broke up with *you* and then *you* ran off."

"Not exactly, no. I left because I wanted to." I snap.

"Mhm. I don't think I believe that. You two were always hot and cold. You made me dizzy half the time."

"Right.... so, *why* is my love life the most pressing topic of conversation?"

"Because your ex is engaged already, but you've got a car in his name in my driveway while you're shacking up with the Alpha's boy."

"How do you know it's in his name?"

"Because *you're* not going to put vanity plates that say "rich boy" on a car like that. Agnes would have taught you better."

A quick glance out the window would prove that, yes. That is what the plates spell out. *Damn.*

"Fine. I found Ethan White in the midst of sticking his dick in someone else, so I left. I took the car as... *compensation* for dealing with his bullshit."

"And Jay?" Athena pushes, fingers laced under her chin, elbows propped on the counter.

"Jay is Jay. Put him and me in a room together for long enough and one of us will fold." I shrug. It's not a lie. He already feels like an itch under my skin, one I'm dying to scratch.

I thought you just needed to get laid. My wolf snarks, apparently satisfied with the conversation as well.

The two things aren't mutually exclusive.

"And that's all? You didn't come home for him?" Athena pushes again, and I have to restrain the urge to reach out and shove her off her barstool.

"No, I didn't *come back for him*. Apparently, everyone thinks that though." I sigh, remembering how Helena had also interrogated me as soon as I'd entered the Packhouse.

"Are you running with us tonight?" Mom asks, using her dusty mom instincts to sense that I don't want to talk about Jay anymore.

"Nope. Not allowed to join." I answer, taking the remnants of my now cold soup to the sink. Not that I'd run with my mom or sister in the Pack run anyway. They're too slow. Too loud.

My mom sucks in a breath, her eyes going round. "*What?*"

"You heard me. I'm not allowed to join in this run. Magnus essentially said that if I wanted to be a *lone wolf so bad*, I could be one for one more full Moon. No one is allowed to join me, either. I'm to run alone while you all run together."

"That's what you get," Athena says under her breath, and I have to push down the sting of hurt. I don't know why I keep expecting her to take my side. It's been *years* since we were on the same side of anything. Even before I left we'd strayed apart. She has a ring around her finger now, and to shift the focus off of my shoulders once and for all, I ask her about it.

"Did you marry whats-her-face?" I knew she had a steady girlfriend before I left, but I couldn't say what her name had been.

"Daisy?"

"If that's who you were dating when I left, sure," I answer, leaning against the counter with my arms crossed.

"Yeah. We broke up off and on for a while but we found our way, eventually." Athena has a soft smile on her face, and I am happy for her.

"Daisy is wonderful. I love her!" Mom adds, and then the two of them start talking about how good of a cook my sister's wife is, cooing over the lamb steaks she makes on occasion.

Apparently, they do *family* dinners now too. Fucking kill me now.

I can't help but wonder what Dad would have thought about all this... about *me*. Would he have understood my inability to join in on another Pack's run? Would he have let me go? Growing up I'd always been his shadow. The Shadow's shadow.

Because that's what Dad had always been. Magnus's shadow. His second.

"What does Magnus mean when he says *'blood debt to your father'*?" I suddenly ask, interrupting their conversation about the menu for the next family dinner, that I've been invited to.

Mom cuts a look at me, before sighing heavily and leaning against the counter. "Your father made Magnus swear an oath, sealed with a blood bond, that our family would always have a place in Timber Hollow. So long as it's Magnus's blood in power. It was his contingency on becoming Beta. He didn't want to get himself killed in a fight, and then have us all be kicked out."

I hate her for how she says everything so callously, without her face betraying even a spec of emotion. But I swallow down my emotions, instead just nodding and letting them go back to their menu planning.

So if there is a blood debt in play, then my punishment is merely that. Punishment from the Alpha for running away.

After making excuses to leave my mom's around three, I head back towards my apartment. The Pack won't start running until nightfall, but they're all over at the Packhouse now. Eating, laughing and just *being* together. A family. Mom and Athena had been talking about going over soon, too.

I can't wait any longer though, I need to shift. I need to *run*.

The time I spent over at my Mom's has only made the need that much more urgent. When I pull into the lot for the apartment, I'm surprised to see that all the boy's cars are still there. Throwing the shifter into first and ripping the e-brake up with probably too much force, I exit the Stingray. I can't go inside.

I can't. I have to run.

My wolf is pacing inside my mind, and I can feel her fur under my fingers, her teeth in my maw. Taking the trail that leads into the forest, I shed clothing piece by piece. First my boots and socks, then my shirt, then my pants. I drop my underwear at the tree line, and then it's just me and my wolf.

I surrender. The words come out as a prayer. I don't mean to say it, but it doesn't matter. In seconds, my limbs all snap and rearrange, and her teeth emerge. The wolf. *Me.*

My paws barely touch the cool earth before I propel myself forward. The Moon isn't even visible yet, the Sun is still too bright— but I feel it.

I feel the ebb and flow of the tide in my blood, a song for the Moon and the Moon alone. Tilting my head back towards the sky, I let the note free- let it reverberate through the woods.

Here I am. Here I am.

Running through the trees, I trace my steps from days and years past. Even when I was young, on full Moon runs I would inevitably find myself separated from the pack, alone under the canopy of leaves. It's not half bad, no, it's just the fact that *I'm not allowed* to join the others. Not allowed to be part of my family for the night we're supposed to be closest.

Noise coming straight towards me disturbs my thoughts, and seconds later, Jay's wolf emerges. The two wolves flanking his either side, a step behind must also be Saint and Dante. I can't tell who is who, other than Jay is in the middle, his silver wolf distinct from the other two.

One is grey, looking like it has been dusted by cinnamon sugar, the color more dense along his forehead and spine. The other is more brown and red, only the points of it grey.

My hackles raise a low growl erupting in my throat. I'm on edge, and I have no idea what Jay is going to do. He takes a step, then another towards me, giving me ample time to read his movements. My muscles tense, locked, and loaded to explode into motion. Then, he brushes his body against my own, a sort of bump hug that would have sent me to my knees if I didn't feel so charged.

Jay has me- hook line and sinker and he doesn't even know it.

I take a tentative step towards the deep forest, checking to see if they are going to follow. Jay's wolfy eyes are bright, and they all take that same step with me. My heart soars.

With a yip, I dash away. Claws digging into the dirt, the boys hot on my tail.

Hours and hours pass, running through the trees with them. The Moon rises, and still we run. Through the trees, jumping over streams, and sneaking behind waterfalls. We run all over the forest until even the Moon sets.

But every step of the way, Jay, Saint, and Dante are with me.

Jay

Resisting Artemis' call is impossible.

Even if I hadn't *known* it was her, that she was *here* there is no resisting the howl she let loose.

I can't believe she's back though. I'd almost given up entirely on her.

Not anymore though. Not a chance. Not when I know how hard her heart races when I kiss her, even if she tries to pretend otherwise. With Saint and Dante following me, I keep sight of the black tip of her tail. I didn't ask them to come, to disobey our Alpha, but they did anyway. *My* pack.

I never had any intention of listening to my father's order when it came to making Artemis run alone, again. Saint and Dante never let me get into trouble by myself, so the party of two became a party of four.

Following her clothes to the treeline like a trail of breadcrumbs set a fire in my blood. Every time she lets me get close, I wonder if I'll be able to pull away. I wonder if I'll tip my hand, and I wonder if she bolts again, if I'll be able to find her.

I've kept tabs on her through the years, once I found her that is. Artemis had dropped off the face of the earth for a few years until one of my buddies in the Nevada Pack said he had a new bartender resembling my high school girlfriend. By the time I'd gotten there, Artemis was already gone. But it was her, the memorial polaroid of her sitting on the bar that was tacked up to the wall behind the top shelf booze now resides on the bookshelf in my room.

A few other packs had contacted me through the years, saying a blonde fitting her description had been there for a few days, gone without a trace. One out in Colorado had sent me a picture of her with both middle fingers up, wearing a cheesy grin.

And then, when her beautiful face showed up plastered across the tabloids, I thought for sure I'd die on the spot. I thought I'd lost her for good. The photographers sure did like capturing photos of Artemis standing next to her fiancé. Learning to let her go was the hardest thing I've ever had to do.

But here she is. Leading me around the woods just like she used to. I'll follow her anywhere. Anything she wants, I'll give to her.

Artemis Hunt. The girl I never got over. She'll be mine again before she even realizes. I'll make sure of it.

15
Body Bag

twenty seven days to full moon

I wake with anxiety already pooling in my stomach, uneasy despite being barely conscious. The house smells like maple syrup and frying bacon, so I manage to roll myself out of bed, and into an oversized shirt before stumbling down the steps. I don't usually eat breakfast, but something about the aromas wafting from the kitchen is making my stomach rumble, even if I still feel like someone is watching me.

When I pass through the living room, peeking out the windows to see that it is only my car, and Saint's Jeep sitting in the lot. He's in the kitchen bustling around, a fresh batch of bacon hitting the screaming hot pan. Saint also has music going quietly, loud enough to be heard over the frying meat but not so loud to make it impossible to hear yourself think. He sees me enter as he's spinning around, spatula in hand and his hair tossed into a bun at the back of his head.

Saint is still singing along to the lyrics as he nods at the island, already assembling a plate of pancakes and bacon. Fresh squeezed orange juice sits in a large jug in the middle, along with a few short glasses with black bottoms. "Do you want some?" I ask Saint as I pour my cup. He nods, still singing, so I pour juice into a second glass, sliding it towards his side of the counter.

It's bright, incredibly flavorful and tart. A slap in the face with vitamin C. Exactly what a wolf needs after spending the night sprinting through the trees after prey. When Saint slings the plate of food before me, my stomach growls. A glance at the clock tells me it's *technically* almost lunch. So really, my rule of not eating breakfast isn't broken.

"Eat up." Saint orders, turning off burners and sitting down with his plate loaded with food.

"*Heard*, Chef," I say, mocking his tone, giving him a two-finger salute. He snorts, before dumping *thick* maple syrup over his pancakes. The sticky liquid comes out in thick ribbons, cascading slowly down the stack. The label indicates it's *real* maple syrup—the good stuff—not the watery store brand.

Saint sees me eyeing the syrup, and with a smirk, he says "You want some, Tiny?"

"Yes, Chef." I sass back, extending my hand towards the little jug. Saint smiles, but passes it to me anyway, along with a fork. I drizzle considerably less syrup over my flapjacks than Saint did, just a couple of passes over them. Saint waits until my mouth is stuffed full to ask how I slept.

"Fine, I guess." A lie. After running all night with the three of them, I would have expected to be exhausted, but it had been the opposite. Once the four of us had come home, tension had been *corded* through me. Jay, Saint, and Dante had all gone against Magnus to run with me. After ordering Jay to go to sleep in my room, I'd expected him to join me last night too...well all nights if I was honest with myself. With daybreak not far off, I'd expected Jay to join me inside, climbing into my bed with me.

He hadn't, instead, the three of them had stayed up even later, leaving me to go to sleep alone.

"Where are Jay and Dante?"

"Dealing with Magnus," Saint answers around a mouthful.

"Ah." My chest pangs, guilt making my stomach turn. I pick at my pancakes with my fork, ripping it into little chunks.

"Jay won't let anything happen, Tiny. Don't worry about Magnus."

"Why?"

"Why what?"

"Why shouldn't I worry about the Alpha?"

"Because Jay won't let anything happen," Saint replies with a look that says he believes what he's telling me.

"Why?"

Saint just smiles and says "Finish your food."

Dante, Saint, Jay, and I are all lying on the couch, sprawled across one another. Saint is leaning against Dante, who has a bag of chips at his side and is in control of the remote. My head is lying in Saint's lap, Jay laying half on and half behind me, his head on my chest, legs tangled with mine. Saint's hands idly trail through my hair as we all hang out and watch some DIY home improvement show.

Of course, we hadn't started this way on the couch, but after about the third episode we'd all sort of....*sank* into the cushions. Ended up in a big cuddle puddle. My eyelids keep getting heavier and heavier, and the will to resist sleep withering along with them. The boys have all been commenting on the show and the design choices of the hosts since the first episode. Eventually, they start asking me questions too.

"What type of house would you build Artemis?"

"I wouldn't build shit," I mumble, not even bothering to open my eyes.

"You know what I meant, Tiny." Saint chirps back, tugging on my hair.

I sigh but tell him the *pipe dream* house of mine anyway. "Big house. With one of those turret-tower things with the curved window seat to read in. Big library. Paint the whole fuckin' thing black. Big windows with powered blinds so I can go bat cave mode whenever I want. A big porch to look at the stars under, lots of big plush couches and blankets. Green. Lots of green." I mumble. "Oh, and a Saint to cook me food all the time. Dante can decorate it. And Jay pays for it."

"Oh, is that all Gorgeous?" Jay chuckles, his head still resting on my chest.

"Mhm. Simple right?" I snap my fingers in a burst of motion. "That's what I'm cashing in on for my bet. *Perfect.*"

The boys all chuckle, and with my eyes closed it would be so very easy for me to drift off into slumber. That is, until my stomach gurgles loudly, making the boys all laugh again.

"Let me up, please," I say to Jay, rubbing the back of his head for a moment.

"No." Jay hums, snuggling closer. It makes me laugh, but then my stomach rumbles again, and Jay moves saying, "Alright *fine.*"

As soon as I leave the tangle of limbs, I'm cold. Goosebumps run up my arm as I make my way towards the kitchen. Through the large window, a glint of chrome catches my attention. A familiar-looking vehicle speeds down the road towards the apartment.

Even without confirmation, I *know*.

Time to face the music, I guess. Ethan has found me. Without a word to the boys, I make my way outside, not willing to let Ethan take even a single step into the house. He would taint it. Ruin the peace I've managed to carve out for myself in the short time I've been here.

Dust billows all around him as he exits the vehicle. He's chosen a Porsche, the ugly canary yellow color making my eyes hurt.

Ethan has one in orange at the Estate, equally as offensive. For a man so concerned with looks, he sure doesn't pick very attractive-looking vehicles to drive. I suppose I should feel some sort of... accomplishment or something since he's come all this way himself.

I'm sure some other women might find it romantic. Heartwarming even.

I see it for what it is, though. He is merely coming to collect something he sees as his property.

"There you are. Knew you'd be shacking up with a bunch of *losers*." Ethan says, brushing dust from his three-piece suit.

"What do you want?" I ask, ignoring his insult.

"You left."

"Great observation skills." I snark, rolling my eyes and crossing my arms. It is going to make Ethan see red, I know, but I'm not his fiancée anymore. I'm not his little plaything, and I'm done stepping on eggshells around him.

"So it's like that?" Ethan says, pouting.

"Yep. What do you want?" I ask again.

Ethan's face contorts, anger making his face flush beet red. "Watch your fucking *mouth*."

"What. Do. You. Want, Ethan?" I repeat, annoyance coloring my voice.

"Sam's dead." He retorts in a flat, emotionless voice. Cruelty glimmers in his gray eyes though, making them shine.

"What?" Silence rings in my ears.

"Your little friend? The one that never liked me? She's dead." Ethan repeats, and adrenaline floods my veins.

"You had her killed?" It's the only thought I manage to give voice to.

"Cute. No, *bitch*. I went there looking for you. She wasn't home though."

My stomach drops, bile rising in my throat. "How do you know she's dead?"

"I called her phone. Someone else answered. Her funeral is next week. Get in the car." Leave it to Ethan to deliver the news that my *best friend* had died like an asshole.

"No." Despite the way my insides tremble, my voice is clear when I answer him. Sam and I chatted on my way home from work again just the other night. There is no way he's telling the truth. I don't believe him.

"I said, *get in the fucking car,* Artemis," Ethan demands, a vein popping out on his forehead.

"No," I reply again, with half a mind to call Sam right now.

"If you want to know anything about her funeral *get in the fucking car Artemis,*" Ethan orders, taking a step towards me when I don't move or say anything.

"Lay a hand on her, and you'll leave in a body bag." Jay drawls, emerging from the dark entryway of the house.

"Who the fuck do you think you are?" Ethan says, drawing himself up to his full height, attempting to look down his nose at Jay. Too bad Jay's a veritable mountain compared to Ethan.

"Go inside, Artemis." Jay orders without breaking eye contact with Ethan. Saint and Dante appear out of the doorway a moment later.

"What? No, my friend-."

"Get inside the fucking house, Artemis." Jay's eyes are wild, and I can see his wolf thrashing against his restraint. The moment stretches between us, but... I trust Jay. And this isn't my friend sticking up for me... This is the Alpha's son, protecting his Pack from an intruder.

"I....*Okay.*" Is all I manage to say, turning away from the group of men on the lawn. What the fuck is with men telling me what to do lately—and me listening?

As the door shuts behind me, I immediately go to the window, pulling the curtain back to watch what is happening on the lawn, already taking my phone out to call Sam.

Sam picks up on the third ring. "*Hello,*" she chirps into the phone, music softly playing in the background.

"Hey. Guess who showed up." I reply, trying my best to read lips.

"Ethan found you?" Sam immediately gasps, and I can imagine her sitting up straighter, dropping whatever she had been doing to focus on me.

"Yep. Tried to get me to go back with him by saying you were dead." I say, watching Ethan's face turn purple, his hands flying in every direction. I don't need to read lips to imagine well enough what he's saying. Threatening to sue Jay, probably.

"Wow. That's a bold strategy. *Clearly,* I am alive." Sam retorts, and I snort.

"No kidding."

"So what's happening now?" Sam questions.

"Jay, Saint, and Dante are outside talking to him. Jay told me to go inside when Ethan was going to touch me."

"*Oouh.*" Sam purs back, and I roll my eyes.

"Yeah yeah. I know. I can't read lips though so I don't know what they're saying out there."

"Bummer. So what are you going to do?"

I drop the curtain and go to the kitchen, my original destination. "I don't know. Wait for my sentencing I guess." I answer, grabbing a handful of blueberries from the fridge.

"And you'll tell your best friend everything, of course?"

"Naturally."

"Okay. Love you *byeeee.*" I chuckle to myself as Sam ends the call, and after placing my phone in my back pocket, I grab another handful of blueberries and go upstairs to my room. Needing a distraction, I grab my book from the nightstand and flop onto the bed. It takes a little while, but Jay does come back and finds me in my room.

"Did you take their heirloom diamond?"

I snort. "Yea, I have the *piss dick diamond*." I can't look at him. My fingers shake around the pages of the book that I haven't really been reading.

Jay chuckles as well, the sound purely surprised amusement. "He wants it back. Do *you* want it?"

"No. It's ugly."

"Then why'd you take it?"

"Bargaining."

"*For?*" The exasperation in Jay's voice is clear, but so is the amusement.

"The Corvette."

Jay makes a noise low in his throat, I get goosebumps. "You want to keep it?" he finally asks.

"Sure would be swell if I could. And the rest of my books that I left behind."

"We'll get whatever you want," Jay answers easily. It makes me roll towards him, finally.

"Do I have to give him the ring?" I ask, already dreading having to see Ethan again.

"Nope. He's never looking at you again."

"My friend isn't dead by the way. I called her. I don't know how much of the conversation you heard before you came and *ordered* me inside." As hard as I fight the small smile, it still wins, spreading across my face.

"Well, that's good. Where's the diamond? He's waiting for it." Jay asks, his eyes never leaving mine.

I make a face, but get up and retrieve the diamond from the depths of my backpack. "Here ya go," I say tossing it to him after opening the small box to verify the ring is still in fact inside.

"Ahh. Makes sense." Jay says, laughing to himself when he lays eyes on the jewels.

"I told you. *Piss dick diamond.*" I say with a laugh.

"Yeah, you sure did Darlin." Jay laughs, hooking his arm around my shoulders and leading me out of the room. His lips press against my forehead for the barest of moments, but I swear I feel it all the way down to my toes.

Jay makes me wait inside while he goes out to give Ethan back his diamond. Jay tosses it through the air at him, making Ethan practically throw himself to the ground to catch it. Pleasure creeps up my spine. The men exchange a few words, Ethan tossing his finger in the direction of the house, or maybe the Corvette I don't know.

Minutes crawl by until finally, Ethan gets back into his ugly ass car and leaves. The boys wait until he's a fair distance down the road before they all come back inside.

"Saint, if you could order a couple pizzas?" Jay asks his friend, steering me back up the stairs with his hand around my bicep.

"What happened?" I ask when Jay closes the door behind us.

"He'll give you what you want, but you have to unblock his number while everything is transferred and answer his calls," Jay says, his jaw tight and his eyes hard. He's *pissed*.

"Okay. That's not that bad." I say, running my hand down his arm.

"Did he always talk to you that way?" Jay demands suddenly, and I have to fight back a sudden rush of emotion. My eyes burn, my chin wobbles. I bite my lip before I answer.

"Not always, no." I eventually answer without meeting his eyes.

"Not always. But most of the time?" Jay asks, lifting my chin, and forcing me to look him in the eye.

"You're not wrong," I reply, making Jay's full mouth twist into an unwilling smile.

"I'm...*not wrong?*"

"Yep. Not wrong." I reply, biting my lip again, my smile stretching across my face.

I know the way Jay is looking at me. I recognize the way his gaze tracks my teeth indenting my lower lip. The way his own eyes darken. He wants to kiss me. *I know it.* Time slips by while I silently beg him to *kiss me*. Please just *kiss me*.

Saint shouts up the stairwell though, effectively ruining the moment. "Pizza will be here in fifteen!"

"Wow. That's fast." I say, pulling my chin from Jay's grasp. "Just enough time for a quick lobotomy then!" I say brightly, grabbing a rat-tail comb from the nearby dresser and offering it to Jay.

Jay laughs, then lowering his lips to my ear he says in a dark voice "If I'm shoving something hard in your head *love* it's going in your mouth."

16
Cookies

After the pizzas were delivered, Jay had to go back to the Packhouse. Apparently, he found it necessary to tell the Alpha about our little guest. Saint went with him, leaving Dante and me alone. He retreated into his room, so eventually, I did the same. And that had been *hours* ago.

I try to pass the time by reading, attempting to finish the trilogy I've been working on but the words on the page don't hold my attention for longer than a sentence or two at a time. Eventually, I give up on that as well, slamming the book down on the nightstand. My mind keeps drifting in every direction, anxiety pooling in my chest. The clock on the nightstand indicates that it's now a little after eleven. Jay and Saint still haven't returned.

Go to sleep, they will be fine. My wolf grumbles at me like I've woken *her* up.

I can't.

Try. She grumbles back, golden eyes disappearing into the black. I roll my eyes at her.

Still, it takes me another twenty minutes of tossing and turning around in bed before I finally toss the blankets off. I need to get up. I need to *do* something. So I grab one of my Coyote Bills t-shirts from the drawer and toss it over my head, making my way down to the kitchen. I asked Ivy for this one specifically, *gloriously* oversized. I think it had been a mis-order or something because I don't think anyone at the bar takes a 4XL.

Cookies. I want to make cookies. Saint likes to cook. I'm willing to bet he has all the ingredients downstairs.

It only takes a moment to gather all the things I need. There are chocolate chips as well as peanut butter chips in the cupboard, so I decide to put them both in the dough. The stove is unfamiliar since I haven't had a chance to cook for myself here. Not that I'm complaining, but it does take a minute to *find* the damned preheat button.

This has to be the fastest I've ever put together a batch of cookies in my entire life. It's been a while, of course. The servants at the Estate always had freshly baked cookies stocked, so I never really had a chance to do it myself.

Twenty minutes after walking downstairs, there are four sheets of cookies in the large, commercial-sized oven. I have nothing else to do than clean up while I wait for them, so I start doing just that. Thankful, at least that the timer isn't annoyingly difficult to set. By the time I'm considering starting the dishes, tossing utensils in the sink I hear the rumble of Jay's car in the driveway.

My heartbeat skyrockets, thudding in my ears, shaking my chest.

Jay and Saint enter the house, and it sounds like Saint is going up to bed. Jay's footsteps are still in the hallway, not on the staircase. And now, I can't help but think of the night I led Jay up the stairs, spent all night next to him, and then woke up alone.

Artemis Hunt, you are in entirely too deep.

When Jay walks into the kitchen, he has his hand on the back of his neck, a tired expression on his face. As soon as he sees it's me in there in the middle of the night, Jay asks, "Hey. What are you doing up?" While tucking his hand back into his pocket.

"Couldn't sleep," I answer, hopping up onto the island counter.

Jay looks around, clearly trying to make out what I've been doing. "Cookies?"

"Yep. They'll be ready soon." I reply, glancing towards the screen that indicates six minutes are remaining on the timer.

"Nice," Jay replies, and I hear the shower being turned on upstairs. The rush of water through pipes in an otherwise quiet house.

"Mhm... how'd it go with Magnus?" I ask, picking the skin around my thumbnail.

"About how you'd expect."

"So how long do I have to leave?"

Jay looks sharply at me, eyebrows lowered. 'Why would you say that?"

"I mean... Magnus made it pretty clear that he's not a fan of my return, and so has Helena, and guessing by the amount of people at her baby shower thing she's relatively popular here, and then Ethan came and made trouble and then you guys went against Magnus to run with me, and-" Once the words start, I can't stop. All of my worries just keep pouring out. Jay walks over to me as I ramble at him, fingers trembling as I pick at a loose thread on the hem of the big tee I'm wearing.

"Artemis. You're not being kicked out of the pack. It's not like humans don't regularly come to town for the festival and the store. It's fine. I told Magnus because the douche canoe threatened *you*. He threatened a member of this pack."

I take a sharp breath, still not enough to fill my lungs. "And what about you guys running with me?"

"That's nothing for you to worry about, Gorgeous. I always ran with you when we were kids, he knows that. Don't worry about us."

"But-" I start to argue, but Jay prevents me from speaking again with a hand cupped around my jaw, thumb held to my lips.

"But nothing. You have nothing to worry about." Jay says, his thumb smoothing over my bottom lip. His hand feels like a brand, sending searing warmth straight to my toes.

Staring into Jay's mercurial blue-green eyes, I bite my lip. The moment feels heavy somehow, my heartbeat thudding in my ears. Jay's thumb shifts again, pulling my lip free from my teeth.

"Don't do that." He says, blue-green eyes flashing.

"Why?" I whisper.

"Because it makes me think you want me to kiss you," Jay grumbles, watching me. Like a slow dance, I widen my legs, biting down on my bottom lip again. Jay doesn't hesitate to shift forward, hips flush to the counter between my thighs. Then he tilts my head back, just a little. My hands find the planes of his stomach, gripping his shirt in fists. "Is that what you want?" He grumbles, eyes shifting.

"Yes." I'm breathless, my heart frantically pounding in my chest. Silently I *beg* him to do more than *just* kiss me.

"All you had to do was ask," Jay says roughly before lowering his mouth to mine. He threads his hands through my hair and kisses me like he's never to see me again. It's all-consuming, without room for anything but *him*. Jay doesn't waste time before he's deepening the kiss, tongue dancing with mine.

Yes, yes, yes, is all I can think about as Jay's hands roam my back, sliding me closer to him. My legs wrap around his waist, hands wandering under his shirt to claw at his skin. When Jay trails his mouth down my jaw and neck, I moan loudly, earning a delighted chuckle from him.

"Yeah, you still like that, don't you baby girl?" He murmurs against my neck, teeth nipping the sensitive spot that sends goosebumps racing down my spine.

"*Yes,*" I moan, tilting my head back to give him better access.

"*Good girl.*" He groans, his hand drifting farther up my thigh, underneath the shirt. Instead of going between my legs though, his hand coasts over my hip, grabbing my ass and roughly yanking me forward. I squeak before Jay reclaims my mouth. I'm barely resting on the edge of the counter, so I settle back on my elbows, meeting Jay's intense kiss. I rock my hips against him, wanting *more*.

My head is nearly resting on the counter, my neck entirely exposed to his exploration. But still, I want more, *more, more*. Jay's hands roam further under my shirt, spanning my rib cage and just barely dusting the edges of the royal purple lace bralette I have on. I'd started wearing matching sets since the full Moon for *this* exact reason.

Shifting my weight to one arm, I tug Jay's shirt over his head, tossing it to the ground. He doesn't waste time before he's covering me again, kissing his way up my neck and resettling in between my thighs. And then, the timer for the cookies dings, making me jolt.

Jay laughs.

"Shut up, I forgot about it." I mummer against his neck, arching my back when he palms my breast in one large hand.

Jay laughs *again* but steps away from me. "What are you doing?" I immediately blurt, hoping he isn't going to stop now.

"Letting you up to check on the cookies." He says, adjusting his jeans, a hungry look in his eye.

"Oh," I say, clearing my throat and straightening my shirt. But, I get up and see that the cookies look perfectly browned but still gooey in the center. It only takes a moment to locate the oven mitts in a nearby drawer and take the trays out. The flaky salt is up on the highest shelf of the spice cabinet, so I have to stand on tippy toes to get it out and sprinkle it over the tops.

I feel Jay's presence at my back before he says anything, the electric charge to the air. "All done?" He asks in that gravelly voice that sends shivers down my spine.

"Yup."

"My turn." He demands, hands on my hips as he spins me in place. In an instant, I'm on him. He lifts me easily, my legs circling his waist once again, our lips already locked together. He groans into my mouth, fingers indenting my ass. Too soon, he sets me back down on the island, this time ripping my shirt over my head, and tossing it to the floor with his own. "Mmh, you're so fucking *hot*," he says, taking in the lacy matching set, his hands coasting down my entire body, making me lay back against the counter. Then he's kissing me again, exploring my body with his hands.

I moan when he palms my breast. He earns a gasp when he bites down on my neck and tweaks my nipple at the same time. Jay's going so slow it's driving me positively *mad*. I can't help but compare it to how we used to be, fast and dirty at every opportunity available. This is like he's *savoring* it.

That particular train of thought will send me spiraling– and I don't want to *think*.

So when Jay starts moving his mouth down my collarbone, I moan loudly again, rocking my hips against the bulge in his jeans. When he hooks his thumbs on my underwear though, I remember where we are.

"Wait-" I say, and Jay freezes.

"We can't-not on the counter." I blurt, legs still locked around his waist.

"That's not an issue."

"I made a huge mess, I should clean up."

"Do you *actually* want me to stop or are you just worried about the mess? Because I'll stop if that's what you want. But if you're just worried about the kitchen, don't. I'll clean it later." Jay says, leaning over me, but his hands haven't moved. He hasn't moved an inch since I said *wait*.

"But— Jay, your friends eat here," I say, but without much conviction.

"I'm going to eat here too." Jay grins, eyes flicking down my body and back up in a heartbeat. "I'll clean it later. If you think I'm going to stop now when you want me? Absolutely not."

"And if one of them comes downstairs?" I question, hoping he doesn't notice the way my heart skips a beat.

"What if?" He answers, unconcerned.

"And gets an eye full of us? Of me?"

"Darlin, I don't do jealousy," Jay says, smirking at me.

"I don't know what that means," I growl back.

"What are you worried about? Do you not want them to see us? Because we can go upstairs, but I don't mind the thought of them seeing you take every inch of me, seeing you cum hard on my dick." Jay says, rocking forward against my center, showing me exactly how hard every inch of him had become.

I moan at the contact, debating for one single second before I say "Oh, just fuck me already Jay."

Jay groans back "That's my good girl" before he rips my underwear free, making me gasp. His mouth leaves hot wet kisses behind as he moves down my body, capturing my nipple under the lace in his mouth. His tongue flicks over the peaked flesh, and I arch into him, giving him more. My nails rasp against his skin, his scalp when I thread my fingers through the short strands at the back of his neck, wishing it was just a little longer like he used to wear it. The movement earns me a groan, Jay still slowly working his way down my body. He kisses my hip bone, then my thigh, then the other one. Then, he hooks my legs over his shoulder and lowers his mouth to my center.

I moan, widening my hips for him, rocking into his mouth. Jay groans back, licking and sucking at my clit. One hand drifts over me, pulling the cups to the bralette down to bare my breasts. The other caresses my hip and ass, his thumb just barely brushing my center.

His eyes are electric from where he peers up at me between my thighs, intense and determined.

"Fuck, Jay-" I moan, dropping my head back on the countertop.

"Oh, I will Darlin'. I will." He murmurs, replacing his mouth with his fingers, rubbing my clit in slow circles before he plunges them deep in me, mouth resealing around my clit. It makes my back arch off the table, a loud moan rolling out of my lips. "That's it, let me hear you."

"Fuck, oh, *fuck* that feels good—*Jay!*" I babble, unable to form anything more coherent, threading my fingers through his hair, and holding him in place.

"Yea? You wanna cum, don't you baby girl?" He rumbles, fingers crooking inside of me to hit a new spot.

"Fuck, *yes,* please, can I cum?" I moan, holding the edge of the counter in a white-knuckle grip.

"Cum for me, pretty girl. Cum all over my face." Jay says, and I moan-nearly scream when he sucks hard on my clit, orgasm slamming through me. "That's a good girl," Jay murmurs, still lapping at my center in slow strokes, carrying me through the aftershocks.

When Jay steps away from the counter and begins unzipping his pants I move quickly, going to my knees before him and taking off the bralette. If my memory is any good, I know *exactly* what he will want next. Immediately, his eyes darken, and I bite my lip.

"Open your mouth." Jay orders, and I obey. He groans when I suck the fat tip of his cock into my mouth, flattening my tongue to take as much of him as I can. His hand grips the back of my head, helping me move up and down the considerable length of him, stroking him with my hands as I move. "Yea, just like that baby girl, just like that-" He groans, eyes fluttering closed with every stroke.

Then Jay is moving again, hauling me up and pushing my spine against the counter. "How do you want it?" he asks, peppering my collarbone and neck with kisses.

The question makes something pang in my chest that I can't define. "It doesn't matter, just fuck me, Jay."

"Impatient?"

"Something like that," I answer, sealing my mouth over his to prevent him from talking anymore.

He breaks the kiss though, saying "Hold on I have to go get a con-"

I halt his retreat by grabbing him by the dick, stoking him slowly. Then I whisper "No, you don't."

Jay's eyes close for half a second, before they're open, and entirely focused on me. "Why?"

"Because I can't have kids. It was one of the first things I took care of when I left." My answer is simple. It's Jay's potential response that fills me with dread. The question of *what if he wants them* blares like an alarm in my mind for one single second before I push it away. Now is *not* the time for that.

"Really?"

I gulp before saying "Really really."

Jay's eyelids lower, that flash of his wolf rising and a lazy smile once more in place. His hand replaces mine as he strokes himself, watching me. "So I can fill you up all I want?"

There's no hiding the rising flush to my cheeks, so I shift my hips answering with a simple *"yes."*

"That's my good girl," Jay says, lining his cock up to my entrance, hooking one of my legs over his shoulder.

"I'm not really all that good, Jay-" I start to say, moaning when his hips surge forward, his cock sliding in inch by *glorious* inch. "Oh, *fuck!*" I groan, seriously wondering how I'd forgotten exactly how *big* he is.

"You look pretty good from here, Gorgeous." Jay chuckles, moving his hips in slow, controlled movements, kissing up the column of my neck, letting me stretch around him.

"Mother fucker-" I gasp, clawing at his back. Jay laughs against my neck, speeding up his movements.

"Yeah, feels good doesn't it, baby girl?" He agrees, kissing up my neck. Then he starts pulling almost all the way out before rushing back in, burying himself to the hilt. At a leisurely pace, he lets his hands roam across my body, caressing my skin–reacquainting himself with my curves and dips. I can't help but arch into his touch, rocking my hips with his slow movements.

"Mmh, yes-" I moan, threading my fingers through the short strands of his hair. Jay groans in agreement, closing his mouth over my nipple, his teeth graze the peaked bud, shivers racing over my skin.

Jay keeps up those slow movements, turning my breathing ragged and making me desperate for him to move faster—*harder*. When I voice the demand, he says "Who said you're in control here, Darlin?" To punctuate his point he pulls back, sliding home *agonizingly* slow.

"Who said you were?" I sass back at him, raking my nails down his back, angling my hips for him when he lets my leg slip off his mountainous shoulder. Even I can't hide how my breath shakes, how my eyes roll back every time he does that.

Jay laughs a dark chuckle that once again sends goosebumps racing over my skin. Then he wraps a hand around my neck, the other cradling the back of my head. "Oh, I think we both know the answer to that, Gorgeous." He says, squeezing my neck and then *unleashing* himself. He's still going slow, but he's going deep and *hard*.

"fuck-" I pant, eyes rolling back.

"Yeah, that's it. Take it." Jay groans, rolling his hips. "So submissive, aren't you?"

I growl *"No,"* eyes snapping open, gripping his arm around my neck. Not to remove it, just because I need to hold on to something.

"Don't look that way from here, you're being so *good for me.*" He groans, releasing the back of my head in favor of circling my clit, dragging his hips out, and slamming back in.

"It's a fluke." I pant, tension coiling in my core, legs locked around his waist.

"*We'll see.*" Is all Jay replies before he picks up speed, giving me exactly what I asked for, squeezing my neck, and fucking me relentlessly. My back arches off of the counter, and he sucks a nipple into his mouth again.

"Fuck- *Jay!*" I moan, release barreling through me like a freight train. Without losing rhythm, Jay captures both of my hands in one of his larger ones, holding them above my head.

"So fucking hot," he murmurs before kissing me, tongue dancing with mine, his hips slowing back down into that agonizingly slow pace. My legs start to shake, another orgasm not that far off if he keeps doing that.

"You're not too bad yourself, big guy," I answer when Jay kisses down my neck, biting on that sensitive spot.

"Are you going to cum for me again, Gorgeous?" Jay asks, hand moving down to circle my clit. I suck in a gasp, moving my hips in time with his movements even more desperately.

"Maybe" I pant, "are you going to make me?" I ask, kissing and sucking down his neck, biting on his shoulder just like he does to me. I want to leave marks on him, see the proof of this on him the next day.

Jay chuckles again and then he's kissing me, pulling a leg back up and over his shoulder. It gives him even deeper access, and he gladly makes use of it. "Fuck, baby girl-" Jay groans, thumb still circling my clit.

"Mmmm-" I moan into his mouth, "don't stop, don't stop!" I beg, completely at his mercy. *And I fucking love it.*

My plea makes Jay chuckle, but he listens–slamming his hips into me, that thumb circling round and round- his mouth trailing wet hot kisses down my neck, biting and sucking. I can't seem to breathe, my lungs frozen in my chest.

"Oh, shit that's tight," Jay moans, feeling how every single muscle in my body had gone tight, squeezing him as I dangled on the edge of orgasm. "Cum for me, baby girl. Do it."

And I do, my head slamming back into the counter, my back arching sharply. My thighs flutter and then Jay's moaning and pumping deep and hard into me. "Yes-yes, yes- give it to me," I pant, clawing at his back when he releases my hands.

Jay captures my mouth again in a deep kiss, his movements even more desperate and then with a groan, his forehead dropping to my chest Jay cums, slamming into me to the hilt one more time.

Neither of us move for a few moments, breathing heavily. When Jay lays his head down on my chest, his ear to my heart he chuckles again, still fully seated inside me.

"What?"

"Your heart sounds like it's going to explode." Jay chortles.

"Compliments to the chef." I sass, shifting my hips. Jay's still *rock*-hard. It's distracting.

"Oh, so you were thinking about Saint?" Jay murmurs, shifting his hips in response.

"No," I gasp when his tongue flicks my nipple, his hips flexing again. "-you idiot."

"Just checking." Jay snarks, withdrawing a little more, pushing his cock back in with force. A groan slips out of his lips, and then he's moving again, coaxing my hips into the same rhythmic movements. "Yeah, you want more, don't you baby girl?"

"Who can blame me when you're doing-" a gasp leaves me when he fucks me hard and deep once before going back to those slow-rolling hips,"-*that.*"

"Well, who can blame *me* when you look like this?" Jay murmurs, kissing up my throat again to capture my lips. And then we're moving again, a different sort of desperation driving our movements.

When he lifts me from the counter, I lock my legs around his hips. My back hits a wall for a few moments, and Jay hooks both my legs over his elbows, pistoning into me with savage precision.

"Fuck- that's deep-" I gasp, clawing at his shoulders.

"You can take it."

"You're-fucking-right-I-can" I pant, my words punctuated by his hips slamming into mine. Then we're moving again, into the living room, where he collapses on the couch with me on top of him.

"Ride me," Jay demands, already moving my hips with his hands.

"Awfully demanding." I sass, but doing as he asks anyway, rocking my hips back as I sink down on each and every inch of him over, and over.

"Yeah, but you like it." He answers, slapping my ass a moment later. "Don't you?" Jay's eyes are electric, dark, and demanding as he drinks down every inch of my exposed skin.

I gasp at the sting, but answer him with a cool "*maybe.*"

"That's what I thought." He says, slapping the other ass cheek, reclining back with his hands behind his head. Still moving his hips in time with my movements, Jay says "Fuck that big cock, baby. Let me see you take it."

"Fuck, that's hot," I mumbled not even meaning to voice the thought.

"Yeah, you are," Jay replies, his blue eyes flashing in the dark.

17
It's all fake

twenty five days to full moon

I wake up alone. That ragged wound opens once again. The clock on the nightstand tells me it is barely past noon.

It's all fake. It's all fake. I silently repeat to myself over and over. Jay and I always used to mess around like this. Hot and cold. It's no different now. We just fucked, Artemis. It's not like before. I repeat the words over and over to myself.

Everything is fine, Artemis. You said it yourself. Put you and Jay in a room together for long enough, one of you will fold.

My wolf is silent. Subdued.

I can smell Saint making food in the kitchen, so I have to assume he's the only one here, yet again. It doesn't matter though, I have to go to work. Slowly, I get out of bed, and into the shower. I ache in all the best places, a vivid reminder of the night before.

After, I dress in a simple low-cut black tank top and black jeans, stuffing my feet into chunky boots. These jeans have a rip right under my ass, a victim of my wolfy claws. I'm willing to bet it will be a good tip night with these on.

I'm in a *really* shitty mood, but still, I swipe eyeliner across my eyelids, a little sparkle to the inner corners. A double coat of waterproof mascara on my lashes. I consider trying to hide the marks along my neck and collarbone, but I quickly dismiss the idea. Not only do I lack the appropriate coverage foundation, but I also lack the patience and willpower to do it. Not to mention the possibility of sweating through it and then having melting foundation running down my chest all night. An easy thirty-five minutes later I'm trudging down the stairs and make it nearly out the door before *someone* says my name.

I turn because of course, I do. Jay's standing in the doorway to the kitchen, one hand tucked into his pocket, the other resting on the frame above his head. My mouth waters. He's wearing jeans and a dark blue tee, the color making his eyes even more intense. I tell myself not to look for marks from last night on his neck, but I do it anyway.

They exist. A vivid path down the column of his throat and disappearing under his shirt.

"Yea?" I respond, hoping he doesn't notice the way my voice cracks.

"Where are you going?" His question is too casual. I hate it.

"To work?" I respond, giving him an *'Are you dumb'* face.

"Hold on." He says, disappearing and reappearing in barely a second. "Put your number in my phone." Jay orders, stalking towards me with one hand rummaging in his pocket and the other holding a can of Redbull.

"Why?"

"Because I asked you to?" Jay responds, giving me a lazy smirk, holding his unlocked phone out to me.

I fight the small smile threatening to pull the corners of my lips up as I take the phone from him and *dutifully* put my number in. "You didn't really ask, big guy." I hate him for making my entire mood feel lighter in 3 seconds flat.

"But you're being a good girl and doing it anyway, aren't you?" Jay whispers in my ear as he tucks his phone back in his pocket. Heat floods my center, my heartbeat skyrocketing.

"You've got me on a technicality. That doesn't count." I simper, trying to keep my composure.

"Sure it does, Gorgeous," Jay responds, offering me the drink and leaning on his shoulder against the wall.

"Whatever you say. Anything else?" I sass, rolling my eyes at him. More than just *heat* floods me as I pop the top of the can—even if it's only to keep my hands busy. Once again, Jay has procured my favorite flavor. *Blueberry battery acid.*

"Yeah. I wanted to tell you that your cookies are delicious. I can't wait for you to bake more." Jay growls, his blue eyes flashing. I swear lightning strikes me down because every single nerve and synapse in my body lights up like a fucking Christmas tree.

I need to get out of here before I do something stupid, like rip his pants off and let him bend me over on the stairs.

So I say "For you? Anytime," over my shoulder, biting my lip as I open the door and leave. Thankfully, I'm able to make it all the way to my car without tripping, even managing to take a swig of my beverage. When I start the Stingray up, I make sure to rev the engine a little, meeting Jay's eyes through my windshield.

I want nothing else than to go back inside that house and bang his fucking brains out, but I know I shouldn't. I know I said I might as well just drown myself since I'm already in too deep, but a girl needs to have *some* self-preservation instincts.

My wolf is riled up, her fur shifting under my skin from all the tension cording through me.

Last night did prove something though. Nobody can fuck me *quite* like Jay Temple can.

Since I don't have to stop for anything on my way to work, it's a quick drive. I have to work tonight, but then I'm off again tomorrow, and then the following day is Fire Night. I don't mind the weird schedule so much as I just wonder how the hell I'm going to fill my time and *not* jump on Jay the second I get home.

Maybe I need to ask Ivy, Angel, and Jill to come over. Have a girl's night or something. As soon as I pull into work, turning the engine off my phone pings with a new text message. I hate the way my pulse jumps, and the way my stomach goes cold at the same time when I read Jay's name in the notification bar.

> I like the way your neck looks with me all over it.

> Thanks for the ride, cowboy.

> Have a nice night, Artemis.

> You too, Jay.

I can't help but feel a little disappointed that he's not coming in like he said he was going to.

You're an idiot, Artemis Hunt. I never should have kissed him, never should have lied and said he was my boyfriend.

Never should have come home. All that Timber Hollow has ever given me is pain. I am a fool to think otherwise.

At least I have caffeine. I grouse to my wolf as I trudge into the brightly lit building that is Coyote Bills.

As I'm tying an apron around my waist she replies. *And we can run later.*

I silently agree with my wolf as I clock and get to work. A smile sits on my face, pulling the corners of my lips up but it's not real. Single-minded focus keeps my hands moving, pouring drinks and counting out change, charming patrons into hefty tips, and cheering on my fellow bartenders as they twirl liquor bottles around their hands. Jill and Angel, are now apparently best friends.

Hours drone by, sweat pooling at the small of my back the more bodies are packed inside. It's a warm night, particularly for October. Somewhere around nine, Ivy finds me as I'm grabbing new bottles of liquor from storage.

"Are you up for the booth tonight?" She asks, helping me carry bottles back to the bar.

"No, I have a migraine," I answer simply, grateful that Ivy doesn't need long-winded explanations. My head does hurt, but it's not migraine-level– just tension gripping my skull. Either way, I really don't want to do the booth. *Astronomical tips be damned.* It would be tonight and my black mood that would end up fucking everything up, like if I were to hit a human with wolf strength.

Some survival instincts, at least, are still intact.

"Oh, I'm sorry. Have you taken anything for it?" Ivy asks, putting the speed pourers on the tops of her bottles.

"Yeah, it's just not doing anything."

"Why don't you take off around midnight then? Me, Angel, and Jill can close up." Ivy orders, patting my shoulder as she walks away, back to do whatever it was she was doing before she found me.

Three more hours. I can manage three more hours.

Around eleven my wolf emerges from whatever black corner of my mind she'd slunk to. Her energy crackles under my fingers, her fur once again tickling my skin. I'll need to hunt something big tonight. Hunt and run until I collapse. She paces in my mind, a continuous loop until I clock out.

I don't drive back to the apartment, instead going down the old back road where the sawmill used to be before it caught fire and was rebuilt across town. The forest has all but reclaimed the space, the remnants of the old charred building covered in moss and vine. I barely make it two steps out of the Stingray before the magic of the shift starts tingling under my skin. Thankfully, I manage to strip out of my shirt and pants before my wolf emerges.

I don't have any spare clothes in the Stingray yet.

A howl rips free from my throat, a clarion call that I know will go unanswered. With our nose to the sky, we sniff, scenting our desired prey. And then we're off nails digging into the dirt, tearing through the forest.

When will I stop running?

18
Pumpkins

six days to full moon

The house is already loud when my eyes crack open. The boys are downstairs doing who knows what, but it's the light streaming through the window landing directly on my face that makes me stretch and sit up.

After running last night, and more specifically hunting whitetail deer into the early hours of the morning I'd driven back to the apartment and slunk up to my empty bedroom. The driveway had been empty, too.

It takes a minute to find my phone, but there are a slew of notifications on the bright screen.

Sam had sent me a picture of tacos and a margarita with a single line of text accompanying it.

> missing you, bitch

> miss you too, bitch

A single chuckle slips free of my lips as I quickly type my response.

The other text thread in my inbox, however, makes my stomach roll. *Ethan*. Ignoring how much my fingers tremble, I open the message. Of course, It's one-line, bait.

> I had the diamond certified.

> Cool. What's your point?

> I had to make sure you and your boyfriends weren't stealing from me.

> Wouldn't put it past you, lying whore and her bitch boys.

> Is there a point to this, Ethan?

This time, he doesn't reply immediately, even though I know he's read the message by the little check marks. When Ethan does reply, I can hear him sneer the words in my head, and see how his face would twist vividly as if he were in the room with me.

> Just keeping you in the loop, as your little bitch boy *negotiated*.

>> Great. Thanks. When will my stuff be delivered?

> When you pay me to ship them to you

>> You're out of your mind if you think I'm paying for a damn thing.

> Guess I'll have the staff donate it then.

>> You're a fucking asshole.

> Be nice to me and I won't.

I have to restrain myself from throwing my phone to watch it shatter into a million tiny pieces against the wall.

We should have killed him.

Yeah, probably. My wolf snarks back.

>> Fine.

> I'll call you when the paperwork is ready for you to sign.

> You'll have to come to the office unless that's a problem for you.

> No. I'll be there.

You motherfucker. Of course, he'd find a way to manipulate me into going back there. The conversation forces me out of bed, and into the shower. As I lather my hair and wash my body, my thoughts turn towards Ethan calling Jay my *little bitch boy,* and then I'm just thinking about Jay.

Picturing how he'd look under the stream of water, How he'd pick me up and slam me against the wall, fuck me fast and thoroughly. And then my hands are moving, slowly plucking a nipple, coasting down the planes of my stomach.

Leaning my head back against the tile, I imagine my hands are his, that it's his fingers dipping into my center, circling my clit. Fucking my fingers in the hot spray, but thinking about Jay moving inside of me, relentlessly bringing me to the brink over and over again.

The sounds of the shower drown out any sound I let slip free from my mouth, but it even takes me by surprise when release crashes over me in what feels like only moments later.

"*Fuck,*" I pant, feeling a lot less tense. Even so, I can't stop thinking about the other night with Jay. Which is about as good for my health as skydiving without a parachute.

Since the water is now merely tepid, edging on cold I get out, quickly drying with an extremely fluffy and luxurious towel. I have no idea what the boys are doing downstairs, but I guess there's nothing to do but go find out. After throwing on a pair of leggings and a cropped long-sleeve, I silently make my way down the stairs.

"Hey, Gorgeous. Invite your friends over." Jay says to me as soon as I cross the threshold to the kitchen.

"Why?"

"To carve pumpkins."

"What if they don't have pumpkins to carve?" I sass at him, rolling my eyes.

"We have plenty. Trust me." He implores, handing me a cold can of caffeinated battery acid. I accept it, hopping up onto the counter, and watching Saint toss dishes into the sink.

"What if I don't have any friends?" I simper, peeking at Jay through my lashes and taking a sip of my drink.

"Tiny! So we're not friends?" Saint chimes in, pouting at me over his shoulder.

"I didn't say that," I reply, feeling just a smidgen guilty for the comment, even if I didn't mean it.

"So invite your friends, Artemis."

I sigh, rolling my eyes at him. "Fine." Setting my drink down, I pull out my phone and type out a message to the group chat for Coyote Bills, inviting them all over. "Are we having food, drinks? Or is this literally just carving pumpkins?" I ask them both, not caring who answers.

"All of the above," Jay answers, closer than he was just a moment ago and in a deeper voice. It nearly makes me drop my phone.

"Oh, a *three-way woot woot.*"

I'm still laughing at my joke, sending out the message when Jay steps closer again, resting his palms down on either side of my hips, large arms bracketing me in.

"Does that appeal to you, Gorgeous?" He grumbles, eyes locked on mine. They're lighter today, complimented by his grey t-shirt. Saint has turned, leaning against the sink and watching me and Jay, *listening.*

"Does what appeal to me?" I stammer, completely caught off guard by the comment, and the intense focus of them both.

Jay smirks, his gaze greedily roving down my body and then back up, snagging on my lips before his eyes are on mine again. "Nothing, never mind Gorgeous." He says, shaking his head, teeth grazing his bottom lip for one second. "You smell *good* today." He adds with a dark look in his eye, running his nose up the column of my throat, and then he's gone, slipping out of the room. I don't miss the smirk he throws Saint before he leaves though.

What the fuck?

I can't help but wonder what the hell he meant about me smelling good, it's not like I changed perfumes— not that I wear one, to begin with— or something stupid like that. I blink at his departure, completely bewildered. It takes me a few minutes to recover, slide off the counter, and go back upstairs to change. If we're having a party, then my leggings won't cut it.

Seeing that all the girls from the bar replied that they would love to come to a pumpkin carving party, I typed out the quintessential girl question, hitting send.

> What are you going to wear?

Almost immediately, the little dots indicating everyone is typing appeared on the screen.

Our group chat had settled on jeans- your favorite ones, tank tops, and flannels. I, of course, chose the same black pair of jeans with the rip under the ass, with a white tank top, black and gray flannel slung over my shoulders. Once the girls arrived, the boys had disappeared into their rooms, reappearing with flannels, too. Angel had shoved all seven of us together to get a picture without pumpkins before the Sun disappeared behind the trees.

Saint loudly declared the picture was going on the refrigerator when he gets it. I hadn't looked at it too long because the small glimpse I got revealed Jay staring at my profile. Hours ago, I'd shed my flannel– leaving it inside when I refilled my drink.

The Moon has long since risen into the sky, our pumpkins now carved and merrily lit with candles all sitting on the steps.

I still can't believe that Jay not only bought the pumpkin I'd picked out but also the grey one that the shopkeep had insisted was too tough to carve. That one has a cute little bat carved into it, the other one of mine has a crescent Moon.

Jay, Saint, and Dante all did their best to carve their favorite characters' faces into the pumpkins, doing surprisingly well.

Ivy, Jill, and Angel all do classic renditions of a jack-o-lantern, triangle eyes, and wonky teeth.

We'd started a fire a little while ago, stacking logs high to get a big blaze going. The boys also apparently have outdoor speakers set up, music playing just loud enough to be heard, and patio furniture arranged around the fire in a loose circle, though no one is lounging in them yet. I truly don't know how I'd managed to find a group of friends and hang on to them. Even in school, my circle mostly consisted of Sarah and the friends of hers she introduced me to.

I wonder what Sarah is up to these days, anyway.

Ask Jay. My wolf replies, again too close to the edges of my consciousness. Even after last night's hunt, she's restless.

Maybe it's the alcohol, maybe it's the wide-open night sky, but I move to do just that. Jay's eyes find mine immediately as I make my way to him as if he'd been aware of my every move even before now. In moments I've crossed the lawn to stand right in front of him, my drink clutched in hand.

Before I can voice the reason I've come over here so abruptly, someone bumps into me, knocking me forward and into Jay's space, where he is perched on the arm of the sofa. His knee goes between my legs, one of his large, warm hands coming around to grip the back of my thigh, the one with the rip in my jeans. Electricity tingles over my skin at the contact.

I tell myself it is just so he doesn't fall backward. That's all.

"Sorry," I chuckle, but stay where I am. Tension stretches between us.

His fingers tighten on my thigh, gripping my flesh and preventing me from backing away. "I'm not." Jay answers simply, eyes flicking down to my lips, then back up.

I shift on my feet, edging minutely closer. Jay's lips part, free hand coming around to grip my other thigh, holding me tight. Fingertips brushing the line of denim under my ass. It's almost as if time slows, feeling my pulse pound, watching Jay's eyes darken when I place my hand on the back of his head, threading through the short ashy brown strands.

Every move we each make is calculated, almost a chess match but I'm not filled with fear of the unknown. This is Jay.

My Jay.

So it is as natural as breathing to lean down, to fall into Jay's eyes. To press my lips against his, to let my tongue dance with his.

I've always been falling into Jay. Why would it be any different now? It might hurt in the morning, but I'm used to the burn.

So I moan softly into his mouth, pulling him closer. He does the same, practically pulling me into his lap. I'm all but lost in the reverie, the warmth that is Jay when he breaks the kiss, keeping me close to him.

"Hi, Gorgeous," Jay says, an unvoiced question dancing in his eyes.

"Hi, Handsome," I reply, fingers still gripping the back of his neck.

"What was that for?" Jay asks, lacing his fingers together at the small of my back.

"Because I wanted to?" For one startling moment anxiety spears through me, like he's upset, and my heart starts pounding, the urge to run, to *bolt* surges. My wolf with it.

"Mmh." Jay murmurs, and I can't tell what is on his mind. "I can live with that."

"Cool," I reply, feeling like a lovesick teenager. Slowly, I step back and out of his hold, and Jay lets me go, even if he hesitates. I raise my drink to him as I back away, turning and downing the thing in one go, dropping the now empty cup on a nearby table. Then, I walk over to Ivy and whisper in her ear.

"I'm going for a run, and I'm glad you came."

Ivy merely nods in return, brushing her hand down my arm as I walk away, returning to her conversation with Dante. It seems like everyone is sufficiently distracted. My steps are quiet as I skirt the edge of the house, around to the front. I could go inside, hide under the covers until dawn, I could strip and sprint through the trees...*or...*

The Stingray is right there. I could leave. Start it up and disappear like smoke. My fingertips tremble, indecision rippling through me.

19
Shut up, Jay

The wind shifts, bringing with it the smells of the forest. Breathing it in, I calmly walk over to the Stingray, parked next to Jay's pretty blue GT. The door barely makes a sound as I open it up, dropping my phone on the driver's seat. My clothes are tossed in next. The door's closing is louder, which is unavoidable. And then I surrender to the pull, the beast within.

My wolf comes rushing forward, my bones shattering on the impact of the two halves of my soul. She tears through everything, leaving room only for the run, the chase—the hunt.

Already, my nose is on the ground, scenting. Saliva drips from my mouth, the prospect of devouring something, ripping through muscle and sinew with my teeth is positively irresistible. There is a warren of rabbits nearby. They're tempting but not enough of a challenge. The bunnies are all tucked away for the night, safely sleeping in the earth's embrace.

My wolf and I? We want something bigger, something that we can *chase*.

And then—there it is. Mouthwatering, and already on the move. The herd of whitetail ahead of me is large, but not moving fast enough. I let them run though, just within my sight line. One of them is smaller than the others, moving slower. As I tear after them through the forest, losing myself in the chase, I hear something—*someone* new behind me. We will not share, not tonight.

Decision made, I make my move towards the old doe. Within a few strides, I've caught up to her, nearly nipping her heels. And then, we're on her. Teeth clamping over her throat, tearing the muscle- ending her suffering. The doe dies with a bleat and my wolf feasts. Ripping the meat apart, devouring our prize.

My nose is deep inside the doe's chest cavity when I hear a twig snapping. A deep growl rumbles out of me as I withdraw my bloody maw from the deer. And then I realize who it is emerging through the dense underbrush.

Jay.

He doesn't move, pristine silver coat seemingly reflecting the Moon's light, while mine *absorbs* it. Jay lowers his large head, growling at me. Baring my teeth at him, I growl back.

Fuck you. This is mine.

The silver wolf circles, prowling around me and my prize. The breeze shifts, bringing with it, the scent of Jay's wolf. It's deep, and musky— and full of sensual promise. Suddenly, my wolf and I aren't so concerned with the doe anymore. When his attention flicks down to the carcass at my feet, I make my decision.

Let's see if he can keep up.

Taking off like the grim reaper is on my tail— and perhaps he is, I tear through the forest. This time *I* am the prey, Jay my hunter. The Moon guides me as I run, every movement promising pleasure. Jay is right behind me, step after step.

When I turn down the gorge, Jay leaps to the ledge above. Without breaking stride he drops down right in front of me, fur raised and a growl rumbling through him. I hear the bones in Jay's body cracking and growing larger, and then he's rising on his hind legs. The Moon isn't full, but on Samhain, my dad always said your wolf is more in control than you are. The two halves of our soul are imbalanced. Something about the magic of the forest.

I've never seen Jay's bipedal form, just his silver Direwolf. When the transformation is complete, he's standing before me at nearly seven feet tall, his face morphed, somewhere between wolf and human. He has sharp canine teeth, but the intense blue eyes staring at me are familiar.

Silver fur cascades down his back and shoulders. The planes of his stomach and chest are bare, as are his bicep and most of his forearm. The backs of his hands are covered in fur, and lethal claws are on the ends of his fingers. Even his thighs are covered in that same silvery fur, all the way down to the wolf-like feet. Tail sprouting from his spine.

When I let my eyes absorb the rest of his body, my mouth waters—heat blooming in my core. The silver fur appears again at his hips in a faint happy trail, down to his cock. It's huge and already hard. The base is thickened–swelling into a veiny knot– a bead of precum dripping off the fat tip.

Without another thought, the same shift cracks my bones, fizzling over my body. I'm not as tall as him in this form, but I am still easily over six feet tall. Black fur covers me similarly to him, claws on the ends of my fingers and toes. My wolf's teeth in my maw.

We're both breathing hard, but time feels paused, somehow.

And then, Jay growls *"Run."* His voice is like gravel shifting. It raises the fur on my back, a bolt of heat sent straight to my core. Of course, I oblige. The added strength and agility in this form are welcome as I sprint away from him through the forest.

Jay lets me run, chasing after me with only a little space between us. I can hear him panting, and smell his *desire.* I'd be lying if I said I don't want this, don't want to experience this with Jay.

Spotting a patch of leaves on the ground, I make an easy decision. It's easy to let my feet slip, stumbling enough to force Jay to catch me. He does, of course, tackling me to the forest floor. He rolls us, taking the brunt of the impact, and then my face and chest hit the forest floor, my back flush to his chest. The earth is frigid against my bare nipples, and Jay already has my hands captured, anchored above me into the dirt. The position puts me completely at his mercy, and, more importantly, my ass pressed against his thick cock.

A whine slips free of my mouth, and I can't help the way my back arches, pressing against him more fully. Aching for contact.

"I've got you now, you know what that means?" Jay grumbles, his wolfy voice thick, chest moving rapidly against my back. His cock twitches against my center as if he's knocking before entering. And *fuck,* do I want to feel him.

"What?" I moan, not even trying to hide what he's doing to me. He has to know, has to smell it anyway.

"I'm going to make you *scream* for me." Jay groans, nosing the line of my neck, letting one of his hands roam down my ribs, across the planes of my stomach, and lower. His claws raise goosebumps in their wake.

"Yes, *please-*" I moan, his fingers carefully dipping into my center.

"Fuck, you're so wet already, aren't you? So ready for me."

"Shut up and fuck me, J-" I start to say, but cut off with a groan when Jay plunges into me *almost* all the way. I can feel the thick base of his cock, the knot against my center, throbbing with his pulse. "Oh, *fuck.*" I pant, my eyes rolling back in my head. I want him to go the rest of the way, want to take every inch of his wolfy cock.

"What was that, Gorgeous?" Jay says, kissing and nibbling my shoulder, pulling his cock out and plunging back in shallowly. I don't have to see his face to know he's smiling.

"N-nothing" I stammer, Jay's fingers move slowly around my clit, his other hand still pinning mine above me. Jay just chuckles, it comes out almost like a growl, the lines between wolf and man too blurred to know which is which.

He rolls his hips, moving my knees apart to grant himself better access. All I can do is deepen the arch of my back, my fingers clutching dirt as Jay fucks me relentlessly. "You feel so fucking good," he grumbles, going harder— deeper. It makes my legs shake, and whimpers leave my throat. "Come on, give it to me, Gorgeous." Jay groans, biting down on the exposed part of my neck.

"Fuck-" I scream, my eyes roll back as release barrels through me.

"Louder." Is all that Jay says, rising, pulling my arms behind my back. Smacking my ass, he pulls me back on his dick as he pistons in, smoothing away the burn with his palm. His claws send shivers up my spine when they rake against my skin.

"Shut up" I moan, rocking my hips with every one of his thrusts. He's not going all the way, the thick base of his knot barely brushing the entrance of my pussy before he pulls back out. It's making me feel crazy.

Jay just laughs, slowing down, rolling his hips, his hand coming around to brush my clit again, making my eyes roll back, a moan slipping free.

"I can do this all night, Gorgeous." He says, pressing my face firmly against the ground once more.

"Yeah? You think you're going to last that long?" I sass, angling my hips to give him better access. I'm fucking *loving* every second of this.

"I'll fill you up as many times as it takes for you to scream for me." Jay pants, lifting us, and pressing my chest against a tree.

With my feet firmly planted on the ground, I move my hips, pushing back down on him deeper, and deeper. I can't stop the moans from leaking out each time he slams into me, the knot at the base slipping in bit by bit.

Jay's claws dig into the bark above me, anchoring himself. He's still restrained though, I can tell by the way he slows, rolling his hips. It makes stars appear behind my eyelids, unrestrained desperate sounds in my throat.

"*Fuck.*" I hiss, wondering how long I can keep this game going, he feels *so fucking good*.

"I thought I said *louder*, Artemis?" He quips, slapping my ass, dragging his claws up the back of my thigh. Shivers creep up my spine, pleasure and *anticipation*.

"I thought I said *shut up*, Jay?" I sass back, pushing against the tree. Jay just chuckles, a clawed hand reaching around to sweep against my clit once. Twice, and then a third time and I *howl* out my release. Orgasm screams through me as I lock down around Jay's cock, still pumping in and out of me, carrying me through it.

"That's what I thought." He chuckles, and slowly starts going even slower, that thick knot slipping deeper into my pussy with each stroke. Jay keeps his clawed fingers over my clit, rubbing in slow circles as he pushes himself in until he's fully seated–the entirety of his knot inside me.

"O*h*- that feels good" I moan, wiggling as much as I'm able to, nipples pressed against the tree. My lungs feel too small like I can't get enough oxygen.

"Mmmhm,' Jay groans in my ear, drawing that thick knot out. Another groan in my ear as he roughly pistons back into me.

"Yeah-" I pant, eyes rolling back in my head, my skin practically humming with electricity.

"Scream for me Darlin" He groans in my ear, kissing and nipping down the line of my shoulder.

"Don't stop, don't stop-" I moan, deepening the arch of my spine, and rising to my toes. I'm hovering on the very edge, everything he's doing is sending pleasure into my veins.

"Didn't plan to, Gorgeous." Jay quips back, panting as he fucks me thoroughly.

"Oh, shut *up, Jay*" I moan, and then he grips my throat in one clawed hand, pulling me down on him as he fucks into me. That's all it takes for me to give him what he wants. A scream rips through my throat that might have been a howl as another orgasm overrides all thought.

"That's a good girl" he moans, his knot plunging in and out of me, ripples of pleasure sending me into another orgasm almost immediately. Jay's breathing in my ear is erratic, his movements frantic. He's close, too.

So I pant "Yes, give it to me, please-" clamping down on his cock.

"Fuck," He moans, stepping a half-step back to let me take over. So I do, moving myself up and down that thick, glorious appendage, using the tree to hold myself steady. "Yeah, just like that." He groans, slapping my ass, his claws scraping against my skin.

My legs start to shake as I fuck him, taking that knot with every stroke. If he doesn't cum soon, I'm going to again. Almost as if I speak the thought out loud, Jay chuckles, his hands on my hips turning my movements more aggressive. His hips snapping up into mine. The tree creaks, wood cracks, and bark falls to the ground at my feet.

"Give me one more Gorgeous, you're so good like this, I want one more" He pleads, his hand back around my throat, the other hand strumming my clit with careful strokes.

"yes, yes yes-" I moan, giving him exactly what he wants. With another few movements, Jay plunges into me, his knot swelling inside of me as he groans out his release.

My heart is thudding in my chest, echoing in my ears. I can hardly breathe like my lungs haven't caught up with me. Jay's chest moves just as swiftly against my back. It takes us a few minutes to catch our breath, to calm our racing hearts.

I almost expect him to do what he did the other night– to shift his hips and coax our bodies into another round. He doesn't though, withdrawing from me when his knot has softened, the reduced swelling allowing him to move.

When Jay does finally step away from me, I turn to face him.

"Well, that was fun." I joke, forcing a smile on my wolfish face. "Go team," I add, raising a clawed hand for a high five.

"Yeah, that *sure was fun,* Gorgeous," Jay grumbles, but gives me the high five anyway.

"Race you back," I say, winking as I will the shift to take me again, back into my fully wolf form. As I tear away from Jay, he lets me leave, standing still as stone where we'd just fucked.

20
The Forge

twenty three days to full moon

My body still aches from the *were-fucking* Jay gave me on Samhain, days later. I have no idea what came over us, but *fuck*. I can't wait for next Halloween. After giving me a headstart, Jay chased me back to the apartment where he'd promptly fucked me in the shower before tucking us into the bed.

Ever since that night, he's taken to sleeping in my bed. I know I invited him, but I hadn't anticipated how much self-control I need to exert *just* to get to sleep. Even after working a shift in the bar, when I'm practically dead on my feet, sleep evades me when I first crawl in next to him. Sometimes, he'll roll over just as I'm settling under the covers and wrap me up in his arms.

When he does that, I have to tell myself it's nothing to obsess over. *He's asleep. It's natural. It doesn't mean anything.*

I still wake up alone, though. Jay is gone to work by then, his side of the bed long since cold.

Instead of joining the Pack on the full Moon run, I'd gone with Aggie, then went out again by myself, just to prove I still could.

This week, I have to go to the Forge and make something for the store. I'd worked my schedule out with Ivy so that I would go in later to the bar, spending a few hours making jewelry before slapping the shit out of some patrons.

I'm to show up at the Forge for work at ten today and get a refresher course. It's been so long since the last time I had the opportunity to flex this particular skill set. The best I ever accomplished as a teen had been a few necklace pendants. So we'll see what happens now, I guess.

Already, I feel tired. I'm only up about two hours earlier than normal, but it feels like *so* much more than that. Driving over to the Forge takes no time at all, even if my knees are jittery as I shift gears, turning the Stingray down streets as familiar as the back of my hand. It's cold today, so I'd dressed in jeans and a long sleeve, this one in a deep green shade. Trusty combat boots on my feet, and a flannel picked up from the floor on my way out complete the look.

There's no dress code at the Forge unless they'd changed that since I've been gone. The brick building is relatively nondescript, with only one sign indicating what the building houses. By the looks of things, they've added on a bit as well.

Good for them.

I don't recognize any of the cars, but I'm not exactly looking, either. I just keep my head down as I walk in, waving to the receptionist. It's a middle-aged man, name tag reading *Dan.*

"Hello, how can I help you?"

"I'm Artemis. I'm to work here— Alpha's orders." I say, stuffing my hands into my pockets. The only people allowed to work at the Forge are Pack members, so I'm not worried about letting out our secret.

"Perfect! Let me get your instructor." He says, picking up the phone and dialing a three-digit code. "Hi...She's here...Yes...Are you sure?... Of course." The receptionist barely taps the button to disconnect the call before he's dialing another three-digit code. "Hi, we need you in the lobby...Thank you." This time he sets the handheld device down on the receiver, turning his attention back to me. "It'll just be a moment. While I have you, why don't you sign a few things?" Dan says, grabbing a small stack of paperwork from various files, and placing them on a clipboard in front of me with a clicky pen.

It's all standard stuff, like my name and address, which I have to look up in my messages with Aggie because I realize that I don't know the actual house number.

How fucking childish. I chide myself, feeling more immature by the minute that ticks by in this fucking town. Within the time it takes me to fill out the handful of forms, my so-called instructor comes through the double doors to my left.

Dante emerges from them, apron tied over his jeans and shirt, sleeves pushed to his elbows. I hate myself for expecting it to be Jay.

"Welcome, to the wonderful world of metalsmithing." He says, spreading his arm wide and holding one of the doors open for me to walk through.

I huff a laugh as I enter the Forge—where the action is— for the first time in at least a decade. It still smells the same, the metallic tang on the tip of my tongue, cloying fire, and just a tinge of burning plastic in my nose. The HVAC system is on over time, recycling the old air with fresh air from outside on a continuous loop.

Everyone seems to have their own station, a desk with a rounded portion to the countertop, and various drawers filled with tools. I hadn't lasted very long here as a teenager. I'd enjoyed the creating part, sure, but the monotony, the constant microscopic attention to detail eroded my patience. I doubt my mom still has the pendant I made her, a purple stone in the center with some fancy filigree around the edges. I had been proud of it, but thinking back on it I don't think the craftsmanship had been... well any good.

Beyond that one, the other trinkets I had made had all been small, simple things. Which is probably all I will manage now. At least I'm not depending on my creations selling to be welcomed back. Magnus just said I have to make something. Not that it has to be good, or *sell*.

Dante leads me around the edges of the room to what I assume has to be his workbench and an empty one beside it. "So. What exactly do you remember?" He asks, handing me an apron.

"To be honest, not a whole lot. I didn't last here very long before I left."

Dante hums and nods his head, rooting around on his desk for something. Eventually, he finds a circle of metal, a silver ring blank. "Start with this. Make something. Don't use what you can't remember how to do, and we'll see what you manage."

I blink at him. "That's it?" I ask, reaching out and taking the ring blank from his outstretched fingers.

"Yep. Show me what you can do without me." Dante says, settling himself on his stool and going back to what he'd been working on before coming to get me from the lobby. I stare at him for a minute, and he staunchly ignores me, picking up a file and resuming his work.

Grumbling under my breath, I sit at the empty desk, opening drawers to see if I can find any tools that look familiar. There's an assortment of files in one drawer, and a series of clamps in another. A different one holds a soldering iron and spools of silver and copper wire. Of course, there are also many ring sizers, clamps pliers, and such in the other drawers.

Dante turns on a Dremel tool, leaning over his piece with a mask on so he doesn't breathe in the filings. I can't help but notice that my desk does *not* have one of those.

"How come I don't get power tools?" I sass, still rifling through the drawers for the file I want.

"You get power tools when I'm sure you're not going to burn the place down." He fires back, voice only slightly muffled through his mask.

"Pft. As if I'm going to *burn the place down* with a Dremel tool." I say, rolling my eyes.

"From what Jay says about you, I would wager that if anyone can manage it, it's you."

"What's *that* supposed to mean?"

"Nothing. Get to work." He barks, and I'm surprised I don't have whiplash.

Hours later, after struggling the entire time with that fucking ring blank, Dante decides that I'm not half bad. "You get power tools tomorrow." He comments as he's cleaning up his desk, a rag in my hand to clear filings off of my station.

"I'm surprised you don't still think I'm going to burn the place down." I fire back, mocking his voice and rolling my eyes.

"If you didn't when you dropped your ring on the ground the tenth or twentieth time, I think we'll be okay." He remarks, cutting me an amused look.

"*Shut up.*" I hiss, fighting back a smile.

"You can keep that– by the way. It was just a test." He remarks, hanging his apron on the small rack, taking mine to do the same with.

"Cool." Funnily enough, it slides easily over my thumb.

"Have time to get a bite?" Dante asks, turning off the little light above his desk, reaching out to do the same with mine, corralling me towards the exit.

"Nope. I have to get to the bar."

"Ah," Dante nods. "Until next time then, Ace." He says, holding the large double doors to the Forge open for me.

"Ace?" I ask, spinning to walk backward in the parking lot.

"Yea. You're *ace* at holding on to things." He quips, stalking towards a lime green motorcycle. His helmet matches the color of the body, sitting on the back seat.

I laugh, saying "Shut up, *Magpie*," as I open up the Stingray.

"Magpie?" He questions, looping the chinstrap of his helmet through the buckles, the open visor allowing me glimpses at his grey eyes.

"Yeah. How many *shiny trinkets* did you buy at the festival?" I sass, raising an eyebrow at him.

Dante's laughter is muffled in his helmet, but his shoulders shake with it. Then he shakes his head, closes the visor, throws his leg over the bike, and turns on the engine.

It's a loud bike, but the Stingray is louder. I can't help myself as I rev my engine a few times. Dante flicks open the visor of his helmet, shouting "Wanna race?" and miming the twist of his throttle.

I shake my head, pointing at my non-existent watch. Dante shrugs back and takes off. I do the same, following him through a few turns until he signals for the road the apartment is on. The rest of my drive to the bar is uneventful, and I quickly change my long sleeve for a tank top, flannel thrown over before I leave my car. As I walk into Coyote Bills, my phone buzzes in my pocket a few times, but I ignore it for the moment, finding Ivy to tell her I'm here but I need something to eat before I do the booth.

Lucky for me, she is in the kitchen with Cook. They're peeling potatoes, but their conversation halts when I enter the room.

"*Aye*, Boss lady! Just the woman I'm looking for." I greet, giving Cook a nod when he mimes eating. The guy's got one helluva' instinct when it comes to feeding people.

"Sounds foreboding. What if I don't want to be the boss?" Ivy quips, smiling at me.

"Oh. It's nothing big. I was just coming to tell you I needed to eat if you don't want me *hulk smashing* my guests because I'm hangry." I give Ivy a bright megawatt smile, trying my best to look innocent while walking backward toward the sink to wash my hands.

Ivy laughs while I scrub my hands, and says "Fair enough." Then, she hands me Cook's abandoned potato peeler. The two of us manage to peel a handful or so before Cook makes a show of plating a pile of fries, sprinkling them with salt and pepper, and a cute little crock of gravy on the side. He hands the plate to me with a flourish, grinning ear to ear, even if he is missing a few teeth.

"Why thank you, kind sir!" I say, accepting the plate. It only takes me a few minutes before the food disappears, the crock of gravy practically licked clean. My phone buzzes in my pocket again, so I pull it out after depositing my dirty dishes in the sink.

I have four messages from Ethan and one from Jay.

Naturally, I go to Jay's first because apparently I just can't help myself.

> Where are you?

> Work?

Three little dots appear and then disappear. He doesn't respond.

My wolf whines in the dark recesses of my mind. With a sea of tangled emotions swimming in me, making my fingers tremble, I open Ethan's message.

> You need to be in the office at 9 AM on the 10th.
>
> Don't be late or the car is mine.
>
> Your disgusting books are being shipped to you.

>> Got it.

> Don't fucking tempt me, Artemis.

>> Wouldn't dream of it.

Turning my phone on silent, I stuff it back into my pocket and shoulder my way through the crowd to the bar. It's rowdy in here tonight, but maybe that's just me. Almost as if I turn on autopilot, I help the girls out in the bar, thinning out the people waiting for drinks. It doesn't take long before I make my way to the edge of the bar where I do slap shots. Out of the corner of my eye, I spot the top of Saint's head, his curls tied back in a floppy bun.

Fuck. That probably means Jay is lurking around here too. Despite myself, I can't stop scanning the crowd.

Still, I keep asking my patrons what they want to drink, and if they want to be praised or otherwise after I slap them. None of my boys join the line for slap shots, though. And it makes my blood boil.

Ivy and Angel close the bar tonight, so around midnight I stalk out the rear exit, walking towards the Stingray in the back lot. I'm watching my feet, wrapped up in my little ball of rage, so I don't notice until it's too late that Jay is leaning against my car.

Almost immediately, the rage is gone, but it leaves this yawning hole in my center, instead. I stop dead in my tracks, a few feet of distance between us.

"Hi." I greet. My voice is flat. Emotionless. At least I have that going for me.

"Hi." He answers, holding my gaze.

The moment stretches, the sounds of the night filling the silence between us. And I can't take it anymore. So I toss him my keys, giving him the barest of warnings. Then I walk around him to drop my flannel in the car. Jay asks "What are you doing?"

I ignore his question, instead giving him one of my own. "Will you take my car back to the apartment?" He's trying to catch my gaze again, trying to get me to look at him.

"When you tell me where you're going, sure."

"Nowhere," I answer, dropping my jeans and phone to the passenger seat on top of my flannel.

"Liar." Jay fires back immediately.

"I'm not going anywhere, Jay," I answer, closing the door and stalking towards the dark trees. I'm going to lose this tank top and these underwear, but at the moment I can't seem to care.

He grabs my arm, stopping me before I can make it more than a few steps.

"Let me go, Jay, or I swear you will never see me again," I order before he can open his mouth. Blue eyes stare me down, flay me down to my soul. Jay doesn't say anything, his fingers trembling for half a heartbeat on my arm before they loosen one by one.

A whine works its way up my throat, but I keep it locked down as I step away and call my wolf forward, shredding through my clothes in an instant. I know Jay watches me leave and can hear it minutes later when the Stingray starts up and drives away. Someone else is driving his car. I can hear *that*, too.

My wolf and I chase the Moon through the trees, more than half her face darkened. We run, and run and run— until the urge to leave Timber Hollow stops shredding my soul. And until the Sun turns the sky violet and pink.

21
Heartstrings

twenty two days to full moon

Eventually, I make my way back to the apartment by late morning. I only have about an hour to catch a nap, grab a quick shower, and then leave again. Still wearing my wolf's black fur, I hesitate at the edge of the tree line.

There is a waffle weave black bathrobe waiting for me, hooked over the end of a broken tree branch.

It smells like Jay.

Shifting nearly sends me to my knees, but even if I don't collapse in the dirt, I still tremble and quake with every step up towards the house, and up the steps. Once inside the door, I hear Saint cooking in the kitchen and try to sneak upstairs to my room. Of course, Jay pops his head around the doorway immediately and spots me. His face is guarded, and I *hate* it.

"Morning, Gorgeous" he immediately greets, coming around to lean against the doorframe.

"Hello, sailor," I grumble, feeling my precious time erode every second it takes to get up these stairs and bury my face in the pillow I know must smell like him and crash.

"What are you doing?" Jay asks, moving to keep me in his line of sight as I climb the stairs.

"Crashing until I have to go to the Forge." I grouse, adding "Who's asking?"

"No Forge today. Bosses orders." He winks, then turns around and goes back to the kitchen. I'm left gaping at his back from over the railing. Does that mean Magnus's orders, the boss at the Forge, or... *His?* Is Jay the boss at the Forge?

"Bosses orders?" I finally manage to shout at his retreating form, which is met with a chorus of laughs from however many of them are in there. *Holy shit, Jay is the boss at the Forge.* It sounds like more than just the boys, so that must mean that Alex and Helena are still staying here.

Honestly, I haven't seen the hide nor hair of either of them since before the full Moon. Good to know they're still around and Jay's presence in my bed is just a matter of convenience.

Nothing has changed.

Everything between us is *exactly* the same as it has always been. I fall too deep, let my heart make leaps my mind knows aren't reciprocated.

Awesome.

At least I have more than an hour before I need to go to Coyote Bills.

My wolf doesn't so much as huff an amused snort at me, deep in the confines of my mind where she sleeps. And now that I'm thinking about it, half my days at the Forge, the other at the bar, sleeping, and then doing it all again doesn't sound too bad. It will make it easy to stay out from under Jay. Easy to do other things than just thinking about climbing him like a tree and fucking him senseless at every waking hour.

Because clearly, this is a game to him. A game I have no way of winning, since *he doesn't 'do jealousy'*.

My chest feels heavy and *tight*. It's what makes me slam the door closed as I enter my room. The clothes from the bar last night are lying folded on top of the dresser, and my phone is plugged into the charger. I ignore the way my eyes burn, the way my chin wobbles.

I don't stop on my way through to the bathroom, showering the forest off as quickly as I can manage, drying similarly. Not even bothering to put on clothes I fall into bed, pulling the covers over top of my head.

My eyes are closed for all of three minutes before I realize I have forgotten to set an alarm. Adrenaline spears through me, my heartbeat skyrocketing. Blindly reaching out of the cocoon of warmth and Jay's scent filling my nose, I grab my phone. The screen's illumination blinds me for a moment as I navigate the apps to make sure I have plenty of time to get ready for the bar. Task complete, I shove the device back onto the nightstand, determined to rest for at least a little while.

My good intentions of waking with plenty of time to get ready for the bar are shot to hell by my repeated snooze alarms. So, when I do finally crawl out of the bed I don't have time to do much other than messy space buns and a quick face.

I smell like Jay. Sleeping on his pillow has made my hair smell like him, and the few pieces of it that I leave out to frame my face waft his scent into my nose with every breath.

Does it make me a masochist to enjoy this as much as I hate it?

The inky black fur of my wolf rustles, before her golden amber eyes peer out at me. *In the broad sense, probably,* she replies.

A snort my mother would chide me for being *unladylike* escapes my throat as I make my way down the stairs.

Of course, Jay meets me at the door.

I don't know how he fucking does this, and I wish I had the common sense to tell him to stop.

It's because you like it. My wolf snarks at me, doing the wolfy equivalent of rolling her golden eyes.

Who asked you?

"Will I be returning your car for you again this evening m'lady?" Jay asks in a British accent, holding what looks like half of a sub and a can of fizzy battery acid with caffeine. I accept the drink, but not the food.

Leave it to Jay to leave out all the tough bits. "Nope," I answer back, swallowing razor blades.

"Would you like me to bring the boys down tonight? Slap us around a bit?" Jay asks, quirking a smile at me.

"Do what you want, Jay." I snap and make my way to push past him. His hand around my bicep halts me in my tracks.

"Hey, what's wrong Gorgeous?" He asks, staring down at me with those unfathomable eyes.

I don't know what takes over me, what makes the words come out, but they do, one after another I croak the words. "What are we doing here, Jay?" This particular question has been lodged in my throat since that party.

"What we always do." Jay's answer is easy. It just rolls off his tongue.

"You mean I lose myself in all your pretty words, and you break my heart again?" My newfound boldness makes the words tumble out. My knees feel like jello, and I taste bile at the back of my throat. I can't look at him, don't want to see the truth that is no doubt written all over his face.

Jay brushes a strand of hair out of my eyes, cupping my chin, tilting my face back up to his. Blue-green eyes trap me, ensnare me.

"No," His breath fans against my eyelids. "This time I'm not letting you go."

The moment stretches, and I find myself searching his gaze for *something*...anything. My wolf whines, and paces in my mind, I know what *she* wants. For this to be real. For it all to be real.

"Yeah. You've said that before too." I reply, tugging my chin out of his grip and walking out of the house.

Away away away.

Artemis Hunt. Always running away.

The tires chirp as I speed off, my limbs shifting gears easily, automatically. Dimly, I register Saint's vehicle chasing after me. Betrayal coats the inside of my mouth, but I swallow it down. It goes well with the flavors of caffeine and heart attack fuel. Too bad my wolfy heart is immune to such things, or maybe the shit would have killed me by now.

If only that invulnerability covered other things. Too bad my heart has always had a Jay-sized hole in its defenses.

My dashboard shows me the image of an incoming call, Jay's number scrolling by.

So if I answer this am I truly a masochist?

*I'm a wolf, what do **I** know?*

Saint's orange Jeep catches up to me, keeping a respectful distance from my tail. In the rearview mirror, I see it's more than just Saint in the vehicle. All of them are packed inside.

I'm grateful, at least that they can't see my face as I push the button to accept the call, shifting gears easily, making the turns to the less traveled back road. It's not my usual route, but it has nice curves to whip through.

"Hello?" I'm grateful, at least that my voice sounds more casual than I feel.

"Artemis, where are you going?" Jay demands, his phone held to his ear, the other hand gripping the handle above his window. His voice fills my car, and I resist the urge to close my eyes.

"To work, Jay. Relax." I sass, breezing through a curve, my feet working in tandem to brake, shift, and press the gas without losing momentum. It's not quite a drift, but I know there will be curves later on the road.

"This isn't the way you usually go to the bar." The SUV disappears from view momentarily, not built for cornering at speed like the Stingray. Or you know... *speed* in general.

"How do you know that?" A peek in my rearview shows me that he's put the phone on speaker, and I hear the boys in the background laughing at him.

"Because I do. What's happening, Artemis?"

"What's *happening*, Jay Temple, is I'm driving to work, in my very fast, very *fun* car and you're being a wet blanket." I sass, throwing my car around another curve, the rear end sliding easily. The next twist in the road comes in a blink, so I have to brake and shift, oversteering to be able to accomplish the tight *s*-curve.

They all suck in a breath–audible even through the speakerphone. It's like they are all holding their breath as if I intend to smash the vehicle.

Laughter bursts free from my chest as the straightaway opens up before me, and I floor it. Pedal to the metal, I open up the throttle, easily reaching a cool 100 MPH in 3.5 seconds. For the first time in my life, I thank the pack's ruthless attention to detail, noting that there hasn't been a single pothole. Even one would *truly* fuck up my day.

"That's so fucking hot, dude." I hear Saint congratulate Jay, a quick chorus of thumps to his shoulders I see in the rearview. Again, the taste of betrayal coats my tongue. I wash down the taste with a quick sip of my drink, having a brief moment to do so on the straightaway.

"Why are you being so reckless?" Jay practically growls into the phone, my eyes rolling on instinct.

"I'm just having fun, Jay," I answer quietly, downshifting to slow down for the reentry to town limits, and reentry to the flow of traffic. It's like he holds the very strings attached to my heart, tugging them every which way. I can only wonder when he's going to rip them out again.

There is nothing else to say, so I end the call with a quick button mash of my thumb.

Saint follows me all the way to Coyote Bills, but none of the boys stop me from entering the building or starting my shift.

I can't tell if I'm happy about it, or not.

22

I adore you

nineteen days to full moon

The next few days I manage to avoid Jay like the plague. I show up early at the Forge, put in my time, and leave before he or Dante arrives. Rinse and repeat. It's in the very few hours that our sleeping hours align that pull me closer to him. No matter which one of us lands in that bed first, I always wake up wrapped in his scent. It's all over my skin, as if we intertwine in the twilight hours.

Cowardice or stubbornness, I don't know which it is that makes it impossible to revoke my offer to share my bed with Jay until his brother is gone.

I manage to make a few things at the Forge. A set of silver cufflinks carved with the face of a wolf is the best of my creations. My other favorite is a single earring, shaped like a dagger. There is a single ruby set into a gold casing, dangling from the carved tip of the dagger. The mate to the earring has eluded me. No matter how many times I try to replicate the design I always end up scraping too deep, gouging into the metal. There are a shameful amount of mistakes in the 'discard' pile contributed by yours truly. That is the only reason the finished dagger isn't my favorite.

When my day off from both places of employment finally arrives, I sleep until three in the afternoon. Of course, It is unavoidable that I run into *everyone* when I emerge from my cocoon, driven by the aromas coming from the kitchen. I don't bother throwing anything other than a flannel picked up from the floor and a pair of thick socks on before I leave the room.

I'm able to pad quietly all the way into the kitchen, observing the three of them interact without anyone noticing. Saint is at the stove, stirring something that smells of garlic and spices. A flick of Saint's wrist tosses the pan, revealing sweet bell peppers and onions frying with *something*.

Dante is standing against the counter, facing the open doorway. He notices me lurking in the doorway first. Jay's back is to me, his large form leaning against the island. Dante doesn't reveal my presence, instead keeps the conversation going as if I'm not being a creep, standing in the doorway. Of course, it only lasts a moment or two.

When Jay's spine snaps straight, like he'd been struck by electricity my heart stops. Then he whips around to face me. Before Jay can say anything though, I burst into motion, marching around the island to perch myself on the counter next to Saint. I figure *he* is the least likely to interrogate me.

I don't want to have intense conversations. Not right now. And not with Jay.

Tension keeps my spine ramrod straight, and not just from the awkward pause of their conversation. Tomorrow, I fly back to California to deal with Ethan. Which sounds about as fun as drinking bleach. But at least then the car will be mine, and I won't have to deal with *rich boy* Ethan anymore.

"Good Morning, Gorgeous." Jay rumbles, watching me lift myself onto the countertop. My bare thighs are in danger of being singed by splattering grease, but I don't really care.

"Hello," I chirp, giving a half-wave to the room.

Keep pretending your heart doesn't skip about a dozen beats just because he says good morning. My wolf snarks, amusement glittering in her golden eyes.

Shut up.

Saint is sautéing Brussels sprouts with the peppers and onions in bacon grease, a well-seasoned piece of chicken resting on the cutting board on the opposite side of the stovetop. It all smells *fucking delicious.*

"You want some, Tiny?" Saint offers, giving me a small wink like he knows why I'm over here. Like he knows that I'm using him like a shield. Jay and Dante go back to talking about their vehicles, discussing some aftermarket parts they both are considering adding on.

"Only if there's enough for me."

"Who do you think this is for?" Saint breezes back, smiling, giving the pan a little shimmy and toss while he sprinkles seasonings over the sprouts. My chest aches, and I return his small smile. I don't know what else to say. "Do you want anything else with it?" He asks, grabbing a plate from the cupboard, slicing the chicken on a bias, and plating the handful of sprouts.

"Do we have juice?" I ask, accepting the plate and fork.

Dante answers, opening the fridge. "Cranberry or orange?"

"Cranberry, please," I answer, stabbing a piece of chicken with my fork.

"Do you want a splash of bubbly in there?" Dante asks, holding a small can of lemon-lime soda up for my inspection.

"That sounds fantastic," I mumble around my food. The chicken is tender, juicy, and flavorful, perfectly paired with the crisp, caramelized Brussels sprouts. "I'm going to *fucking* die if you ever decide to stop cooking, Saint."

That comment makes everyone laugh, and I have to fight the smile threatening to break out across my face. It's so easy here, so easy to just *exist*. The boys go back to talking about their cars easily enough, Saint chiming in here and there about a new lift kit or getting bigger tires for mudding while I devour the rest of my meal. Dante's drink suggestion washes everything down perfectly, the added bubbles tingling my nose.

I find Jay's eyes on mine when I set my now empty plate down, so I ask "What?"

"Want to go for a ride with me?"

"To where?"

Jay smirks, but shrugs before he says "It's a surprise."

My mind whirrs with all the possibilities as I look him up and down, but eventually, I answer with a shrug of my own "Sure. Why not."

Jay's wolfy eyes glow from inside, primal satisfaction evident all over his face. "Go get dressed." His eyes linger on the lengths of my legs as he orders me out of the room.

Excitement bubbles up as I follow his command, and I am grateful for the distraction. Even if it means spending more time with him than I should, getting pulled into Jay's orbit.

Before climbing into bed last night I'd showered off the bar, falling asleep with my hair still wet. It means the lengths are fairly wavy already. A few strands are kinked weirdly though, so I twist them around the end of my comb after spritzing with water. The result is questionable but good enough. I end up just pushing the strands behind my ears.

While I decide what to wear, I wash my face with a bit of cool water and then swipe a moisturizer over my cheekbones. A second glance into the mirror makes me swipe a few coats of mascara over my lashes and a dusting of shimmer to the inner corners of my eyes. Then I grab a tinted lip balm glazing my cupid's bow without much thought behind it.

Jay hadn't been wearing anything specifically fancy downstairs, so I tug my favorite jeans over my legs, and a black long-sleeve tee over my shoulders. The same flannel I'd been wearing goes overtop of that. November in the woods is easily as muddy as spring sometimes, so I also grab my boots before leaving the room.

Jay is once again waiting for me at the bottom of the stairs. I don't know what that look in his eyes is, but it sends a shiver up my spine. "Ready?" He asks as I make my way down to him.

"Yep. Do I need anything else?" I have no idea what we're doing, but I have some money tucked into my flannel pocket. The one with the button. I leave my phone behind, knowing that if I tempt fate I'll end up shifting, leaving it behind.

"No?" His reply is a question all by itself. I just smirk and push my feet into my shoes, sloppily lacing them. When he leads me through the doors, dusk is already upon us.

"I hate daylight savings." I grouse. Losing daylight at barely 4 pm has always felt like the short end of the stick.

"Yeah, but then we get more time with the stars," Jay replies, tugging me by the hand toward his pretty blue GT.

"Sure, that's one way of looking at it." Giggles want to burst free as he pushes me into his car, a smile on his lips. My lips feel stretched to their limit when he does a silly jog around the vehicle and hops into the driver's seat.

"That's the best way of looking at it. Everything going dark isn't so bad." He says, shooting me a quick grin as he backs out of the lot and begins driving.

I roll my eyes. "Sure, Jay. Whatever you say."

"What do you want to listen to?" Jay asks, holding out the AUX cord. When I take it from his outstretched hand, anxiety bubbles up, unbidden.

"What do *you* like to listen to?" I ask, thumbing through the music player on my phone.

"That's not what *I* asked. You pick, Gorgeous." He says, refocusing on driving through traffic in town.

Picking music seems like an insurmountable task right now, all that I can think about is how often Ethan would make snide remarks, mock the music I would choose or just outright say it was awful. Ethan's voice in my head plays on repeat as I try to make a selection.

"Where are we going?" I ask if only to fill the silence so that it doesn't seem weird that I'm taking forever to choose a song.

"I told you it's a surprise." Is all that Jay has to offer me. My eyes roll automatically. Finally, I end up just putting my music on shuffle, deciding just to see what happens. If nothing else, maybe he'll be a dick and make it easier for my heart to let him go.

You are in far, *far* too deep, Artemis Hunt. I grouse to myself, and my wolf stays silent.

A half-hour later, with nary a stray asshole comment about my music choices, we're still driving. The sky is pitch black, the tops of the trees disappearing into the sky. The headlights of Jay's car illuminate the night, but our eyesight is far superior to a human's. I wouldn't go so far as to say we don't need them, because driving without headlights is just plain dumb.

I start singing along with the music when a favorite comes along. I pretend not to notice the way Jay sneaks glances at me.

He makes my head whip towards him when he starts singing along with me though, my mouth falling open. I can't tell what I'm more shocked about— that he's singing, or that he likes the same music I do well enough to know the words.

"What's wrong, Gorgeous?" Jay asks, picking the notes of the song back up.

"I—um, nothing," I say brightly, going back to staring out the windshield. Jay chuckles, grabbing my hand and pressing a kiss across my knuckles. My stomach bottoms out.

"I adore you," Jay says it like he's said it a thousand times. He says it like he means something else. Something I don't allow myself to dwell on.

"Yea?" I answer, turning to look at him. It's a mistake. We're apparently at our destination because he pulls over, and turns off the car. And *now*, I have his full attention.

"Yeah."

"Since when?"

"Always."

I don't know what to say back to that. So I open my door and get out, looking around. We're at the scenic overlook, the one that looks down the valley. You can see almost the whole town, lit with an amber glow, shrouded by the trees.

But the *sky* is what grabs my attention. The vast expanse of black is dotted with stars, twinkling against the light of the Moon. She's creeping up on half full, but hanging so low in the sky that it pulls my wolf to the surface.

"What are we doing out here, Jay?" I ask, face still tilted towards the expanse of black.

"This." His mountainous shoulders rise and fall in my periphery. "I wanted to come out here, you looked like you could use a break. That's all."

"Why do you come out here?"

"To think. It's quiet. I like the stars." Again, those shoulders rise and fall.

There are a thousand things I could say, to steer this conversation toward subjects I *actually* know how to navigate, but I don't.

Instead, I just grab his hand, giving his fingers a gentle squeeze. "Thank you, Jay." His pulse jumps under my fingers, and he returns the small squeeze before my hand slides out of his.

"Anytime." Jay's eyes are still on me, and I think I might spontaneously combust if he doesn't stop looking at me like that, so I again break the nice moment with a question.

"So are we just gonna stand around, or are there chairs or what?"

Jay smiles, but retrieves a blanket from the backseat, laying across the grass with a flourish. "Ta-da."

Laughter bursts out of me, catching me by surprise making my belly ache, and tears leak out of my eyes. This side of Jay is one I used to see all the time when we were kids. Before we blurred the lines between friendship and *more*.

"Oh, my mistake." I chortle, taking a seat on the blanket, and leaning back on my palms. The town seems far off, even though

I know it's not. We're still within town limits, *technically*. It's just the part that stretches into the forest.

Jay leans back on his elbow, stretching his legs out before him, one knee bent. Comfortable silence stretches for a few minutes before he speaks again. "So are you ever gonna tell me where you went for all those years?" He asks like we're talking about the weather.

"You never asked," I reply, looking for constellations. The light from the town would make them impossible to spot for a human, but with my wolf so close to the surface of my soul, I can see better. Can make out the glow of the stars burning light years away.

"I'm asking now." Jay's reply is immediate, and I can *feel* him burning a hole into the side of my face with his eyes. But I know if I look at him I'll notice the way his muscles bunch in his long sleeve pushed to elbows. I'll notice the patch of skin at his waist left exposed just above the line of his jeans. The line of the fabric of his boxers. I'll notice his hands, and start thinking about how they feel roaming all over my body.

"Well." I take a deep breath, letting it out slowly. "I had a bunch of money saved from random jobs and graduation... So I bought a bus ticket to the farthest place on the line and found a Pack.

They let me work in the diner for a while. Rinse and repeat until I turned twenty-one, then I moved on to bartending."

"That's rather vague."

I shrug, catching my lip between my teeth. "It was simple. I just wanted to get out."

"Was being here really all that bad?" Jay asks, and something in his voice makes me want to turn my head and look at him, but I don't.

I know deep in my bones that there are people out there who have suffered far *far* worse than me. I had a roof over my head. Food. A family. I can't help how I had felt so very alone in my mom's house growing up, despite being the fourth one living there though. Maybe that is why being a Lone Wolf hadn't ever bothered me. I've always been alone. *"Bad? No..."*

"Bad enough to make you drop off the face of the Earth for seven years." Jay counters.

I snort. "I didn't *drop off the face of the Earth,* Jay. I was in California. Well, at the end anyway."

"The land of eternal Sunshine," Jay says in an old-timey voice, waving a hand in the air.

"More like the land of endless dickheads. Except Sam. She's cool."

"Shifter?"

"Yea. Anaconda."

"Sexy."

"Extremely. She plays for the other team though." I reply like I'm consoling him, reaching out to pat his arm.

Jay smiles, capturing my hand to press a kiss across my knuckles again. "I think I'll survive," he says, soft lips pressing another quick kiss to my skin before he lets me go.

One single giggle slips through my lips, turning my entire face red with embarrassment. I flop back on the blanket, laying fully on it to hide my face. "That's a relief." I find myself saying.

"Yea?"

"Sure."

Jay lays down with me, our shoulders touching. "Which one is your favorite?"

"The Dragon," I reply, pointing to the space between the Big Dipper and Polaris. "Yours?"

"The wolf, obviously. Can't see it here though."

"You would pick a constellation you don't get to see."

"Sounds like me, yeah. Picking things I can't have."

"You should probably stop doing that."

"Nah."

"So how come you guys don't all have your own place?" I ask, curious about why the boys had all been renting with my cousin.

"Saint, Dante, and I are waiting for our house to be built." He replies, tucking an arm under his head.

"Like, all three of you are building your own houses or...?" I ask, turning to look at him. It's a mistake. Jay practically hums with power, with sensual promise. I know it would only take trailing my fingers through his hair, a graze of my teeth over my lips and he would give me everything I ask for. If I gave him the go-ahead, he would ravish me right here under the stars.

Is that what I want though?

Or I could tell him I'm going to California tonight. But then we'd be talking about Ethan.. and I don't want to do that.

"Nope. Think of it like the Packhouse. It's going to be big, our own space but still together. They'll be my Betas when I take over."

"And none of you want to live *alone*, apparently?" There's a teensy drop of teasing in my voice, a smile threatening to crack my calm and cool facade.

"Both of them came from packs that abandoned them," Jay says, and my heart wrenches for Saint and Dante. "If left on their own for long enough, the part of their wolf that remembers what it was like being abandoned emerges. It's hard to reason with them when that happens."

"Oh...How long were they alone?" I ask quietly.

"Not as long as you, but long enough to do permanent damage," Jay responds, locking his blue eyes onto mine.

"So that is why Magnus was so paranoid about my wolf."

"Yeah."

Turning back to the skies, I made a mental note to make sure that Dante and Saint both know that I value their friendship. I truly hadn't realized how much I had missed being part of a Pack. And that is what Jay, Saint, and Dante have become.

My Pack.

"How long until your house is done?"

"A few months still. The walls are up but some materials aren't in yet to continue."

"What is Dante going to do when it snows? Does he have a car in storage somewhere?"

"Magnus is rather anal-retentive about keeping the roads clear from snow." Jay chuckles quietly. "When it does snow, which isn't much these days, it's cleared within the hour. Dante drives his bike or rides with Saint."

I only hum back in response, watching the red and green dots of an airplane flying overhead.

"I'm sure they'll be happy to know you're worried about them."

"Only a little. Don't ruin my ice queen mask." I fire back, a grin now firmly in place. I just can't seem to help it around him.

"Wouldn't dream of it," Jay responds, blue-green eyes roaming all over my face, lingering on my mouth.

As much as I want him to kiss me, I push up from the ground. Staying here with Jay any longer is dangerous for my heart.

"Would you like to make a wager, Jay Temple?" I ask, looking down at him.

"You have my attention, Artemis Hunt." He replies, a smile creeping across his face.

"Do you think you can make it home before me?" I ask, stepping towards the woods, tosing my flannel into his face. I've undressed in front of Jay thousands of times, but *this*... leaving my clothes for him to pick up before I shift feels different. *Intimate* somehow.

"In the car? No, probably not." Jay's voice is thick, and he audibly swallows when my jeans hit the dirt.

Looking at him over my shoulder, I toss my bra and panties into his lap as well. Then I say "You should try," before letting my wolf free and tearing through the forest.

Jay does *not* in fact make it back to the apartment before me. By the time he gets home, I'll be halfway to the airport.

There's no way I'm backing down from Ethan. No way that I'm giving him back the car.

The flight isn't too long, but I'll be able to sleep a little, at least. It's an overnight flight, taking off at eleven pm here, and landing at two am there. For once, the time zones are working in my favor. From the airport, I'll catch a cab to Sam's apartment to use her shower and her closet. And then from there, I'll head to Ethan's office.

I'm suddenly really glad that I'd left my phone at the house when Jay asked me to go for a ride with him. Otherwise, this entire process would be impossible without my flight itinerary. Well... not impossible but exceedingly more annoying.

Ivy is taking me to the airport, having been there while I looked over the documents Ethan sent my way. Of course, the arrogant bastard is sending me the White's private jet, but he's made my boarding time as inconvenient as possible for me. If this is what it takes to keep the car and keep him off my back though, I'll deal with it.

And anyway, he still doesn't realize I stole twenty thousand dollars from him. So who's the real winner here?

After I sprint up to my room and dress quickly in leggings, a tee shirt, and a hoodie I find my backpack. In it, I toss my toothbrush, my wallet, charger, and a change of underwear. A quick glance at my shelves is all I need to select a book to read at the airport.

While I make sure I have everything I'll likely need for the next 48 hours, I tie my hair up in a messy bun with a big silky scrunchie. The notification chime from my phone tells me Ivy is here.

23
My Pack

Jay

My phone rings as I speed down and around the curves of the back roads. I'm going well over the limit, and it's no surprise whose name the caller ID reveals. The Bluetooth connection takes a moment to connect the call, but when I do, I greet him with a simple "Father."

"Any particular reason you are speeding haphazardly around the back roads?" Magnus asks with a sly tone to his voice, so he probably already knows, but I'll be damned if I give him the satisfaction.

"I like to live vicariously."

"Sure you do, Son. Come to the Packhouse." My father disconnects the call without another word.

"Mother fucker. Cock sucking dick balls MOTHER FUCKER!" Anger seeps out of me like a poison. There are cameras all over the roads in TImber Hollow, installed as an automated solution to surveying Pack lands. Before that, enforcers would patrol every hour of every day. There are still Pack enforcers, but their job is less *be a wolf twenty-four-seven* and more to teach the young wolves *how* to be wolves these days. How to meet the two halves of your soul and balance them.

So, obviously Magnus or one of the enforcers saw me on the cameras. Likely saw Artemis in the car with me on the way up. There's absolutely no way I'm making it back to the apartment before, or in any way close to Artemis now.

Dutifully, though I turn down the appropriate roads toward the Packhouse, rather than ignoring him like I truly want to. The big brick building is lit up, the parking lot just as illuminated as the interior.

Magnus is standing at the pool table, watching Nero, his Beta line up a shot. Nero had been Beta with Artemis' dad before his death. In other packs, Virgil's death would have opened up a spot for another wolf to become Beta, and the competitors would fight for the position. There are even some packs in the south that still fight to the death. My father had never replaced him though. Never even mentioned it.

"Hello, Son." He greets me simply, bending to line his shot up. Nero nods his head in my direction, folding his hands over the top of his stick.

"Father," I answer, giving Nero a similar nod.

"What were you doing at the lookout?"

"Why?" I'm squeezing my jaw so tight I think my teeth might crack. My phone buzzes in my pocket, but I ignore it. I hate to, but I have to for the moment.

"Call it a father's curiosity." He says, blue eyes swiveling to me as Nero takes his turn.

"I took Artemis up. She seemed like she could use the quiet." I finally respond.

"Why do you give that girl the time of day?" Magnus' back is to me once again, so I can't see his face but I hear the inflection in his voice, the implication that she's scum, *unworthy*.

"Because she's *Pack*," I growl.

"She hasn't been in years. *She* disappeared, remember?"

"Artemis Hunt has always been, and will *always* be **my** Pack." I snarl at my father's back, feeling my wolf rise.

"Ahh. I see. And where did she run off to this time?" He answers, turning to face me.

"Back to the house. She was racing me. *That* is why I was speeding, *father*." I practically spit the words at his feet.

"So you say," Magnus replies simply.

"What do you mean?" My heart feels like it's going to pound out of my chest, my stomach dropping immediately.

"Artemis was picked up from the apartment."

"She left?"

"Yes."

Immediately, I pull my phone out of my pocket. A message from Dante greets me.

> Artemis left the house. She has a backpack.
>
> Didn't say where she was going. I'm following.

"Fuck. Fuck. *Fuck!*"

"Where is she going, Son?"

"I don't know." I'm walking down the hall and away from my father before I realize it.

The Alpha only orders *"Control your wolf!"* as I exit the Packhouse.

The drive over to Aggie's cottage seems like it takes no time at all. I know that Artemis wouldn't leave without telling her. Or...at least I *hope* she told Aggie. It's my only hope of finding Artemis again. Artemis' aunt greets me at the door, my knuckles only rapping once against the pink wood.

"Jay! What a surprise. What can I do for you young man?"

"Where did she go?"

"What?" The woman blinks at me, brown eyes blinking rapidly.

"Artemis. She left town maybe forty minutes ago. Where is she going?"

"California. Are you going after her?"

"Yes." Aggie halts my spin away from her with a gentle hand on my arm.

"Take my phone. She's sharing her location with me. Passcode is her birthday." Artemis' aunt presses her device into my palms, patting my shoulder. "Bring her home young man." Then, she's nudging me down the stairs, closing the door behind me.

Before I leave Aggie's driveway, I check Artemis' flight itinerary. "Fuck!" She's on a private plane. I can't buy tickets for her flight.

"Fuck, Fuck *FUCK!*" Throwing the car into gear, I speed down the roads towards the hangar. This land was once grazing pastures for dairy cows, but it now houses the new addition to the town. Which will come in handy, tonight. *Very* handy.

Magnus originally purchased a little Cessna to spray crops, but the addition of the six-seater is relatively new. It's the large rolling doors for the six-seater that I push open. There is *absolutely* no way I'm leaving California without my girl in one of these seats.

Ain't no fucking way.

24
Coffee

Artemis

Being back in the city feels like a thousand fire ants are crawling across my skin, my wolf pacing in the dark corners of my soul. And the taxi ride to Sam's feels like it takes a whole year to complete. I should consider myself lucky that it isn't closer to the full Moon.

Maybe then I really would bite Ethan's hand off. My snort of amusement makes the cab driver give me a scathing look in the rearview, but he doesn't comment as he pulls up to Sam's apartment complex. Sam's lights are on, and the ones in the lobby are glowing softly as well. After I unlock the door with her spare key, I send a quick text to Ivy, letting her know that I've landed. A moment of hesitation makes me also send one to Aggie.

Neither of them responds, but it's barely six am over there. I'm sure when they wake up they'll ask for another update.

By the time I make it up the elevator to Sam's apartment, she's waiting for me at the door.

"Hey. You look like shit." She greets me cheerfully, closing and locking the door behind me.

"*Thanks,*" I respond, rolling my eyes.

"You're welcome!" Sam chirps, giving me a bright smile. "Are you showering now, or in the morning?"

"Now. I feel gross from the plane."

"Cool. Couch or cuddle?" Sam knows me well enough to understand I don't always want to be touched.

"Couch, please," I answer, giving her a small smile.

"Alright. I'll get it set up while you're in the shower. What time do you have to be at the dickhead's office?"

"Nine."

"Alright. I'll make sure we're up. I'm coming with you, I hope you realize."

"I can't ask you to do that, Sam," I reply quietly, my eyes burning with unspent tears.

"Who said you had a choice in it?" She breezes back, squeezing my hand gently.

"Thank you, Sam. I don't deserve you."

"You deserve the world, Artemis. I'm only glad you're getting out." I can't do anything other than nod, emotion clogging my throat. "Go get in the shower. I'll see you in the morning." With that, Sam turns and sets off to find linens, leaving me to walk into her bathroom, leaving the door cracked open.

My shower is quick and efficient. Sam doesn't skimp out on personal hygiene products, so there is an array of different shampoos to choose from. When I leave her walk-in with glass doors, I notice she has laid one of her large tee shirts just inside the door for me. The girl in the mirror looks different than I remember. She has more light in her eyes. Less weight draped across her shoulders.

Sam has already retreated to her bedroom, the lights all dimmed out in the living room. There is a soft glow from the hallway where her room is, letting me know that she's still awake, even if she's giving me privacy. The big green couch has a sheet thrown over the bottom cushions, and a plush blanket overtop complete with one of Sam's big fluffy pillows.

She's even set the TV remote and a glass of water on the coffee table.

"I do *not* deserve you," I say quietly to the room, truly wondering how I'd gotten so lucky to have a friend like Sam.

In the silence of my friend's apartment, curled into a ball on her couch, my mind drifts—inevitably, to Jay. Why did I leave like that? Why didn't I tell him?

Why?

My wolf has nothing to offer, subdued in the dark corners of my soul. Sleeping, or waiting I can't say.

Is it even going to matter, though? Will Jay do *anything?* Probably not. Laying here thinking about him is...making me feel alone. So very alone.

Leave it to me to create an art form of running from problems, only to make it a bigger mess in the end.

Fuck.

I can't stop thinking about how much of a fuck up I am. Can't stop wishing I had told Jay about this so he'd come with me. Then maybe I'd find out if sleeping in my bed was anything more than a convenience for him.

That's when I realize that despite how many times we've slept in the same bed, Jay has never taken advantage of my proximity. When he leaves the bed in the morning, sometimes he wakes me slightly by untangling our limbs. So I know that even if we're laying flush hip to hip, he never lets his hands roam.

I know I'm a fool for silently wishing he would.

We fuck, but Jay never really makes the first move. When I'd been in the kitchen making cookies, it was me who kissed him. At the party, *I* kissed him. Led him on a chase through the trees. Begged for what he was giving me.

My cheeks are wet before I know it, and my hand is clamped around my mouth to stifle my cries. I've known since I left all those years ago that Jay just doesn't feel that deeply towards me... It's just... I can't seem to let him go.

How do I tell my heart that he's not mine? How do I let him go?

Sam wakes me in the morning with the rattle-rattle-shimmy-shake of an iced coffee in front of my face. She's gorgeous, even in the morning without a drop of makeup.

Her honey blonde hair is like a glowing halo around her head with the Sun streaming through the high windows.

My eyes feel crusty like there is sand beneath my eyelids. I guess that's from crying myself to sleep. "Good morning!" Sam says, grabbing her drink from the coffee table when I accept the one in her outstretched hand.

"Morning," I mumble, rubbing my face. "What time is it?" The iced coffee is *delicious*. Caramel notes but not too sugary. I drink almost a quarter of it in one go.

"Seven. We have plenty of time to get over there." She answers a grin painted all over her face.

"What's with you?" I ask, gesturing to her entirely too cheerful expression.

"Why didn't you tell me you have a bodyguard?"

"Huh?"

"He could have come up to the apartment. He didn't have to sleep in his car." I swear she's saying words but they do *not* sound like English.

"*Huh?*" I repeat.

Sam blinks at me twice, and then an even larger grin stretches across her face. She takes a delicate sip of her coffee, inspecting her manicure before deigning to reply. "Go look out the window."

I blink back at her, my not-awake brain just not understanding what is going on. "*Why?*"

"You'll see." She sings back, looking at her nails and taking another sip of her coffee. I glare at the side of her face but she doesn't say anything else. So, before I get up I stretch out my muscles, arching my back and pointing my toes.

"*Fine.*" I finally answer, after taking another sip of my coffee. The California Sun is bright and merry even this early, and I have to blink and squint against the glare as I make my way over to the large window that looks down on the street.

My stomach practically bottoms out, my knees going so weak that I have to let the window sill take my weight.

"Jay, *motherfucking* Temple." I breathe, and Sam cackles. "Did you do this?" I ask, staring down at his broad form leaning against the hood of what has to be a rental.

"Nope!" She hoots, "He was there when I woke up, saw me through the windows, waved, and then ten minutes later coffee arrived."

"So he's been out there all night?" I ask, unable to look away from him. I can't make out his expression, but I can tell he's looking at the apartment. Looking at *me*.

"Yep! Brittany- that's the neighbor-" Sam pointed towards her door, and the neighboring apartment before continuing. "-sent me a screen recording of her camera. You show up and then a little while later he shows up, parks there, and doesn't move."

"I have no idea what he's doing here," I admit to Sam.

"You didn't tell him to come?"

"I didn't even tell him I was *leaving* town for a few days."

Sam gasps, then starts laughing in earnest. She says "Call him. I'm going to get in the shower." She passes me my phone on her way through, still chuckling to herself.

As I search for his contact and press the little button to call him, my stomach does somersaults. What the fuck am I going to say to him? Jay's phone barely rings once before he pulls it out of his pocket, raising the device to his ear.

"Good morning, Gorgeous." He says, raising his hand to wave at me in the window.

"Good morning, Handsome," I answer back, placing my palm against the pane.

"Whatcha doing?" Jay asks his voice light and teasing.

"I could ask you the same thing."

"I asked you first." He answers, and I don't have to think too hard to imagine the expression on his face.

"I'm here for the car," I eventually answer, turning away from the window to pace.

"Ahhh," Jay replies, and then asks "Well did you at least enjoy your coffee?"

I snort. "Yes, Jay. *I am enjoying my coffee.* Are you going to come up?"

"If you're asking, sure."

"That *is* what I just did, isn't it?"

"Which apartment?"

"Go up the elevator. You'll see me." I reply, ending the call. It only takes Jay a few moments to come up, elevator doors whining open. I'm already standing in the doorway, Sam's large door propped open. His face is too stoic, too closed off for my liking. "Whatcha doing, Jay?" I ask again after closing the door behind him.

"You wanted to race. I just assumed this was part of it." He jokes, giving me a sly half-smile.

"*Ha-ha*. Really, what are you doing?"

Jay takes his time responding, staring down into the depths of my soul. His eventual answer is "Just making sure you're okay." The muscles on either side of his jaw clench and unclench rapidly.

"I'm *great!* I'm about to get a free car." I reply, painting a bright smile on my mouth.

The bathroom door opens, and Sam emerges just as Jay opens his mouth. She's dressed in a pretty green asymmetrical dress, an assortment of chains around her neck and wrists.

"Sam, this is Jay. Jay, this is Sam." I say, introducing the pair.

"Nice to meet you, Jay. Thanks for the coffee." Sam says, raising her hand out for him to shake.

"Nice to meet you too. And, it's no problem." Jay responds, lightly returning the gesture.

"Artemis, can I talk to you for a minute?" Sam asks, laying her hand on my arm.

"Sure," I reply, furrowing my brow. What could she possibly need? She leads us over to the kitchen, pulling us partially out of Jay's line of sight.

"I got a text from one of my clients while I was in the shower, they're throwing a fit and I kind of need to handle it. Will you be okay with Jay going to the office with you? I feel awful bailing on you like this."

"Why do you think he's going with me?"

"Come on, Artemis. He flew across the country after you." Sam insists.

"That doesn't mean anything." Sam levels me with a flat look before she asks again if I'll be okay without her. "Yes, Sam. I'll be okay. Go. I'll text you later." I answer, accepting the hug she pulls me into. She's a flurry of movement as she gathers her things up to go, reminding me to lock up when I leave.

And then it's just Jay and I in Sam's apartment, and a thousand questions on the tip of my tongue. I doubt I'll ever ask them.

"So... I need to go get dressed. And then I need to go to Ethan's office to sign the paperwork. You're welcome to uh.. hang out here or whatever. I'll be gone for a few hours. "

Jay pins me with an arched eyebrow, a stupid smile pulling the corners of his mouth up. I want to smack it off his face almost as much as I want to kiss him.

"Go get dressed, and then I'll drive."

I swear he should be bursting into flames with how hard I'm glaring at him. But I do go get dressed, grabbing my iced coffee on my way to steal something from Sam's closet.

25
Bitch Boy Ethan

eighteen days to full moon

After getting dressed and borrowing some of Sam's mascara and eyeliner to do a quick wing, I walk back to where Jay is waiting for me.

Jay *motherfucking* Temple is waiting for me in my friend's living room. In California. Despite the anxiety of going to see Ethan, my stomach is doing somersaults. What is *happening?*

I'm a little taller than Sam, so I opted to grab one of her dresses from the extensive closet. It's black, which is the only reason that I chose it if I'm being honest. The dress hits me around mid-calf, with a long slit up my thigh. Spaghetti straps hold the dress up, suitable for the California Sun—and Sam's apartment, but I know Ethan's office won't be hot, if anything it'll be air-conditioned within an inch of life, so I'd also grabbed a soft black cropped sweater with a chunky knit. Borrowed cross body bag slung over my shoulder. A pair of heels I apparently forgot here at some point clutched in hand, but I honestly wish I had my boots.

Jay turns from the window as I enter, eyes hungrily drinking down every inch of my skin that is exposed. But he doesn't say anything other than "You look nice."

I give him a small smile, saying "Thanks, it's Sam's clothes. She has expensive taste."

Slowly sliding my feet into her heels, I sigh deeply. The sneakers I'd thrown on before leaving the apartment won't go with this dress, and if I admit it to myself, Ethan's mother will surely say something about them... if she's there. This interaction needs to go as smoothly as possible, and I really don't want to add something to the mix that will give them the opportunity to be annoying.

"It's *really* not. Why are you upset?" Jay replies without missing a beat.

"I don't want to wear these heels. I *can* don't mistake me-" I say, raising a finger in his direction. "-but I really don't want to. I was just thinking that I wanted to wear my boots."

"Sam doesn't have any?"

"She does, just not any that I want to wear right now." I turn just in time to see Jay's smile. "What?"

"I may have brought something with me."

Narrowing my eyes at him, I ask "What?"

"Well, you *did* leave your clothes. We were racing." Jay's smirk makes me want to smack him silly. Or maybe grab the hair at the nape of his neck that will curl if it gets long enough and kiss him. Neither are viable options.

"You're telling me my boots are out in that car right now?"

"That I am, Gorgeous."

"I could kiss you," I say without thinking. Jay smirks and my cheeks heat.

"Anytime, Darlin'."

A laugh titters out of me as I turn away from him. Before I do something else incredibly stupid, I go back to Sam's closet to return the shoes and grab a pair of socks. I can't stop thinking, and can't help but wonder how it's possible that the best and worst-case scenario being that *Jay* was who ended up as my *fake* boyfriend.

So, when I reenter the room, I blurt "How is it possible you're single? All you gotta do is talk to someone like you talk to me, and you're golden. So what gives?" I'm smiling at him, but the question is genuine. *And* he said he's been single for a while.

Jay shrugs, tucking his hands into the pockets of his jeans. "Haven't found anyone."

Again, that just doesn't sound right. Jay is practically as handsome as they come. Strong jawline, full lips. *Delicious*-looking shoulders. Kind eyes. Not to mention he kisses like his life depends on it. And... he takes care of his friends. His Pack.

"Sounds like they're pretty dumb then."

"If you say so," Jay responds, staring straight through me with those eyes that never can decide on blue or green.

"I do. You ready?" I ask, grabbing my keys and phone to stash in the bag. I'm going to walk down to his car barefoot, so I also tuck the socks in too. Jay nods, so I lead him out of Sam's apartment, locking up behind us and into the elevator. Just before I step out of the building, Jay stops me with a hand on my shoulder.

"What?"

"You're going to walk outside barefoot?"

"*Yeah?* You think I'm scared of a little concrete?"

"No, but you're going to get your feet dirty."

I can't do anything other than blink at him, because I have never heard *anything* so ridiculous in my entire life.

Jay moves before I can formulate a response, picking me up and throwing me over his shoulder. His hand clamped around my thigh keeps my dress from exposing my ass to the world, but it also makes my heart race. And then, he's marching across the street, depositing me securely into the passenger side of his rental. As promised, my trusty boots are in the foot space.

When Jay goes to his side and slides into the driver's seat, I demand answers. "So, how did you know where I was anyway?"

Jay grins, depositing a phone that was lying in the cup holders in my hand. The pink case is an immediate giveaway. "*You went to Aggie?*" I practically shout the question at him.

"Sure did. So where are we going?"

As I rattle off the address for Ethan's office I stuff my feet into socks and my boots, lacing them tight. Why would Aggie have helped Jay? I'll have to talk to her when I get home. I can't keep avoiding even thinking what we're going to do though, so I turn my thoughts to Ethan.

I know Jay's presence will set Ethan off, likely making the encounter even more charged. But... I'm still glad he's here.

"Why did you go all quiet?" Jay asks me sometime later, about halfway to Ethan's office.

"Just anxious." I shrug, watching the city roll by. Leather creaks and I notice Jay's knuckles tighten on the steering wheel.

"I hate that you dealt with him for so long."

Again, my shoulders rise and fall. "I never claimed to make sense."

Jay snorts. "Yeah. You're a regular mystery."

"Eat your heart out." I snark, giving him a wide grin. It makes Jay chuckle, and a smile takes form on his face.

And then, the GPS pings that we have reached our destination, so I direct him to the parking garage across the street. Ethan's office has a valet, but I don't want to depend on someone retrieving Jay's car to leave. Inside the concrete monolith is much cooler, eternally shaded from the brutal Sun. I don my sweater as I exit the vehicle, about to turn and tell Jay I'll be back in a bit when I hear his door close, and the chirp of the door locks.

"What are you doing?" I ask, gripping the strap of my bag with white knuckles.

"Coming with you?" He replies, squinting at me like I'm dumb.

"Why? You don't have to do that."

"If you think I'm going to let you walk into some place that you're *clearly* anxious about *alone* when I'm here you're absolutely out of your mind," Jay says simply, crossing his arms in front of his chest, making the black t-shirt cling to his shoulders and bicep. My throat goes dry.

"Really though, It's okay. You don't have to be involved." I croak. My wolf cracks one amber eye open deep in the confines of my soul.

Jay just rolls his eyes and says "You're Pack. You don't do things alone anymore." The breeze rips through the pillars suddenly, blowing my hair across my face. Jay tucks a strand behind my ear, saying "If you want to do this, then let's go. If not, we can be on our way back home within the hour."

***Our* way *home*.**

Resisting the urge to cuddle deeper into his palm, I swallow and say "Okay. Let's do this." The urge to bolt, to run is easier to manage with Jay looking at me like that, pressing the warmth of his palm into my face.

"That's my girl," Jay says, smiling at me.

I chuckle, and say "Shut up." Jay laughs too, following me out of the parking garage.

The receptionist recognizes me as I enter the building through the large glass doors. "Welcome back, Miss Hunt. Mr. White is waiting for you. Oh! And your guest must sign in, please." Once she sees Jay, she pulls out a fancy clipboard for him to sign his name in.

"Thanks, Juliette. Where is he?"

"The conference room."

"Thank you." The office is a mixture of all the businesses, different floors pertaining to the different aspects of the White portfolio. Ethan's office is on the fourth floor, the upper two levels for Stephen and the shareholders. It's the button for the fourth floor that I mash as Jay and I enter the elevator. A barrage of memories where Ethan would press me into the corner and paw at my body, despite me telling him to stop assaults me on the quick ride up, and I have to suppress a shudder, feeling incredibly dumb once again for dealing with him for so long.

Jay lays a hand on the small of my back as he leans in close, asking "Do you know where we're going?"

"Yeah. I've been here a time or two." Jay nods, removing his hand from my back. Tension winds through my body, my spine ramrod straight, shoulders back. It takes a monumental effort to keep my breathing calm and even as we walk through the building. I've always hated the carpet. It is a somewhat grey color that contrasts with the dark baseboard wood trim. To me, it looked like prison grey.

I suppose, though, that was more due to my own feelings of being trapped. Trapped in a life I didn't want, with someone who didn't love *me* so much as just the *idea* of me. Finally, after a few minutes of stalking through the offices, the double doors to the conference room appear before Jay and I. My steps falter just as I lay a hand on the bronze door handle, my heart racing.

This is it. After this, I'm done. No more calls, no more texts.

You can do this, Artemis Hunt. The mantra repeats, and the door handle clicks as I open the door. Ethan's lawyer—more specifically, *Stephen's* lawyer— Mr. Dunkirk sits at the table with a stack of paperwork before him. Ethan stands at the window, his back to the door. When the door swings shut behind Jay and me, he turns. His smirk immediately turns into a scowl, seeing that I am not alone. Without saying a word, he moves toward the other chair on that side of the table.

"Hello, Artemis. Ah, Mr. Temple, is it?" Mr. Dunkirk greets, "Thank you for joining us today. Please have a seat."

"Mr. Dunkirk," I nod my head and give him a small smile as Jay pulls the chair out for me, seating himself to my left. The lawyer hasn't ever been a dickhead to me, was quite nice whenever I saw him. Jay has positioned us so that I'm in front of the lawyer, and he in front of Ethan.

"Are we all ready to get started?" The lawyer asks, looking towards Ethan for confirmation, who nods. I do the same when he looks my way.

"Mr. Temple, can you tell me why you're joining us? I don't believe you have a stake in these proceedings." Ethan asks Jay, a snide smirk on his face. He's taken to wearing his hair slicked back, the gel shiny in the fluorescent lighting.

"I'm here to ensure my friend doesn't get bullied into an unfair arrangement," Jay says simply, glaring daggers at Ethan.

Mr. Dunkirk clears his throat, tapping the manilla folder before him twice. "Okay. So, Miss Hunt, earlier this year, you signed *this* agreement-" out of the folder comes a prenuptial contract, bound in a pale blue. "-which also details what would happen if the engagement were to be canceled. In this, it states that if either party wishes to end the engagement, certain monies would need to be discussed. Now. First of all, were either of you unfaithful to your engagement?" The lawyer flips through the pages of the agreement, looking for the relevant pages.

I raise a pointed eyebrow at Ethan and wait for him to admit it. He doesn't, of course, so I have to do it for him. "The night I left I saw him and Cassandra having sex. They were clearly *familiar* with the act. *That* is why I left."

"Is this true, Ethan?" Mr. Dunkirk turns to look at his client. Ethan, being the bitch boy he is, doesn't say anything. Merely nods. "In that case, the contractual agreement in these pages states that Miss Hunt is owed a sum of—" The lawyer rifles through the papers again for a moment before saying "-fifteen thousand dollars. Is there anything you'd like to add?"

"She gets the car," Ethan says, glaring daggers at Jay. The amount of testosterone in this room could kill a bull, I swear.

"Ah, yes! How could I Forget." Mr. Dunkirk rifles through his folder again, procuring the papers for the Stingray. "One Black, manual transmission Corvette Stingray, free and clear of liens and loans. If you could sign here, and here, Ethan. " Ethan takes the pen from his outstretched hand, signing in the indicated places. Then, the lawyer passes the pen and papers to me, designating where to put my signature. Another paper comes out, indicating that this transaction would register as *non-taxable gifts.*

The lawyer goes through a few stipulations about what I can or cannot take from the manor, but honestly, the only thing I want is the books I left behind. When I say as much, Mr. Dunkirk passes a sheet of paper indicating their shipment.

"Your possessions are currently in transit. Mr. White arranged for them to be delivered after this meeting. Is there someone at the address listed that will be able to sign for them, if you are still in California at their arrival?"

"Yeah. There will be someone there." Looking over the shipment confirmation, I see the delivery date is next week. We'll be home by then, so I'm not even a little worried. I don't miss the way Ethan's lip curls though, his disgust clearly written all over his face. He doesn't say anything, actually. None of us say anything else other than Mr. Dunkirk as he goes through all the legal mumbo jumbo for transferring the funds to me. I loathe giving Ethan any of my information. Managing to give the lawyer my bank details by reminding myself that Ethan won't have direct access. It makes my skin crawl to even think about the fact that Ethan even knows where I live now.

At the end, Mr. Dunkirk says, "Now, Miss Hunt, our business is concluded. I feel it is my professional duty to inform you before you go that not all agreements are such as the one you had with Mr. White. Stephen and Cordelia added the infidelity clause to their heir's prenups— that is to say that it is not standard practice to award monies if the infidelity occurs *before* your vows are said." Mr. Dunkirk then gives me a searching look, one that I don't understand.

Ethan doesn't leave it up for debate. "He's telling you not to go around getting engaged to your betters just to earn a quick buck." His eyes rake down my form, making me feel dirty. *Unclean.*

"Ethan, please. That is not what I'm saying-" Mr. Dunkirk says, clearly flustered by Ethan's outburst.

"It's fine. That *is* what you were saying. Are we done here?" I ask, gathering my copies of the documents I'd been handed.

Mr. Dunkirk clears his throat, then says "Yes, all of our business has been handled. Mr. White?" Ethan nods.

"Great. Thanks. See you never." I say, getting up and leaving the chilled conference room. Jay follows me out the door, but we only make it a handful of feet before Ethan's voice rings out again.

"Glad to see you're not hiding how much of a whore you are these days, Artemis."

Before I've even turned all the way around to tell Jay to ignore him, to just keep walking, he's marching straight towards Ethan. "Oh, Fuck." I sigh, knowing that we're not leaving now.

Jay grabs Ethan by his pressed collar, slamming him against the wall. "If you *ever* say anything about her again, you're dead. If you *ever* contact her again, you're dead."

"Sounds about right that she lets her new boy toy fight her battles for her. How long has she been warming your bed, huh? She likes to play hard to get, but she likes it rough, don't you, *Whore*?" Ethan glances away from Jay just long enough to look right at me when he says the insult. The insult doesn't land, though. He's called me that too many times for it to sting.

Jay slams him against the wall again, "Don't look at her. Look at me. The next time I see you, you're *fucking* dead. Think about her again, you're dead. Artemis Hunt is officially *out of your reach*. Hear me?"

Ethan gulps, he must have caught sight of Jay's wolf in his eye, the predatory glint in his too-white smile. I let the shiver of pleasure, seeing Jay defend *me* like that, sit in my chest for one single moment, before I push it away.

"She's got you wrapped tight around her finger, doesn't she?" Ethan says, puffing out his chest, Jay still holding his collar.

"You're a piece of shit." Jay growls, and before I can intervene, Ethan opens his dumb mouth again.

"I bet she laid down for you without you even asking, huh? Was she still full of my cum when you ate her out-" Ethan's words are cut off as Jay slams his fist into his jaw, standing over him as Ethan crumples to the floor.

"JAY!" I shout, tugging him towards the elevator. All of his muscles are clenched tight, his fist already red. I know he'll be fine, but with a hit like that, he could have broken bone. "Fuck, Jay."

"Sorry." He grumbles, shaking out his fist as the elevator doors close.

"Did you break him?" I ask, suddenly wondering if Ethan is going to make me pay hospital bills for a broken face.

Jay sighs, then says "No, I don't think so."

"Good. Alright. Well. Thanks for punching him. I've wanted to for a long time." Adrenaline makes me ramble at him.

Jay chuffs a laugh, then says "No problem, Gorgeous."

"Are you hungry? I know of a great sushi place." I ask, looking up at him as the elevator doors reopen.

"Yeah, I could eat." He says, a small smirk pulling his lips up, a hungry look in his eye.

"Well, then let's go, Big Guy," I say, grabbing his hand and tugging him away from the dregs of my old life.

After Jay and I get back to his rental, he drives us to the restaurant according to the GPS narration. "How come you're not just telling me how to get there?"

"Because I am not who you want to trust with navigation."

"Artemis. You drove your Corvette *all the way* home. I think you could manage."

"I drove all the way home with *GPS navigation,* Jay. I could wing it, or we can make it there in a reasonable amount of time. Can't do both." I retort, resting my elbow on the center console and propping my chin on my hand. Waiting for him to acknowledge defeat with a smug smile plastered across my face.

"I'm never going to win with you, am I?"

"Sure you will. You've got those blue eyes. You blue-eyed mother fuckers always win in some way or another."

"Yea?"

"Sure! It's bound to happen at some point." I chortle, fiddling with the music.

"I adore you." Jay laughs, turning into yet another parking garage next to the restaurant. And suddenly, I feel lighter than I have in *months*. Maybe even years.

When Jay parks the car, he turns the engine off, but I don't immediately move to get out, so neither does he.

"What's the matter?" Jay asks, voice much softer than I've heard it in a long time.

"Feels surreal. It's over. I'm done. For a while there I thought that was going to be my life forever. Just need a minute to process, I guess." If there was one person on the planet *uniquely equipped* to uncover my secrets, it would be Jay *mother fucking* Temple.

"Take all the time you need, Gorgeous. I'm not going anywhere." He replies, grabbing my hand and giving it a gentle squeeze. His knuckles are still red, but I know he probably doesn't even really feel it anymore. Ethan on the other hand...

My wolf's amusement is palpable. We'll be reliving that moment for a long time, I think.

"Thanks... for it all." I eventually say, pressing a kiss to his middle knuckle, the one that is the most discolored.

"You don't need to thank me."

"Sure I do. You've made everything... so much *easier* for me since I came home. So, I'm paying for dinner."

Jay opens his mouth to refute it, but I silence him with a wide smile. "I just got fifteen thousand dollars. Not to mention another little *something-something* I took before leaving. I'm handling dinner, and that's final."

Jay's expression turns from stern to perplexed, and he asks "What did you take?"

"I *may* have opened his safe while he was between someone else's legs," I reply, biting my lip, trying to contain my smile.

"He told you the combination?" Jay asks incredulously.

"Don't need a combination if it's left unlocked." I tease, the battle of containing my smile, lost.

Jay laughs, practically howls with it, clutching his rib. Once he gets his laughter under control, he opens his door, chortling "Wow. He is a *fucking* idiot."

"Sure is," I reply, and Jay gets out of the car, doing a little jog around the back to open my door.

"Which way to the restaurant?" He asks, tucking his hands into his pockets.

26
No take backs

eleven days to full moon

Since getting back home, I have barely had the time to do anything other than eat, sleep, and go to work. My books were all delivered yesterday while I was at Coyote Bills, various boxes stacked in the halls and living room just waiting for my attention to put them on my shelves. Today is my first day off since getting back to town, and of course, I've been playing phone tag with just about everyone I know.

First, Sam calls to tell me she's ending her lease agreement, and moving. Miss *hot-stuff-neighbor* is actually kind of crazy. Like, the bad kind of crazy. Sam hasn't decided where she's going to move yet, just wanted someone to listen to her complain, which I was glad to do after all the ways she's helped me over the years.

Since it was in the middle of the night for her, she lost steam within fifteen minutes, claiming to need to crawl into her bed.

Before I even manage to sit up, Ivy calls. Of course, I answer it, greeting her with a simple "Morning."

"Morning? It's like Noon." She chortles.

"Shh, I'm barely awake."

"That's fair. Can I ask you to pick up a few extra shifts this week? We're down a coyote now."

"What happened?" A yawn interrupts the rest of my sentence. "And yeah, sure. Not today though. I need more sleep."

"I had to let go of Jill. George caught her taking money from the till last night after you left."

Immediately, I feel *so* much more awake. "Holy shit."

"Yep. So I'll be looking for a new bartender. If you know anyone, send them my way." She says, and I hear the clanging sound of her keys as she unlocks the doors to the bar.

"For sure. How many do you need me to pick up?" Can't say I'm that upset, more shifts equals more money. Which is always helpful, insurance on a sports car is exceedingly expensive— as it turns out. Luckily I can pay for a year's policy and get a discount. Otherwise... I don't think I would be able to keep the beast.

"Literally as many as you can. I know you just started, but I trust you." Ivy says, a thread of vulnerability in her usually confident voice.

"Of course. I'm here if you need to talk, about *anything,* you know that, right?"

"Did you know the night you left I was visited by a certain *Dante Kincayd*?" Ivy takes my offer to gossip, immediately.

"Wait, you were? Why?"

"He kept asking where you'd gone on that plane. I didn't tell him, but he was *quite* determined."

"What did you do to him?" I chortle, knowing if the roles had been reversed I would have tortured the poor bastard for asking or even thinking I'd spill my girl's secrets.

"Oh, nothing much. I don't think I'd mind it if he followed me home again though." She says, and I can *hear* the smile on her face.

"Oh, it's like that huh?"

"I know you have eyeballs, that man is fucking *eye candy.*"

"Yes, yes he is. Did you give him your number?"

"You're a menace."

"Sure am. Did you though?"

Ivy can't hide her giggle. "Yes. He's even sent me a contact photo. Of him. On his bike. With his helmet on…"

"So you're into masked men, huh?" I chortle at her, absolutely unable to resist teasing.

"A MENACE I TELL YOU. You're a *menace*." Ivy says, laughing. "Alright, I have to go and get the bar open. I'm covering Jill this morning and then Angel is coming in. But I can count on you for tomorrow right?"

"Of course."

"Thank you so much, you're a lifesaver," Ivy says, then hangs up after we say goodbye.

Finally, I manage to crawl out from under the covers and into the shower. I don't have the patience for an *everything* shower, but I do at least wash my hair and deep condition it, scrubbing last night's sweat from my skin.

When I leave the bathroom, I dress in loose sweatpants, and a cami with a built-in bra, flannel tossed on overtop. The house is uncommonly quiet, and if it weren't for the sound of running water coming from one of the other rooms I would have said I am alone.

And of course, as soon as I step foot into the kitchen, my Mom calls me.

Immediately, my lighter mood from talking to Ivy is ruined.

I barely utter a "hello" before my mom starts in.

The first item on the docket, I suppose, is just to bitch at me."Hello to you too. How come I haven't seen you more since you came home?"

All I can do is blink at the abrupt audacity of my Mom. "Sorry, I've been busy I guess with work."

"Not too busy to spontaneously fly back to California, from what I hear." She says, and then for the next forty-five minutes she carries on, and on about it, and how she only heard from Aggie that I'd left *after* I was already home.

According to her, I'm a very ungrateful daughter who likes to worry her, just for the fun of it. Of course, she doesn't say so in so many words. The message is still received loud and clear though.

"It wasn't really *spontaneous*, I had some things to deal with. Again, I am sorry for worrying you."

She jabbers in my ear louder than required again. "I just don't understand why you don't talk to me about things anymore." My mom signs heavily into the phone, making me wince. "Okay. Well, I better get going. Your sister and Daisy will be here soon for dinner. Can I expect to see you, or are you too busy?"

Cradling my forehead in my palm, I say "I don't know Mom, it's been a long few days."

"Figures. Well, you're welcome to come. Love you, Bye."

"Bye, Mom," I say hollowly into the phone. "Love you too." I parrot the words back to her, the echoes of her tinny voice coming from the speaker. When I end the call I let the phone drop to the counter below me with a clatter. I just barely resist the urge to smash my forehead against the counter as well.

"Why did you come home?" Jay asks from the doorway, and I have no idea how long he's been standing there... watching me as I rub my temples in slow, soothing circles.

Any conversation with my mom leaves like this, irritated, and inexplicably sad. Jay's question throws me off guard, and ridiculously, raises my hackles. I'm so tired, but even that doesn't distract me from how delicious Jay looks, and how much that gets under my skin. His eyes are more blue than green today, and the grey shirt that he has stretched across his shoulders accentuates the blue of his iris.

"For shits and giggles," I reply, closing my eyes. I can't cope with his all-seeing stare, not today. He's always peering down into the depths of my soul and seeing *far more* than I intend to let him.

"Answer the question." Jay demands, a quick glance through my lashes tells me he is now standing still as stone against the counter.

"Why do you care?" I snap, not meaning to, but I'm just exhausted.

"Artemis."

"*What?*" I growl, snapping my eyes open, not even needing my wolf to create such a sound.

"*Answer the question.*" He commands, the flash of his wolf making mine rise.

Fuck that. I shove away from the island and start to walk away.

Always running away. My wolf says, inky black tail twitching.

Be **quiet.**

"Baby Girl," Jay says, halting me in my tracks with a shiver running down my spine. He is still leaning against the counter, though his arms are now crossed. I can't decipher the look in his eye, the small smile curving his mouth. "Answer. *The*. Question."

What little control I have over myself, over my galloping heart and delusional hopes *snap* in an instant.

"*What do you want from me*, Jay?" I holler, feeling like a volcano, finally exploding. "Do you want me to tell you all my *sad little secrets?*" I spread my arms wide. "Do you want me to tell you all the little ways I've had my heart broken? That I was sad and just wanted the comfort of the trees I knew?" Tears leak out of my eyes, unbidden.

The heat in his eyes ignites the more I lose control of my emotions, the flash in his eyes telling me his wolf is raging.

"Do you want to hear about all the ways I've let other people chip away at me? How I didn't even *fucking care* until I woke up with you in my bed? That I didn't even notice how lonely I was until I came home?" I take a deep, ragged breath. Jay still doesn't move.

"Or did you want me to tell you that when I left I was *angry* and lost but most of all I was *heartbroken?* So I packed up and I *ran* and *ran* and kept running until I couldn't tell which way was up, " My chest feels like it is cracking wide open, and there stands Jay, against that fucking counter *not moving*.

"Ask me why I left." I fling the words at him like arrows.

"Why did you leave Baby Girl?" Jay's voice drops lower, not like he was afraid to ask, but... there is *something*.

"Because I fucking *heard you*. Heard you talking to Brandon and Mike about how I *make this sound right before I cum* and how *dick whipped* I was," I threw up quotation marks around my words, mocking Jay's lower voice. I see the flinch, how he tries to mask it. But I still see it. "I turned around and left that night. Walked back to my house, packed my shit, and then I was *gone*."

The sound of my ragged breathing fills the kitchen, marking the passage of time.

"How long did it take you to notice I was *gone*, Jay? Did you even notice at all?" The silence stretches, and the itch to leave, to shift and run is tangible.

"Right. Got it." I say when he just looks at me, swallowing my grief, just like I always do. A heartbeat, then another echoes in my ear. I'm sure that my heart is going to burst, that it will explode right here and I'll be left hollow- forever. I make it exactly one-quarter turn away from him before Jay finally speaks.

"Ask me why I said those things." He says, arms now uncrossed but the white-knuckled grip on the counter betrays his calm facade.

I can't say what possesses me to ask, but I do, unable to raise my voice above a whisper. Braced against the inevitable- that he'd meant those things, I ask. He's going to say that he wasn't sorry. That whatever *this* is that we've been doing for the last few weeks was going to end. That it'd all been a lie.

"Because I was young. And stupid. And I thought it made me sound cool. I shouldn't have said it. I'm sorry, Artemis." Jay says, unflinching. A shuddering, heaving breath fills my lungs.

"And for the record, I noticed right away. I went looking for you when I saw the stands letting out and found Sarah who'd said *you'd* gone looking for *me*. Didn't even cross my mind that you might have heard the conversation. And then I figured I'd see you at the party, and you never showed. Then when days passed without a word from you I figured your mom had taken your phone again and then *I* had to go."

I remember all of Jay's texts. One or two at first, and then when he had to go to his grandparents he sent one last message- that he was leaving. And he'd miss me.

I never did respond to any of them. Had I managed to keep that phone these last seven years I think those messages would still be in my inbox. I hadn't ever been able to bring myself to delete them. And when I'd lost that phone on the banks of the Colorado River after a full Moon run and romp that I'd promptly regretted, I'd been devastated. Not for the loss of the phone, but because that had meant I'd lost my last tenuous connection to Jay.

"Eventually I took the hint that you didn't want to talk to me," Jay shrugs his shoulders, the motion loosening some of the tension in his grip. "But that never lasted long before so I decided to wait. But *you* never came back. Until now." The ticking of the clock is the only sound in the house for a moment.

"Are you still waiting?"

"Waiting? No." Jay says, and my heart shatters like glass. I could swear the cracking sound was audible. "But I'll give you the world if you let me." My breath catches in my throat.

I don't respond right away, needing a minute to process that *this is actually happening* and not all in my head. "What if I don't want the world?"

"I'll let you go if you can tell me that is what you *actually* want. Tell me you want me to stop and I'll stop. But you can't lie to me, Artemis. I've lost you once, I can manage it again, if that's what you want. So don't spare my feelings. Tell me what *you* want."

"What if all I want right now is this? Whatever this is?" I blurt, gesturing between the two of us.

"I can work with that."

Neither of us moves for a moment. The muscle in his jaw feathers, then he pushes away from the counter, taking slow, measured steps around the island that I'd been leaning against during my phone call. I swear my feet have grown roots, anchoring me to the spot while Jay stalks towards me.

I'm not running this time. Not anymore. Not from Jay.

Jay raises a hand, warm palm wrapping around my neck, and he continues walking, guiding me back against the doorframe. Pushing his hips into mine. His thumb caresses the line of my pulse, so I know he can feel just how rapidly my heart is pounding.

"No takebacks." He says quietly, blue eyes searing into me.

"No takebacks," I whisper a promise I'd made a long time ago, renewed.

Jay kisses me, deepening the contact immediately. I'm lost, lost in the feeling of him, of not having to hide how much he affects me anymore.

"I've missed you so fucking much," Jay says, lifting me into his arms. I wind my legs around his waist without hesitation.

"I missed you too."

"I'm fucking, *glad*, Gorgeous." He says, sealing his mouth over my neck.

"Yea?" I moan, tilting my head to give him better access.

"Fuck yes. I don't know what I would have done if you didn't want this. Us." Jay says, pulling back to look at my face as he says the words.

My heart feels like it's going to explode, so I say the only thing I can think of. "It's always been you, Jay."

"Always?" He asks, throat bobbing.

"I gave you my heart a long time ago, and you never gave it back," I admit quietly. To myself, and him.

"Never going to," Jay says, moving us. He walks us up the stairs, and into his dark room without breaking stride.

"Sounds a little selfish." I laugh when he tosses me to the bed, breathless as he stands over me.

"When it comes to you, Darlin, I'm the most selfish man in the world."

"Yea?"

"Absolutely."

"But you don't *do jealousy?*" I tease, referencing what he said the first time we had sex in this house, propped on top of his bed on my elbows.

"Nope."

"What does that even mean, anyway?" I ask, watching Jay crawl over his mattress in the darkened room to me.

"I don't do jealousy means I don't care if you think someone else is hot because I'm the one in between these thighs and I'm the one under your skin and we both know what *that* means, Gorgeous," Jay says, holding himself above me, watching my face.

"You make good points," I murmur, laying back on the pillow, pulling his shirt up to access the planes of his stomach.

"Do I?"

"Mhm. Now come here and show me how much you missed me, Big Guy." I say, grinning up at him. With a quick tug of my fingers, his shirt comes off, dropping to the floor somewhere behind him.

"Thought you'd never ask," Jay smirks back, lowering his mouth to mine, his body now flush with every inch of me. A slow rock of his hips into mine when he deepens the kiss coaxes a gasp from my mouth. Jay waits only a few more minutes before he's pulling my tank over my head, spanning my ribs in his palms.

Then he's trailing hot kisses down my neck, my collarbone to my chest, swirling his tongue around a peaked nipple. I moan, scraping my nails across his shoulders. Jay groans back, resuming his path down my body. He barely pauses before he's tugging my sweats off, baring me to him. Then he's lowering his mouth to my center, locking his blue eyes onto mine.

Immediately, I moan, widening my legs, tilting my hips. Jay lets his hands roam all over my body as he sucks and laps at my clit, pulling more and more desperate moans from my mouth. When he dips two fingers into my pussy, I gasp, rocking my hips in time with his motions.

"Fuck, that feels good-" I whimper, grabbing onto Jay's hair. Jay groans in response, sounding more animal than man, making my nipples tighten painfully. It seems like it's barely taking him any effort at all to coax pleasure from my veins, making my skin feel alight with ecstasy.

"That's my girl, you want to cum, don't you?" Jay murmurs, slowing his movements, adding a third finger.

"Yes!" I gasp, my back arching—my orgasm barely contained.

Jay's chuckle against my clit makes me whimper. "Go on then. Cum on my face like a good girl." A crook of his finger, and then *rapture.* Orgasm blows through me like a hurricane, making my legs shake and my breath stall in my lungs.

"That's my girl," Jay groans with approval against my skin, withdrawing his fingers, and moving up my body. Then he's lining up his cock, slowly pushing into me. Jay catches my gasps with his mouth, kissing me as I stretch around him.

"Fuck-" I moan again, clawing at his shoulders.

"Relax baby, it'll fit, we know you can take it." He murmurs against my neck, and I'm so full, so sensitive that just a small shift of his hips, sending that big cock deeper into me makes pleasure spark up my spine, earning him another whimper.

"Fuck, I love that sound-" Jay groans, trailing hot kisses down my collarbone.

"Jay- *please-*" I moan, pulling him in deeper.

"Please, *what*, Gorgeous?" Jay quips, winding a hand around my throat.

"I want it all," I demand, kissing down his neck.

Jay smiles, then hooks one of my legs over his shoulder, resting his forehead against mine. "Anything you want." The new angle gives Jay all the room he needs, rocking in and out of me over and over again as he kisses me madly like I'm the only thing he needs in the world to survive.

Again and again, Jay moves inside me, thrusting deep and slow. And again, and again he sparks pleasure everywhere he touches, everywhere he kisses.

It's *perfect*. When he reaches down to rub my clit in slow circles, I see stars, moaning into his mouth "Yes, yes yes-" Jay moves his hand around my throat, rolling his hips plunging in and out nearly all the way.

Jay's breathing turns ragged, wild and I can't do much else other than wiggle my hips, but I'm desperate for him— for this, *us*. It only takes a few more strokes of Jay's *delicious* cock for my orgasm to fizzle over my skin. Then Jay's movements turn jerky, his thrusts harder and harder, until he plunges deep into me to the hilt, groaning.

With our ragged breathing filling Jay's room, he slowly withdraws from me, collapsing on the bed beside me. After a moment he says, "Artemis," softly. I turn my head to look at him, scrunching my eyebrows together.

"I love you," Jay says simply, making me feel like my heart is going to burst right out of my chest, my eyes burning like tears are going to leak.

So I say "I know. You didn't have to say so," I swear my teeth are going to pierce my lip with how hard I'm biting it to contain my smile.

Jay scoffs, then rolls halfway onto his back before I'm moving, pushing him the rest of the way over, straddling his waist. *"Jay,"* I simper, giving him my best angelic smile.

"Artemis?" He replies, eyes guarded.

"I love you." And then he's smiling, cheeks flushed, chest gleaming with sweat.

"Yeah?"

"Yeah," I respond immediately. His smile turns devious, and his cock twitches under me. Jay shifts, hands traveling up my thighs to rest where they join my hips. When I shift in return, sliding along the length of him I am rewarded with a gasp from his lips.

"You know what I want?" Jay says, a desperate thread in his husky voice.

"What's that?"

"You just like this." He replies, moving me, stroking himself with my still-soaking center.

"Say please" I gasp, pleasure sparking up my spine.

"Please" Jay immediately groans, "*Please*, Artemis," Jay begs, "please ride me, baby." With him beneath me, a new fire alights in my blood. All it takes is a quick shift of my hips. Rising, then sinking down on the full length of his cock in one fell swoop.

"Fuck- I gasp, Jay moans, his fingers indenting my hips with bruising force.

And then we're moving again, no longer desperate, but every touch of his on my body sends pleasure ratcheting higher and higher.

Jay and I stay locked up in his room until the Sun sets.

27
Perfect

six days to full moon

This morning, Jay wakes me with a cup of coffee, light streaming through the windows. When my eyes blink open at him, I don't know how to formulate words or even complete thoughts. He's wearing only sweatpants, slung low around his hips, the red hat on his head flipped backward.

The past few days have been relatively the same as before, but now we're *really* in a relationship. So he wakes me up *in his bed* with a coffee and forehead kisses. Previous mornings have resulted in me tugging him back into bed without much effort. I have half a mind to do that right now, with the way his pants are riding low on his hips. Begrudgingly, though I get up. Jay can make a mean cup of joe.

"Good morning, Gorgeous." He says, waiting for me to pull myself fully upright before handing the mug to me. After I came home from the bar last night Jay had carried me upstairs and fucked me silly. I'm sure I am a sweaty, raccoon-eyed mess. The thick stickiness around my eyes is all that remains of last night's mascara. The heel of my palm comes back blackened when I rub the sleep from my bleary eyes.

I have not seen the hide nor hair of Alex and Helena, they'd apparently left while we were in California. Instead of retreating to my room, Jay has taken us to his room every night. He has cool red sheets on his bed, and a thick grey comforter dangling off the edge haphazardly. He's got a set of bookshelves too, though considerably fewer books than in my collection. One singular spine sticks out like a sore thumb on the shelves. I'm very familiar with the title, and all the creases. It was one of my favorites that I gave him in tenth grade. It sits proudly on the shelf nearest to his bed.

There's a Polaroid of me sitting on that shelf too. I have yet to ask him how he got that particular photo.

I have to clear my throat before I manage to speak. "Good morning."

"How are you?" Jay asks, still standing next to the bed, a self-satisfied smile on his face as he lets me ogle him. There's sweat lingering on the planes of his chest, telling me he must have been up for a while, getting a morning workout in. I've learned that, *apparently,* that is a routine of all of the boys.

Morning workouts all around! *Not.*

"Barely awake," I reply, blowing steam off my coffee and taking a delicate sip.

"You need to get ready for work." He says eyes that are more green than blue today roaming over my form half covered by the sheet.

"So it would seem," I reply, glancing at the clock.

"Go get in the shower, I'll be right back." Jay orders, leaning down to press a quick kiss to my lips, leaving without another word.

What the fuck is up with him today? I do what he says though, because I do need to shower. I simply do not have the energy for an *everything* shower, so I skip washing my hair. I'll put it up for tonight. Afterward, I march down to my room and slip on a pair of black underwear, a matching bralette, and fishnet stockings.

My clothes have ended up strewn between my room and Jay's, and after going through what seems like my entire wardrobe for something to wear to work, I come up empty-handed. I end up going back into Jay's room and stealing one of his large black t-shirts. Once it's over my head, it's *almost* long enough to act like a dress. This means, unless I want to show the entire bar my ass, I need the black spandex shorts that should be *somewhere* around here...

Jay reappears before I've found my shorts. He doesn't say anything, just leans against the doorframe. That self-satisfied smile is still on his face, making it impossible to resist tormenting him. Teasing Jay is one of my favorite pastimes.

"Stop staring at me," I order, smirking over my shoulder at him. "Aha!" I woop, finally uncovering my shorts.

As I step into the shorts, pulling them up over my hips and ass Jay groans "But you're so *hot*." My pulse skips a beat at the desperate tone of his voice.

"So is the Sun. You wouldn't stare directly into it." I snark back, grabbing a pair of tall socks from my pile. Winter has yet to rear her ugly head, and I'm taking full advantage for as long as possible.

"If you were the Sun I would," Jay says darkly, jaw muscles flexing.

"Shut up, you would not." I huff a laugh, rolling my eyes.

"Would too."

"No, you wouldn't. Because then you'd go blind and then you'd never be able to look again." I sass, feeling smug. I've already done my makeup, so I'm basically ready for work, other than throwing shoes on my feet before I leave.

"So your beauty would be the last thing I see?" Jay replies, a lazy smile stretching his face. He looks so absolutely *mouthwatering* leaning against the doorway like that. He's replaced his sweats for a pair of jeans slung equally low on his hips, that backward baseball cap still on his head, no shirt in sight.

"For fucks sake!" I groan, throwing my hands up. "Always have something to say, don't you?" I don't even bother trying to hide my smile.

"Even going blind I win that one, Baby Girl." Jay rumbles, giving me a look that makes me feel hungry.

"Your logic is questionable, but I'll give it to you," I answer, crossing the small space between us, palms smoothing over his bare shoulders. His thick arms fold around me easily, like he doesn't even have to think about the motion. Like holding on to me is second nature.

"Are you closing tonight?" Jay asks, staring down at me.

"Mhm," I hum, more than slightly distracted by the look in his eye, and the way his arms feel around my ribs.

"Is Ivy working with you?" Jay asks, eyes tracking my lips. One of his hands roams down my back, over the curve of my hip. His fingers slip through the openings of my stockings, following the line of my ass.

"Yeah, she still hasn't replaced Jill." My voice comes out breathier than it was a half second ago before his hands were touching my bare skin.

"How much time do you have?" He asks, glancing towards the alarm clock next to the bed, down my face, and then back to my lips all in a half second.

I grin. "*Enough*, Big Guy."

Jay *moves*. He spins me, walking me forward until I am pressed against the door frame. Shorts I'd just pulled over my hips hit the floor next. Jay kisses and bites down the side of my neck, suckling that spot beneath my ear that makes shivers erupt down my spine. I arch my back, pressing my ass into his groin. His fingers indent my hips, coaxing little moans from my mouth.

I gasp when he rips my stockings, making an opening.

The door opens downstairs, the top of Saint's head visible as he moves from the living room to the kitchen, and back through the rungs on the railing. When Jay pulls my underwear to the side, fingers deftly swirling over my clit, he hums in delight. I'm *loving* every second of his.

I moan, louder this time, grinding back against him. The buckle of Jay's belt rattles, fabric rustles as he frees his cock from his pants. He drags his fingers back through my folds, a sound of appreciation coming from him when he discovers just how wet I am.

"Fuck, you're so good, Artemis. So good." He murmurs before he's lining up his cock to my entrance, roughly sliding home.

"Please-" I gasp, desperate for him to start moving. Jay gives me what I want, sliding his cock in and out agonizingly slow at first. When my breath turns ragged, he picks up speed, ripping his shirt over my shoulders, but my arms get caught.

Jay chuckles, and instead of freeing my arms, he wraps the t-shirt tighter around my wrists.

With my chest pressed against the doorframe, my arms pulled behind my head I can't do anything other than take it.

And fuck, does it feel good.

"Fuck, you look so perfect like this. So good." Jay's voice is hushed, sending shivers up my spine the closer I speed towards release.

"You feel *so* good, so *big-*" I moan, eyes fluttering shut.

When Jay's free hand wraps around my throat, I know he's going to make me see stars by the punishing pace he's setting, pounding into me.

"Fuck, yeah, Just like that Baby Girl. Just like that." He moans, and then my phone rings. The annoying ringtone tells me it is Ethan. And if that's not a surefire way to ruin an orgasm, I don't know what is. "Do you need to get that?" Jay pants without slowing his pace.

"It's Ethan, so no. But I don't want to listen to the phone ringing either."

A dark laugh rumbles out of Jay, and to my surprise, he leans back to where my phone is lying on the bed. He presses the green button to accept the call and places it in the space between my shoulder and ear without a word.

"What do you want?" I growl into the phone, still pinned and impaled on Jay's cock, who *hasn't* stopped moving even with my phone against my ear.

"I want you to come home," Ethan orders, and Jay smacks my ass.

"What?" I gasp, half from shock and half because of what Jay is *still* doing behind me. Fucking me relentlessly.

"I want you to come home," Ethan repeats. "I miss you."

"You've got to be *joking?*" I screech, the end becoming a moan when Jay circles my clit with a deft finger.

"What are you doing?" Ethan's voice turns sharp, suspicious. And that is when Jay decides to take the phone from me, mashing the button for the speakerphone.

"Do you hear that?" Jay says, smacking my ass again, making me cry out, thrusting his cock deep in me over and over. "That's the sound of Artemis Hunt cumming all over my cock." Jay reaches around and circles my clit again, and it's so hot– so demanding that I do exactly that. Orgasm blows through me, Jay's name falling from my lips.

"Don't ever call her again. Don't ever think about her again. She's not yours." Jay says into the phone, throwing it to the floor beside him.

"Such a good girl, Artemis. Can I have another?" Jay asks, slowly untangling my arms from the shirt.

I don't leave for work for another twenty minutes, the remnants of Jay and I's diversion slipping down my thighs as I walk to the Stingray.

28
Open at the Close

three days to full moon

Today, the Packhouse is alive with people. More so than normally, as this is my official welcome back into the fold. The Pack. I can finally say I'm home again.

When I left this place, I thought I would never return. Magnus is currently chatting with my mom, what about I can not even begin to fathom. He towers over her, though that's not hard for anyone over five-six. The party has been going on for quite a while already, but I haven't indulged myself like I would have otherwise. I still have to go to work, which is unfortunate but the full Moon run is a few days off yet. So there will be another Pack party, and in my opinion, even better— a Pack *run*. Even so, I will admit that they decorated the place very nicely.

Strings of light are hung between branches and illuminate the lawn in a soft, warm glow. A few fires are going on the outer edges of the large plot, groups forming around them. People have some drinking games going, and the area around the speakers holds dancing teens and couples.

Jay, who disappeared for a short while after retrieving our drinks, is now striding towards me. He has this small smile on his face, a grey long-sleeve shirt pushed up to his elbows stretched across his frame.

He's up to something. My wolf mumbles from the confines of my soul.

Definitely.

"Hey, Handsome." I greet him with a smile, running my tongue along my teeth, and pressing against the points. My mouth runs dry when he smiles at me, free and open.

"Hey yourself, Gorgeous," Jay replies, hooking an arm over my shoulders and pressing a kiss to my forehead.

"Where have you been?" I ask, taking a big gulp of my soda.

"Checking on some things. Are you ready to skedaddle? I need to show you something."

"Sure, we can *skedaddle*." I tease. "Are Dante and Saint coming?"

"You'll see them at Coyote Bills," Jay replies, steering me out of the lawn of the packhouse and towards where our cars are parked.

"Are you going to tell me where we're going?" I ask, fishing keys out of the pocket of my trusty black jeans.

"Are you riding with me?" He fires back, giving me a knowing smirk.

"*No,*" I grate, narrowing my eyes at him. I don't like being at work without a vehicle of my own. Don't like having to rely on him—or anyone else for that matter— to leave. I know I can always shift, but... I prefer having my own car available.

"Then nope." Jay quips, pressing another kiss to my forehead, another one of those wide, open, and free smiles on his face. It doesn't falter even as he opens the door to my Corvette, ushering me into the seat. "Follow me, Gorgeous?" he asks, blue-green eyes bright.

"Always," is my hushed reply.

Jay's smile burns brighter, searing into my retinas. His steps seem lighter as he closes my door, and gets into his vehicle. He leads me out of the parking lot at an unhurried pace, cruising through the streets of my home. It's only a few minutes later that he pulls into a long paved driveway. It leads up to an almost-finished house, and I can't help but take in its appearance. The middle roof is the tallest, with large windows covering the front-facing wall. There's a wrap-around porch, one that is just *asking* for a hammock strung between posts. And, on the far side, I see one wall has a tower. A large curved window is currently being installed on the second level.

My heart starts pounding, and my knees are more than a little weak as I exit my car. Jay is already out, leaning against his fender— staring at me.

"What do you think?"

"What do *I* think? What do you mean?"

"This is our house," Jay says simply, that open smile is no longer present, but his expression isn't guarded. It's *pleased*.

"Our?"

"Yeah. I told you that the boys and I were building a house right?"

"Yes..."

"Well, we talked about it. We want you to come live with us when it's done." Jay says, looking down at his feet. For a moment, I can't think, don't have a response.

But it doesn't take long for me to know that I would miss them, *all* of them if they were to move out. But Jay's not looking at me, which I know must mean he's asking me if I want to live with *him*. Decision made, I stride over to him and lean into his frame, his arms immediately wrapping around me.

"Do I get my own room, or is this a *sleep in your room until you're sick of me* situation?"

Jay gulps before responding. "You can have your own room if that is what you want."

"Is that what *you* want?" I ask, playing with the hair at the nape of his neck that's starting to curl.

"No, I want you next to me, under me every night. I want our bed to smell like you, I want to hold you all night. I'm never letting you go, Artemis."

"Never?"

"Nope. Never ever."

"Never is an awfully long time, there Big Guy."

"So let's start with forever." Jay quips and I know he's *so proud* of that response by the smile that stretches across his face.

"Yeah, I might be able to pencil you in for *forever*," I answer, failing miserably at containing my grin.

Jay groans, dragging my mouth to his while he mutters "You're a brat." His hands drift to my ass, pressing me into his groin.

"You like it," I answer, meeting him kiss for kiss, stroke for stroke. I'd climb on top of him and the thick bulge rising in his pants right here and now if I didn't have to go to work—construction crew be damned.

"Yeah, I do. Fucking love it." He says when we separate, my ass still gripped in his palm.

"Race you to the bar?" I ask, backing away from the only man who's ever understood me, more than I've ever understood myself. And, I suppose... the only one who's loved me throughout my entire life. "I'll give you a head start," I add, winking at him as I open my door.

Jay chuckles but gets into his car, and starts driving away. When we're both on the road once more, his phone number comes through the caller ID on my phone.

"If you're a simp say what." I greet as I answer the phone.

"What?" Jay asks, his confusion clear even through the speakers.

"Nothing," I chortle, then ask "What's up?"

"You know these roads are all monitored right? Magnus is going to see us racing *again.*"

"Good for Magnus." I quip, shifting gears and easily passing him on the smooth, straight road.

"I thought you said you were going to give me a head start?" He groans, and I hear his car rev behind me, the shine of his headlights overtaking my rearview.

"I guess I lied." I giggle, speeding away and mashing the button to end the call. His car disappears in my rearview as I take turn after turn, gliding over the road.

I sure do appreciate Magnus' attention to detail with the roads though. Hot damn, this is fun.

When I pull into the bar's parking lot, I see Saint's Jeep parked next to Ivy's, and grin. Dante's bike is missing, which must mean he came with Saint. Right then and there I decide I am going to make Ivy do the slap shot bar with me, if only for these three knuckleheads.

Before coming home, I truly had no idea exactly how far the depth of my loneliness ran. How much I had missed my pack.

Now I have a little Pack of my own. Within Timber Hollow, *these* people are my pack. Jay, Saint Dante, Sam, and Ivy. *They* are my family.

And Sam... I hope she is okay with whatever she has going on in Cali. She always lands on her feet though, so I try not to worry too much. She'll call me if she needs me.

Jay's blue Nissan pulls into the parking lot just as I reach the door to the building, so on impulse, I flash my ass at him before entering. His car stalls out as he pulls into the parking space, and I laugh all the way to the register to clock in.

Angel and Ivy are behind the bar slinging drinks, so while I tie an apron around my waist I ask where they want me. Ivy directs me to the sinks, where they need glassware. And so, my shift starts. Working here doesn't really even feel like work.

The girls and I all dance to the jukebox as we perform our duties. I join them slinging drinks at the bar, alternating between that and bussing tables now and again.

Finally, though, it's slapshot hour. I pull Ivy to the side of the bar where my station is set up, and the boys are waiting for me.

"Hello, Boys." I grin, propping my elbow on the bar, chin on my knuckles. "What can we get you this fine evening?"

Jay's eyes are on me as he says "Two Anjeo." He looks *hungry*. Hungry like a wolf. My blood heats, pulse jumping.

Saint says "I'll have what he's having." While jabbing Jay's rib with his elbow. I chuckle.

"And you, mister *silent and broody?*" Ivy asks in a husky voice. Inwardly, I hoot. This is going *exactly* like I wanted it to.

"Johnnie Walker. Three." Dante says simply, staring straight into Ivy's eyes.

"Pay up, bitches." I sing while pouring Jay's and Saint's tequila.

All at once, hundred dollar bills are pulled from wallets and slammed onto the bar. "You boys are such show-offs." I chortle, depositing their change *directly* into the tip jar.

"Alright boys, when I say?" Jay, Saint, and Dante all have a shot glass within fingertip reach, ready to down their shot after getting slapped. A glance at Ivy tells me she's ready as well, rubbing her palm.

"Three, two, one!" I count down, using one hand for Jay, and the other for Saint. The crack of my and Ivy's hands against the boy's cheeks reverberates in my ears, and they all groan, downing their shot.

"Again!" Saint cheers, slamming his shot glass down on the bar.

Another countdown, another chorus of slaps. Jay and Saint's cheeks are bright red, but their eyes glow, and they are grinning.

"Pleasure doing business with you, Big Guy." I wink at Jay, giving Saint a "Who's a good boy?" for good measure, ruffling his shaggy blond hair.

Dante still has one round though, so the other two wait while he gets his last one. Ivy doesn't hesitate, using her other palm to smack the opposite side of his face. The muscle in Dante's jaw feathers and then he's downing his last shot of whiskey, gray eyes flashing.

Someone randomly howls along with the music in the crowd, making the four of us laugh– and then we all throw our heads back, and howl.

Bonus

graduation

"Have you seen Jay around?" I ask Sarah, following her as the crowds seated in the bleachers start leaving the lacrosse match. We won, defeating the Warriors 22-9.

It isn't hard to see why though, our team looks *jacked* in comparison to the Warriors from where I sat with Sarah in the stands. It was the last match of the year.

Shifters, even teenage ones, look different than our human counterparts. We have longer limbs. Fuller, thicker hair. Larger eyes that seem to peer down deep into the depths of your soul.

A predatory gleam in a too-white smile.

Small things, but the signs are there *if* you know what to look for. And our school is full of them. *Entirely* full, to be exact. Timber Hollow houses the largest population of Direwolf shifters on the Eastern seaboard of the States. Not that the population of the states is aware of us. The wolves of Timber

Hollow are special, even amongst shifter-kind. Our wolf form is bigger than our brethren.

And we have another form. One crafted by the tether between wolf and man. Becoming something more akin to what the humans called a werewolf.

The Warriors are from Clarksville, another small town about 45 minutes away, and while they are a shifter school, the Timber Hollow wolves still stand at least half a foot taller than they do. The small town of Timber Hollow is neighbored by a few different packs, and our school districts are all in the same division.

Not everyone is a Direwolf within the ranks of the Timber Hollow Pack, but it affords you some privilege if you are. *Namely,* eligibility to receive part of the profit share from the logging business the founding members of the pack- *Direwolves-* created. It's like a right of passage, all the teenagers in Timber Hollow typically end up with TH Logging as their first job. Spend your days learning how to cut down trees—sustainably– and making carvings from stumps.

Or, spend a summer at the Forge creating artisanal jewelry.

"I think I saw him and Brandon go down under the old bleachers in the final quarter," Sarah replies distractedly, scanning the crowd for her boyfriend- Lucas. He is a middie, number 3—-the only reason we were in the stands in the first place. She'd find him, soon enough. Lucas doesn't stray far without her. Sarah's family are Jackals, and Lucas is a coyote.

"I'll see you at the party, yeah?" I say to her as the crowd begins pushing us in different directions, down opposite stairs. I toss my paper bowl containing the remnants of nachos in the trash bin as I pass it.

"Hell yeah! Graduation weekend, baby!" She hoots, darting down the stairs when she spots Lucas' blonde hair among the blue and gold jerseys.

Alone, I wander down the track towards the baseball bleachers. The Lacrosse field got new ones- and the old were recycled down there. We don't have a football team. The sport brings out shifter aggression too easily. A few decades back the school made the switch to Lacrosse, and we have had substantially fewer mid-game fights break out since. Baseball isn't as popular, but there are enough kids that wanted to play so the school added another field, making three sprawling across the grass before me.

I don't see anyone playing in the fields, so I use the small worn dirt path to go behind the dugout. There is an equipment shed back there too, and it forms a little hide-away corner.

Some kids go behind it and smoke. Some use it to just sit somewhere and skip class. Jay and I use it often enough to skip class. And do *other* things.

I slow my steps when I hear boys talking. I know who it is as soon as I hear them.

"Are you guys staying together through summer?" Mike Boutche. He had been friends with Jay for a while, though not as long as Brandon Laack.

"Nah, dude. I'm leaving in a few weeks. She knows that." Jay says, and someone scuffs their sneaker in the dirt. The smell of burning tobacco through the air. My heart begins to race in my chest. I *do* know Jay is leaving, but he was only supposed to be gone for a few weeks. Not...*forever?*

"Then why are you always at her house bro? We see your car there almost every night." *Brandon*. Teasing, but... not.

"She asks me to come over. So I do." Jay says. I can almost see him shrug his shoulders like it isn't any big deal, can imagine him running a hand through the grown-out ashy brown hair.

Brandon is right though. Jay is at my house nearly every night. Or I am at his house. But since I don't have a car, no one would know I was there unless we told them.... Which means that Jay never told *anyone* I was there.

The sinking feeling in my chest feels like someone is pouring acid into my veins. My wolf paces in my mind, her golden eyes flashing in anger, far within the depths of my subconscious.

Jay's friends let out a chorus of "*Whipped! Pussy whipped!*"

"More like *dick* whipped. She *begs* me to come over." Jay hollers over his friends' voices, his *bros*. And I can picture the smile I adore so much on his face as he begins to tell them what we do when he comes over. My stomach rolls, and I almost lose my nachos right there in the dirt.

They all high-five. Brandon and Mike congratulate him. I've dated both of them, in the midst of one of Jay and I's many breakups. Never went further than intense kissing with either of them.

Neither of them was *Jay*. My Jay.

"Artemis makes this wonderful sound when she-"

The tenuous control I have over my wolf is eroding. I am *livid*. Practically foaming at the mouth.

I turn around and quickly walk away from the dugout. I can't believe this. When Jay and I had talked about after graduation not that long ago.... neither of us had said anything about breaking up.

I can't breathe around the knife in my ribs as I walk home, to the house I share with the only sibling of mine that has stayed past graduation, Athena, and my mother.

That night I skipped the graduation party that was being held in the back fields by Dave Campbell, where I was supposed to meet up with Sarah. Instead, I quietly Pack my room up, only taking what I can carry in a backpack and a duffle bag that I've used for hundreds of sleepovers at Sarah's.

Toothbrush, toothpaste. Underwear. Clothes. Then I raided the stashes of rolled coins lying all over. Took my graduation money from the card Aggie set on my nightstand and left.

No one saw me. Not even my mom, who was home from her 12-hour shift watching her programs on the TV as I passed. Lit cigarette held between fuschia-painted nails.

I am the child of hers that she'd never worried about a day in her life. Which means that I can slip out of town unnoticed, and unbothered.

Acknowledgements

Thank you, dear reader, for reading and loving Artemis & Jay. I hope you also loved the rest of the Wolf Pack, you'll see them in upcoming projects.

To my friends, Taylor, Mady, Kiera, and Shana, I want to say thank you so much. You guys keep me going when I feel down, and when I feel like giving up. I could not have done any of this without you.

To my family, who I love dearly.

A very special thanks goes to my Wolf Pack for all their support. To Allison, Amina, Callie, Chelsey, Grace, Janice, Kat, Keeks, Kennedy, Mady, Taylor, Rachael, Rishita, and Strawbs. I appreciate you all so much. Words cannot accurately express my gratitude.

Sharp-eyed readers will notice the quote Jay reads out loud to Artemis in Chapter 12 is from my debut series, the Child of the Veil. If you haven't read it yet, go take a peek. Mazikeen and Artemis would be fast friends, I think.

If you read Timber Hollow and thought that some of the scenes felt familiar, you should know this book was in large part inspired by two movies that my sister and I would watch together growing up. The movie Coyote Ugly, which I now know to be inspired by the book "The Muse of the Coyote Ugly Saloon" by Elizabeth Gilbert inspired Ivy's bar, Coyote Bills— no surprise there. And, character inspiration as well as the second chance romance plot gives many nods to Noah in The Notebook by Nicholas Sparks.

Thank you so much for reading. Keep an eye out for the rest of Artemis' Pack and their stories.

AWOOOO

About the Author

I've been an avid reader of all things magical, fantastical, and everything in between since I was a teen reading YA's and the stray romance novel found on many drugstore bookshelves. The spark for the love of reading has never died in me, only burned stronger the older I got.

Somewhere between imagining I was the feisty main characters I read about, -they were always feisty, and sarcastic – and dreaming up scenarios and different endings with the characters I read about, I decided to create my own stories. Now that I have breathed life into worlds, and universes of my own, I have a much bigger appreciation for all of the stories I've read and loved along the way.

When I'm not writing, I am a wife and mom to two beautiful girls, and spend my days in between the trees of New York with my dogs daydreaming about the possibility of a magical world, and listening to music that makes me feel feral.

Also By

Books in this series:

TIMBER HOLLOW

Other series:

CHILD OF THE VEIL

Mazikeen: Hands Of Fate
Mazikeen Stormborn
Mazikeen: Queen of Fate

Endnotes

1. Scene is from the book Mazikeen: Queen of Fate.

Milton Keynes UK
Ingram Content Group UK Ltd.
UKHW020645100924
448088UK00017B/304